TORCH

D. GRIFFITH WHITE

TRILOGY

Torch

Trilogy Christian Publishers A Wholly Owned Subsidiary of Trinity Broadcasting Network

2442 Michelle Drive Tustin, CA 92780

Copyright © 2021 by David Griffith White

Trilogy Christian Publishing/TBN and colophon are trademarks of Trinity Broadcasting Network.

For information about special discounts for bulk purchases, please contact Trilogy Christian Publishing.

Trilogy Disclaimer: The views and content expressed in this book are those of the author and may not necessarily reflect the views and doctrine of Trilogy Christian Publishing or the Trinity Broadcasting Network.

Manufactured in the United States of America

10 9 8 7 6 5 4 3 2 1

Library of Congress Cataloging-in-Publication Data is available.

ISBN: 978-1-63769-860-0

E-ISBN: 978-1-63769-861-7

"The light shines in the darkness,
and the darkness has not overcome it."

John 1:5

For my magnificent seven—Hannah, Solie, Talya, Josu, Lily, Elias, and Seven Mercy—and my lover, Rosie—keep shining bright!

This book is for you!

TABLE OF CONTENTS

TORCH

RHYTHM

Thump…thump…thump…thump…thump…ever louder, faster.
Thump…thump…thump…thump…thump…ever louder, faster.
Thump. Thump. Thump. Thump. Ever louder, faster.

The rhythm is building. It is growing louder, faster as it does every morning. The most intense, the most sacred, the most awe-inspiring wake-up call.

Pounding. Pounding. Pounding. Ever louder, faster.

Like the building of a great storm, a magnificent tempest, it was growing. Beating, pounding, exploding!

Faster now!

Louder now!

It is crying out! Calling out! Demanding everyone's attention.

Beckoning all who hear it to wake up! Dawn is approaching. Light is breaking through the darkness. It is glorious. It is magnificent. It is morning. It is time…for action.

Eyes beginning to twitch. Ears slowly recognizing the faint beating of the drums. Heartbeat stepping in line with the rhythm. Growing in speed and intensity. Fluttering as if to lift me out of bed.

Not sure what I am hearing, I just want it to stop! I am not a morning person, and the last thing I want is to get woken up this way. How about the sweet sound of a mother's voice whispering in my ear that it was time to get up? Or how about the smell of French toast and bacon wafting through the air? Nope, I get drums. Pounding, pounding, pounding. I, tossing and turning in my bed, am not used to this wake-up call, but as foreign as this is to me, it is strangely familiar. There is something compelling, almost soothing to it. As I said, I've never, ever, never been a morning person. That is…before I arrived here.

Where is here? The city of Lucent. I arrived a few days ago along with some other boys. We were part of a rescue mission. So, I'm new here, and although I'm new here, a stranger, Lucent just feels right. Like I belong. Like I've always belonged. If the rhythm hasn't been enough to get me up (yet), the pillows being hurled at my head are. What? Who? While I am trying to get my bearings in the dimly lit room, the pillows are simultaneously followed by laughing, no, howling from across the cramped room, where my new "brothers" are hurling pillows.

"Get up, T! You are *the laziest*! Get up! You're going to be late, and you don't want to be late."

They were right. You didn't want to be late to first light. Shaking off the cobwebs, I jumped up to get dressed. The room was sparsely decorated but adequate for the five boys who slept there. We each had our own bed and a small storage bin under it. We didn't have much in our bins because we didn't need much.

Other than the bed and the bin, there was a table and a chair for each of us in the middle of the room. No pictures on the wall. No artwork. Nothing to indicate that five teenage boys lived there except the beds and the bins. Hewn out of rock on the side of a mountain, if you didn't know better, you'd say we lived in a cave. A stone room? Yes. A cave? No. Right now, I just referred to it as home. And the other boys in my room? Newly acquainted? Yes. Brothers? Time will tell.

Throwing on my tan tunic, I slipped a simple white rope belt around my waist and slid on my sandals. Wanting to prove, once again, that I was the fastest in the room, I took off running toward the door at breakneck speed. In one swift motion, I bounded across the stone floor and reached out to grab the door handle, when, instead of grabbing the handle, something grabbed me from behind and pulled me back. Whirling around, I was ready to throw punches. But when I turned to see who grabbed me, I immediately began to shake inside. Not because of who grabbed me but because of my reaction. The old life, old self, old ways, rising to the surface far too easily. And the hand that grabbed my shoulder, that could only be one person, Salam.

The strongest of my brothers, he was an imposing figure with a dark complexion, a head of curly midnight black hair, and a muscular physique. His chiseled nose matched his chiseled biceps. Intimidating? Yes. Powerful? Yes. A teddy bear? Yes. But as powerful as he was on the outside, Salam's real strength was inside. He didn't say much. He didn't have to.

Salam was from a large family far away from where I grew up. He said that his people were from some arid land with lots of sand, few trees, and the pangs of thirst, a steadfast unwelcome companion. When Salam spoke about his family, it was brief, and his words seemed pregnant with pain. And yet, he was strong. A rock.

"Aren't you forgetting something?" said Takeshi sarcastically. He was small in stature but big in sarcasm. And if you didn't know any better, you'd underestimate him. I made that mistake the first time I met him, and my aching jaw reminds me that it's better to have Takeshi fighting with you, not against you.

Takeshi was tan but a few shades lighter than Salam. He was flexible and strong, very strong. Wiry, lean, and agile is also how I'd describe him. His size was very misleading. Very. His flexibility and strength were awe-inspiring. Growing up as an orphan, Takeshi was "street-smart." He had to fight to survive. If you asked him where he was from, Takeshi's response would be, "I'm from around here" (wherever "here" might be at the moment). Besides being coy about where he was from, Takeshi wore his emotions on his sleeve. Just one look at his face, and you could tell what he was thinking/feeling.

"Hey, T, *think fast!*" came a shout from behind me. Out of the corner of my eye, I saw something rocketing toward my head. I turned to swat at the object like a bee. I flailed my arms in a wild motion clumsily, awkwardly trying to knock it away before it hit my…My nose took the brunt of it and immediately began to run and swell. *I hope it's not bleeding*, I thought to myself. How embarrassing would that be to have my nose bleed in front of my "brothers"? Not to mention the mess it would make to my tunic. Fortunately, just a bunch of clear snot, a slight bit of swelling, and a little bruised ego were all it cost.

Bending over to pick up the object was Twitch, the thrower of the object. Twitch was the life of the party, the class clown, and always ready with a one-liner. He stood a head taller than me but outweighed me by at least a hundred pounds. His cheeks were round, and his ears seemed especially small for his enormous head. He didn't have much stamina, but he was just, well, like a mountain. Not a chiseled mountain like Salam, but more like an oversized snowman kinda mountain. We're not really sure what his real name is (no one is ever named "Twitch" on purpose), but he wouldn't answer to any other name. Besides, the name was fitting. Twitch had a twitch. Not all the time. Just randomly. Unexpectedly. Usually, when he was under stress. The more stress, the more twitching. That's why he liked to joke. He wanted to keep things light-hearted.

Twitch was born in the region of Aphotic, where it is rumored that giants still roam, which fits: someone like Twitch would be from a region of giants. According to Twitch, he still has family there, most notably, his twin brother, Twinge, and his mom. He can't stop, won't stop talking about Twinge and his mother. He dreams of a day when they, too, will be rescued and reunited. A couple of times a day, Twitch says, "Man, I miss my mom's cooking! I could really go for some of her fried chicken right now [or whatever food he was craving at the moment]! You guys would love her cooking!" And from the looks of it, Twitch very much enjoyed plenty of good meals.

"Way to go, T! Or should I say, loser! You couldn't catch anything even if your life depended on it!" came the sarcastic barb from across the room. Still sitting on his bed, Cain looked at me smugly as he did everyone. Arrogant and cocky, Cain was angry. Very angry. Of all of us, he was the only one born in Lucent. The only one who knew where his family was. He didn't need rescuing like the rest of us, but he needed it nonetheless. Cain couldn't believe that he was assigned to our group.

He was pure (or so he thought), his parents were established here, and he wanted us to know it. He was better than us.

Cain was about the same height as me, with very indistinguishable features save for his bright white hair. Even in darkness, his hair almost radiated light. Unfortunately, this didn't translate to his heart. He really was good in just about everything—strength, agility, speed—but that was it. He was good; some would say even average. Probably the only remarkable thing about Cain besides his phosphorescent hair was his forked tongue. He spent most of his waking hours, and probably some of his sleeping hours, thinking up cutting remarks for each of us.

Twitch handed the object to me, and as I took it in my hand, I inspected it and marveled at its beauty. About three feet long and tapered at one end, if you didn't know any better, you'd think it was simply a bat or a club, but you'd be wrong. Very wrong. Made of the finest, most precious wood on the planet, Obsidian Macassar, the object of craftsmanship was stunning in a simple and understated way. Not a single piece of material was wasted in its design. It was elegant and fierce at the same time. Depending on which side you were on, it was either peaceful or deadly. Warm and cold.

The fatter end was slightly rounded but with a straight cut on the very end. This end was also slightly hollowed out. The narrower end angled down perfectly to embrace the steel handle, which fit my grip perfectly. It was my weapon. All that I needed for protection. All that I needed to fight. It was my torch.

I know what you're thinking. Really? A torch? Why not a sword or a bow and arrow or maybe even a whip? But a torch? But let me warn you…don't underestimate it. I did. I do.

But enough about that and enough about my new "brothers" (we'll get back to them later…much later). We've got to get to first light.

Opening the door to our room, I step outside, and once again, like every day since I got here, I have to catch my breath. You see, even in this dawn-breaking hour, with silhouettes and outlines filling our view, the scenery is almost too beautiful to comprehend. Too majestic to describe. It is the city of Lucent. The city of light. And the rhythm is calling us.

TORCH

RUNNING

Thump…thump…thump…thump…thump…ever louder, faster.
Thump…thump….thump…thump…thump…ever louder, faster.
Thump. Thump. Thump. Thump. Ever louder, faster.

The rhythm was blaring. It was jarring. It was growing ever louder, faster as it did all day, every day. Hammering the ominous rhythms of the blackest of days and the darkest of nights. The most fierce, the most hypnotic, the darkest pulsing rage.

Pounding. Pounding. Pounding. Ever louder, faster.

Like the building of a great storm, a horrific tempest, it was growing. Beating, pounding, exploding.

Faster now.

Louder now.

It was shrieking! It was piercing! Demanding everyone's attention.

Beckoning all who hear it to join or flee! Darkness enveloping. Blackness overtaking, breaking, devouring any remnants of light. It was ominous. It was foreboding. It was the worst kind of evil. It was time…for despair.

Running. Fumbling. Tripping. Dodging. Heavily breathing. Aching side. Desperation.

Wheezing getting closer. Terrifying shrieks getting louder. Scampering sounds of hooves and claws rumbling and shaking the ground. Branches breaking. The wind biting. The darkness blinding.

Thorns ripped at my skin. Branches raked across my face. Or were those claws? Or teeth?

A shriek from the darkness. The sounds getting closer. Terror coursed through my veins. Thinking? No, just reacting.

From where? Eyes darting, mind racing, feet frantically moving. From where? Where to hide? Where to escape? The evil was gaining. But from where? Gotta keep moving. Gotta keep running. Push aside the pain. Push aside the hunger, the thirst. Push aside the fear. Push aside the horror. Push aside surrender. *Keep on moving.*

The wheezing and shrieks were close now.

Evil was near.

The air was pungent with the smell of death. The biting wind drove the smell of rotten, decaying flesh into my nose and mouth. The kind of stench you can taste. The kind you don't forget.

Ever. The closer the evil got, the more I felt sick. The smell was nauseating. The stress was unbearable. The fear was overwhelming.

Evil was near.

My head whipped back and forth, looking this way and that way. In the darkness, I could only see different degrees of blackness. Silhouettes and outlines created a distorted view of the landscape. Was that a tree? A boulder? The edge of a cliff? Multiple layers of blackness. But I was determined to escape. I had to escape. I couldn't…

The searing pain coursed down my back. Was it a thorn? A branch? A claw? A sword? It didn't matter. Blood began to flow. My knees began to buckle. My feet were unsteady. Tripping over a stump, I cascaded into the base of a tree, sliding on my shredded back. The searing pain was so excruciating that I actually barfed. My breathing was labored and erratic. And it was at that moment I caught a glimpse of my assailant, and I had every right to be terrified.

What I saw was a creature that was enormous, at least nine feet tall, hairy, and built like a bear. An evil bear, not a teddy bear. Bad bear. But its face was changing back and forth from looking like a bear to looking like an enraged, psychotic man. It was muscular, with large fangs protruding from its mouth, and the end of its hands were clawlike fingers. And when it breathed, it wheezed, coupled with intermittent shrieks…shrieks like someone was trapped inside and was trying to escape, being tortured. It was the embodiment of evil, of darkness, of death. Camouflaged in the darkness, I caught a glimpse of huge leathery wings cascading almost completely around this creature like a robe. At certain angled points on the wings were tiny clawlike hands, each moving independently of each other, each acting as if they were trying to rip apart some imaginary object. It smelled of death…my death.

With the pain becoming unbearable (no pun intended) and the evil closing in, I began to feel myself drifting. My body grew heavier and heavier as if being pulled down, down, down into the blackness. *I give up* was the last thing I remember thinking.

TORCH

FLUTTERING

       Shuffle…shuffle…shuffle…shuffle…shuffle…slowly.
   Shuffle…shuffle…shuffle…shuffle…shuffle…slowly but closer.
       Shuffle. Shuffle. Shuffle. Slowly still, but here.

Dust kicking up. Warm breath, shallow breathing. Still more shuffling. Shuffling turned to scampering. More dust being kicked up. Darkness, dankness, and dirt. Something colossal was here.

Fluttering. Twitching. Blinking. Ever faster.

Thick fog. Damp air. Cold. Really cold.

Fluttering. Twitching. Blinking.

Faster now.

Thick fog. Fading fog. Dissipating. Unfamiliar sounds. Sniffing. Shuffling. Something brushing. Something tickling.

Brain neurons kicking on.

Fluttering. Twitching. Blinking.

Slowly waking. Fog was lifting.

It was time for…what?

Trying to stand, breathe, think—all at the same time. Feet failing, head pounding, the world spinning. Gotta get up. Gotta run. Gotta fight. Eyes fluttering. Twitching. Blinking. Catch up, brain! Stand up, feet! Paralyzed, I lay there, trying to will my eyes focus. Something grazing my cheek. What was that? Was I imagining things? Was it a spider? A feather? It felt like a whisker. A giant whisker, like of a rodent.

I thought to myself, *Is this what it looks like? Is this the end? I mean, the real end? Getting eaten by a…a…an oversized rat?*

I began to shake, waiting for this monster to tear me into bite-sized pieces. Whiskers grazing my other cheek. A cold, wet nose sniffing in my ear. Breath like rotten potatoes. I could hear its teeth chattering involuntarily. This is definitely the end.

My eyes flickering, I was still trying to gain full vision. *C'mon!* I kept telling my eyes, *Focus!* More sniffing. More whiskers grazing my body. Up and down almost methodically. Was that a tongue smacking, like the way you do when you're about to eat your favorite meal?

My mind was still scrambling for a way out. What is the universal rule when confronted by a large, wild rodent? Play dead (which wasn't difficult in my present condition since my body still wasn't responding to any commands from my brain). Laying as still as I possibly could, I barely cracked my eyes, straining to look for an escape. Hopelessly, all I saw, besides oversized teeth, cold nose, and whiskers, was fur. Smelly, stinky fur. This is definitely the end. My end. No, wait, *its* end. The hairy rat had turned around, its bum in my face. This was my chance. With much effort, I tried to stealthily and silently swing my legs around and make a mad dash to freedom but, instead, ended up in a clump and an "umph" on the floor. Whirling around in one motion, the creature seized my shoulders with its disgusting hairy claws. Sweat flowed freely down my face, and my breathing quickened once again. I felt my body begin to convulse, fear taking over. Leaning in toward my face, the creature poured its hot, sticky breath once again on my face, and I turned my head and braced for the worst. And…

It…

just…

stared…

and breathed.

And stared and breathed for what seemed like an eternity! Still shaking, heading spinning, I couldn't take it anymore. My throat was dry and scratchy, but I mustered up as much breath as I could, and I "yelled" (more hoarsely than in an actual yell),

"Dddddddddddddddoooooo iiiitttt!"

Clearly shocked, the colossal rodent eased its grip on my shoulders but only slightly. It leaned back as if to get a better look at me. Maybe he was trying to figure out which end to eat first?

"Wha—wha—what did you say?" came the reply from the still shocked rodent, who was clearly confused.

Was I hearing things? Did the jumbo-sized rat just talk? Did it just ask me a question?

"I asked you a question. What did you just say?" the rodent demanded, leaning in closer to my face and retightening its grip on my shoulders.

Shaking and still in disbelief, I blurted out, as bravely as I could, "*Do it!*"

His beady eyes locked onto mine as the rodent brusquely demanded, "Do wha?"

"You know," I replied, stammering, "eat me…" my voice trailing to a whisper.

"You know? You know? Wha do you know? Eat me? Eat me?" asked the rodent both incredulously and rhetorically. Gaining some steam, he continued, "Why on earth would I eat the likes of you? No self-respecting Mild Ole Little Vegetarian would eva eat a Milky White. We likes 'em darky if you know what I means?" And it just paused, staring at me awkwardly.

I think that was a joke, but I wasn't sure. Wait. Am I having a conversation with an oversized, what did he call himself, "Mild Ole Little Vegetarian"?

Finally, I broke the silence. "So, you're not going to eat me?" I asked, a bit hopeful.

"Well, not right now. I just ate. Finking about a midnight snack, though."

My shoulders slumped, and my head dropped.

"Naw, Milky!" he then exploded in what I assumed was laughter. It bordered on fast wheezing and hiccupping. "I'm a good MOLVE. I eat my veggies at every meal. And the occasional grub. But mostly veggies."

"What kinda name is 'MOLVE'?" I asked, once again relieved that I was not for dinner but once again wondering how it was possible to be talking to an oversized rodent.

"First of all, MOLVE isn't my name. It's what I am. A 'Mild Ole Little Vegetarian.'"

"So, what is your name, then?" I asked.

"Keith. The name's Keith," the rodent replied.

"Keith?" I asked skeptically.

"Well, not really, but I like the name. It has a kinda regal quality about it. Us MOLVEs just usually go by, well, 'molve.' As in, 'Hi, molve, how ya doin'?' and in reply, I'd say, 'Good, molve. How you doin'?'"

"Seriously? Your name is what you are? MOLVE? Not very original," I asked, shaking my head.

"That's why I chose the name, Keith," he replied. "I'd never met a Milky White like yourself until I met Keith; God rest his soul. But I admired him so much in the short time I got to know him. I miss Keith; God rest his soul." The molve's body seemed to immediately appear sad, somehow.

"What happened to Keith?" I inquired tentatively, not sure if I wanted to know the answer.

"Welp," taking a deep, wheezing breath, the molve started, "I met Keith when, like you, he fell right through the roof of me house," pointing up at the ceiling as he said this, for effect. "He said he was on some sort of a rescue mission when he was attacked by the evil. His team was ambushed, and he had to run for his life. I assume this is what happened to you too?"

"I wasn't on a rescue mission," I replied. "But I was running for my life from something evil. Very evil. What, I'm not completely sure, but all I know is that I never want to see it ever again!"

"Did you see what was chasing you?" Keith asked, extremely concerned.

And then, all at once, I felt myself getting light-headed. Everything that I had been through had suddenly come flooding back to me, and I wasn't prepared for it.

Sensing this, the molve, aka Keith, released his grip on my shoulders. "Look here," he said in a comforting tone, "why don't you get some rest, and when you wake up, we'll continue our conversation over supper?"

But I had soooo many questions. "I need to know more about…" but that question and the countless others I had would have to wait. Now, sleep had won.

TORCH

FLICKERING

"*Mom! Mom!*" I yelled.

"*Run, T! Run!*" Mom screamed at me.

My mind was racing. Frantically firing thought upon thought. Trying to sort out which thought to listen to. What? No. I can't run.

"I'm not going to leave you!" I yelled back in reply.

The evil had a grip on my mom, throwing her over its powerful hairy shoulder like a rag doll. That was when it noticed me and began to turn.

"*T, run now! You have to go now!*" she pleaded. As she said this, she looked me dead in the eyes. And then, as if it were her final earthly request, she mouthed the word, "Please."

Frozen, I looked at my dear, sweet, fearless mom in the clutches of the evil beast. Stuck between wanting to fight a beast I had no way of overcoming and running to save myself, I glanced into the pleading eyes of my mother once again. That was it.

I turned to run as the evil turned its attention fully on me and made an attempt to grab me with its free hand. I stumbled, trying to get my legs and feet to respond to the rapid demands I was sending them. And I was off. Running through the darkness as fast as I could, I only stopped when I heard the beast let out a bloodcurdling roar.

The evil let out a hideous roar that briefly stopped me in my tracks. I turned back to see a wave of evil creatures enveloping the once serene countryside, like a swarm of locusts, destroying everything in their paths.

Darkness was flooding the sky as they made a beeline right toward me. The evil had summoned them. I took a final look at my mother and, with all the anger, rage, fear, and adrenaline that I had coursing through my body, I yelled out to her one more time, "*Mom!*"

I felt something on my shoulder shaking me.

"Milky White, you okay?" Keith asked.

Sitting up with a start, I felt immense pain in my back, so much that I almost passed out. I was suddenly reminded of my encounter with the evil. Steadying myself, I let my eyes slowly focus on my surroundings. The day before, I was too tired, sore, and overwhelmed to do much noticing. What I saw now was an enormous cave dug out of the dirt. Maybe not so much a cave but a tunnel. The roof and some of the walls of the cave had what looked like tree roots coming through them. I had been sleeping on a large rock with a few leaves sprinkled on top to make it softer. It didn't work. Except for one item on the wall, the cave was very plain. Something both peculiar and fascinating was hanging from a mass of roots on the far wall. From where I was sitting, it looked like a glowing stick, but it didn't at the same time. It was more. It was also the source of light that allowed me to take in my surroundings and finally get a good look at Keith.

"Milky White, you okay?" Keith asked again. "You haven't gone all mad, have you? Sometimes the evil will drive people to stupid."

Collecting my thoughts and breathing through the pain, I responded, "T. My name is T."

"What on earth kinda name is that?" Keith retorted. "T isn't a name; it's a letter!" he continued. "And you was poking fun at me name yesterday? Humph."

"You asked me what was chasing me before I passed out," I said, interrupting Keith. "As I said, I'm not sure what it was because I've never seen anything like it. Imagine a creature from the worst nightmare *ever*! It was huge and resembled a bear mixed with a dragon and a demon. Ya, a demon is a good word to describe it. A grizzly bear demon. But the most horrifying part is that it looked as if a man was trapped inside of the creature. A deranged man trying to escape," as I said this, I realized that my heart began to race and my breathing labored.

And with that, Keith started to mumble under his breath about names and letters, seemingly forgetting that I was sitting there. I could hear him say, "No, no, no, not good at all!" still mumbling to himself. He was extremely distressed. But then, as if an alarm had gone off, he snapped back to the present and remembered something.

"You must be starving," Keith said. "You've been asleep for almost a week."

"A week? What? Yes, I am starving, but I have so many questions—"

"Shh, shh, shh," Keith said as he put one of his long clawlike fingers up to my lips to silence me. "We'll have time for questions, but first, let me scrounge up some food." He turned to leave, but I wouldn't let him. I grabbed hold of his slick, hairy tail and demanded.

"What was chasing me?"

He whirled around unbelievably fast and had a gnarly rodent finger in my face. I could smell his breath, his fur, and his fear. In the scant light of the torch, an ominous shadow highlighted his face.

"What was chasing you?" Keith started sternly, anger and terror dripping from every word. "I've only heard rumors of that kind of creature. Stories that I've picked up. Like a prophecy mixed with a fairytale. That creature is called many different names like 'Cacodemon' and 'Incubus.' Some legends give it the name of 'Hellhound' or 'Succubus' if it appears female. After listening to the stories, I call these creatures Chaos because that is their intent: confusion, fear, and destruction. It was a bear mixed with a dragon this time. Another time, though, it could be a lion mixed with a bat. It changes based on the person it takes over," he paused to let this sink in. Leaning in close to my face, his breath warm and pungent, Keith began again, this time in a raspy whisper, as if someone or something might be listening: "The legend also states that in the end times, when the evil makes a final attempt to overtake the Light, Antioch, author of the darkness, will unleash these demonic creatures on humanity. They will be cloaked in things like money and sex and power, easily luring away those who have forgotten about the light. Or, in some situations, have traded it away for the illusion that these things will bring happiness and peace. Instead, in their pursuit of these things, they sacrifice everything: marriages, friendships, jobs, children. It comes with a price and when Antioch says, 'Pay up!' you pay up. So they are transformed into a ghastly creature like the one that chased you and captured your mom. This is not the creature that was chasing Keith. This…this is far worse."

And with that, he turned and scampered off, seemingly to find food.

This left me all alone sitting on the leaf-covered rock. My mind was fatigued. My heart was heavy. My body was broken. And every time I closed my eyes, I remembered the pleading look that my mother gave me as she was taken away by the beast. It was that look that gave me the only purpose I had for living. So I sat there in the dimly lit cave, the home of an oversized molve named Keith, wondering what happened to her and the others. And once again, my eyes were slowly drawn to the stick with fire on the end of it, which was hanging on the wall. I felt like it was calling to me, beckoning me to come closer. I stood up, taking time to steady myself, and painfully made my way toward the light. I wasn't exactly walking. It was more of a crawl. Each step was agonizing, reminding me of my still shredded back and deep cuts and bruises on my legs. I limped-crawled my way ever so slowly, trying to stifle the pain. But it seemed like I wasn't making any progress. I had underestimated the size of the cave, and the light was further than I imagined. Not sure if I made a good choice to get up off the rock, I thought about turning around, but again, the light seemed to be calling out to me. In fact, it almost seemed like it was speaking to me. Calling to me by name but without words. It was a feeling I'd never had before. It wasn't just a mental thing. It was as if the light was communicating directly to my heart. *Wait a minute*, I thought to myself, *It's just a light on a wall*. No. It was more. Much more. And the closer I got, the louder it spoke, the greater the pull was. This was no ordinary light. The pain that was so overwhelming a few minutes before seemed to slowly be dissipating each step closer. Don't get me wrong, the pain was still there, but in the presence of this light, it was bearable. While I was inching closer and closer, something else occurred to me. I began to shiver. A deep-down shiver that almost makes your knees buckle and your lips begin to quiver. It was a sensation that I had never felt before, the transition from cold to warm. I had been cold for so long that I never realized it. It was just part of who I was. But now, now in this cave, under the ground, with an oversized molve named Keith, here in the unlikeliest of places, I was, for the first time, experiencing a sensation that was so hard to describe other than enrapturing bliss. It was warmth accompanied by a sense of peace and something else that was hard to initially pinpoint…Power. And it was calling me.

Gazing at the light, I felt like it was reaching out to me. I was so mesmerized that I wasn't sure if I was breathing or not. The undulation of the flickering light was hypnotic, and slowly, as if on cue, I began to breathe, really breathe. To take a deep breath after a deep breath. My lungs filled with air as if I'd almost drowned and was taking that first life-giving gulp of air!

This was the first time that I heard the rhythm. The beating. Slowly, quietly as the flame danced in front of me, it began to dance inside of me. Breathe in—flicker. Breathe out—flicker. Breathe in—crackle. Breathe out—snapping.

Was I imagining things? Flames on a torch don't talk. They don't call out to you. A flame doesn't match your breathing with its flickering. Or stir a rhythm in your chest. Or make you feel powerful. Or…or does it?

Inching ever closer, I reached out my hand to touch it. For some reason, I *had to touch it*! Noticing the finely crafted handle, the intricate details that a master carver had spent hours shaping and shaving and sweating over, I was about to grab it when…

"*Milky White, Milky White!*" I heard my name, the silly nickname Keith gave me, being bellowed, waking me from my trance. Partially blind from the radiant light, I turned, and from some unknown direction, Keith came scampering toward me. Shuffling to a stop near me, Keith, slightly out of breath, exclaimed, "Oh, there you are, Milky…er um…T! Wachu doin'?"

As he spoke, I got a better look at Keith's face. In this light, I noticed that he couldn't see. He had eyelids that incessantly fluttered, and what I could see of his eyes, they appeared to be, well, milky white. For someone not being able to see, he could see quite clearly.

"What is this?" I asked, pointing in the direction of the light (as if he could see where I was pointing).

"Oh, that. It's nothing. Just something that Keith left behind. Now, enough about that. Let's eat!" He scooped me up in one of his ginormous hairy arms and carried me back toward the rock I'd been sleeping on. Back toward the darkness. Away from the light.

"You know, T, Keith was a nice fellow, kinda like you. He ended up here after running from the evil," the molve said as he set me down on my sleeping rock. "Keith," he continued, "was in bad shape when I first laid eyes on him. He looked a bit like you, but worse. Much worse. To be quite honest with you, I didn't give him much of a chance to make it."

"What do you mean by making it?" I asked a little uneasily, a lump in my throat.

Keith had scrounged up some food and was about to hand it to me when he froze at my question. It was like he was whisked back in time, and lunch was momentarily forgotten. In the dimness of the cave, I couldn't make out his face. I didn't have to. His voice said it all. This normally jovial rodent was carrying deep sadness.

"Well, you know," Keith said quietly, emotionally, "I didn't think he'd live. Every day for weeks, I would wake up and wonder if he'd made it through the night. I wondered the same thing about you. When you have as many injuries as he did, you don't survive. But he did."

"So, he got better and left?" I asked hopefully.

"*No!*" Keith snapped, putting his oversized rodent face in mine. "I...I don't know where he is or what became of him. Better. Yes, he got better." The molve took a step back, and I heard a heavy sigh come from him.

"I...I...I'm sorry," I stammered. "I didn't mean to upset you. I was just curious to know..."

"No," Keith interrupted, "I'm sorry. Sorry I wasn't here when they came for him."

"Who?" I asked. My mind was wondering what in the world creature would end up down here. In my time in the rodent's cave, the only creatures I'd seen beside the molve was an occasional bite-sized bug that made the mistake of getting a little too close to escape, being eaten by Keith, usually without hesitation or warning. Besides that, there were the ominous sounds that you might expect from a dark cave: random scratching, scampering, squeaks, and the ever so infrequent shriek. These never alarmed Keith, so I didn't let them bother me…too much.

"*Who?*" Keith's voice began to rise again. "*Who?*" He sat down beside me to collect himself. We sat there for a long time. Silent. Not a word. Just silent in the dim, flickering light. Breathing and thinking.

He was shaking when he reached over to hand me something. His oversized paw opened up and dropped what appeared to be a rag. A tattered rag. It was hard to tell, but it looked like it might have blood on it. Was this dinner? Was this what molves thought that humans ate? A dirty, blood-soaked rag? Disgusting.

"What is this?" I said, finally breaking the silence.

"That," the rodent said, still solemn, "is all that is left of Keith. That and the torch on the wall. I found them both deep inside one of the tunnels when I went looking for him. This was wrapped around the handle of the torch. The torch's flame was very dim."

"Can I ask you something personal?" I asked.

"Ask away," Keith responded.

I gulped as I asked him, "Are you blind?"

Sitting there for a moment as if processing my question, he finally answered, "That depends on your definition of 'blind.' If by 'blind' you mean if I can see with my eyes, well, no, I can't see with my eyes. So, yes, you'd assume I'm blind. But being able to see and being able to *see* are two completely different things. I can see more clearly than most creatures. Take yourself, for example. You see what's in front of you. Maybe you even use your hearing to determine your surroundings. *But*, me, on the other hand," he stood and began to move around a bit, talking with his hands, "I can hear, see, and feel things that you have no comprehension of. Right now, above our heads, through layers of dirt and tree roots and decaying matter, I can hear the scampering of creatures, big, small, and in between. I can feel the vibrations, and I can tell how many and what kind. I can also feel the emotions of these creatures. I knew you were coming before you knew you were coming. I felt the pain, anguish, and fear racing through your body, and I knew I had to help. It was the same way with Keith."

"So, if you can't see with your eyes, how did you know about the torch?"

"I could feel its warmth," the molve started, "but it was more than that. It was like Keith left a part of him burning in the torch, and when I found it, I knew I had to keep it safe for him just in case…" the rodent's voice trailed off momentarily. "Well, that was a few years ago now. I don't think he'll be coming back for it. I always had this feeling, though, that if it wasn't for Keith, there was a bigger reason to hold onto it. Something I can't explain. Almost as if…" Again, his voice trailed off.

"As if the torch communicates with you?" I finished his sentence.

"Ya!" Keith said. "Weird, isn't it?"

"Weird, for sure," I agreed. And then I ventured again to find out what happened to Keith, the human. "So," I began, looking down at the bloody rag in my hand and remembering how hungry I was, "what happened to Keith? I mean, what you know or what you think happened?"

Turning away, the rodent flatly said, "The Offspring. The Offspring happened."

"The Offspring?" I asked, the lump returning to my throat.

"That's right. The Offspring. You know the evil you were running from? Well, the Offspring are like its demon children that come behind to devour anything in their path. They get rid of any loose ends. Like the Chaos, they, too, used to be humans. They owed debts to Antioch that they could not pay. So now they are hideous, vile creatures. They have hair all over their bodies, and they have long, sharp claws extruding from their hands and feet. Their teeth are gnarly and protrude from their mouths like tusks, and their eyes are bulbous and manic-looking. They tend to run hunched over, appearing to look hunchbacked, on all fours like wild animals. Protruding from their backs is a pair of wings, which they keep well concealed. The Offspring are indebted to Antioch for all of eternity, and they were looking for Keith. On the day he disappeared, I went to find us something to eat, and when I came back, Keith was gone. The only thing left was the smell of rotting flesh. I had to leave, to move. To get out. I couldn't live there anymore. The stench was so overwhelming that I was sick and retched for days. This is not my original home."

And then, as if our stomachs were in unison, the oversized rodent molve named Keith and I both remembered how hungry we were.

TORCH

THE LAST SUPPER

As hungry as we were, it felt appropriate to have a moment of silence before eating. So, we sat there still, quiet, thinking, remembering. Keith remembering Keith. Me remembering my mom and others. So many others…

In the darkness, my mind was still racing…images of people, loved ones, friends, teachers flashing through my head. The torch on the wall flickered, and with each dance of the flame, another image flashed. Mom (*flash!*) sister (*flash!*)…So many, it was almost too much. And there were the questions. Questions upon questions. I was shuffling a foot on the dirt floor and waiting for the images and questions to silence. I turned toward Keith.

"I don't remember much about the day the Chaos showed up," I said, breaking the silence. "It's like a fog. Something happened to my little sister, Em. She was somehow lost, even though that doesn't seem quite right. And then my mom and I were running for our lives in the woods. I have no idea where they are or how to rescue them, but I must try." I said the last sentence, trying to sound confident.

"The mines," Keith said flatly. "The mines. That's where they take them. Your Mom. Keith, if he's still alive. The others. They are slaves forced to work for the evil, Antioch. From what I've heard, it's in a place called the Veiled City. That's where Keith was heading when he ended up here. He was on some sort of a rescue mission looking to meet up with a team of others."

"Where?" I asked, "Where are these mines and the Veiled City, and who are these 'others' that Keith was meeting up with?" my curiosity fully peeked, and my voice higher pitched than I intended.

"I don't know where the mines are. I've just heard about them before and what I've heard is that they try to break people there. Break their wills. Break their minds. Break their souls! Those who don't embrace Antioch's twisted dogma are also turned into the Offspring. And as for who Keith was meeting up with…Well, he wasn't quite sure. He said they'd find him when the time was right."

Processing what the oversized rodent was telling me, again, I had more questions than answers, and I didn't know what to believe. What I knew was that my mom was gone, dragged away in front of my eyes. My sister was missing. I was all alone, in a cave, with an oversized rodent and a…torch. A torch that at this moment seemed to bring comfort… to somehow dull the pain of loss. A torch with a flame that was dancing around as if singing a soothing song.

At first, I thought that Keith might be crying again, getting emotional, and then I realized that no, he wasn't getting emotional: he was getting down with some grubs! One thing I hadn't expected was how grotesque-looking a molve would be while eating. The slurps. The burps. Grub juice running down his chin and elbow. *Yuck*! Whatever appetite I had was gone, maybe to never return. But I couldn't help but stare.

I guess Keith felt me staring because, as if reading my mind, he turned toward me (giving me the full view of his disgusting, goo-covered face), stopped in midbite with a mouth full of grub, and defensively said, "What? I'm an emotional eater! You can't tell me you've never overeaten because you're stressed? Oh, wait, sorry. How rude of me. I know you're starving." With that, he handed me a couple of my very own grubs.

With the grubs in one hand and the bloody rag in the other, I tried to think of how to politely get rid of the grubs. The thought came to me to quietly wrap them in the rag, but then what? Hold onto them for later? Have them squish all over the rag? They smelled horrible, like they'd been fermenting for weeks. I don't know what was worse, the thought of eating one or the way they smelled. Probably the smell, definitely the smell.

From across the cave, I looked up to notice that the torch's flame was no longer singing a soothing song with its flickering. No, it was beginning to pulsate. Rhythmically pulsate. Faster now. Faster still…

That's when I realized that Keith had stopped eating. He wasn't moving except for the tip of his nose, which, incidentally, had a mind of its own.

"Are grub worms always this bad-smelling? They smell so bad I can taste it!" I asked, trying to understand why the emotional eater was suddenly full and fighting back my urge to vomit.

"No, T," he whispered, his nose lifted higher in the air and moving frantically. "No, T," he repeated in a hushed, guarded tone. The flame on the torch wasn't flickering now. It was throbbing. Almost pleading.

But what did it mean?

"*Run!*" screamed Keith. "*Run! Move! Now!*"

I tried to do as I was commanded, but my legs still wouldn't work. My back was still on fire, and my body was still broken. Although my mind was alert, it couldn't think fast enough. *Run!* I implored my legs as I tried to will my body to move. I rolled off of the rock I'd been sitting on and onto the cave floor.

"*Run, T!*" Keith repeated.

I tried. I couldn't do it. The best I could do was crawl. I needed to move faster, but how? And why? Whatever it was that I was "running" from was surely going to overtake me. I had this sense, though, that if only I could get to the torch…

The ground began to shake violently. Dirt and rocks began to fall from overhead. I tried to stand to my feet again but with no success. And then, along with the violently shaking cave, came the smell, like getting punched repeatedly in the face by an unseen opponent. Smelling it. Tasting it. It wasn't the smell of grubs; it was the smell of death. The smell of the Offspring.

If my mind was racing before, now it was about to explode. The smell, the violently shaking cave, and then the sound. It was ear-splitting, high-pitched screeching that penetrated my thoughts, making it nearly impossible to think or move. It was like a paralyzing force. A strategy, I would find out later, that the Offspring used to stun their prey before going in for the kill. I had to keep moving.

In a panic, Keith ran. When I noticed him, he was almost to the other side of the room. Feeling utterly hopeless and desperate, I screamed out his name, "*Keith! Keith! Keith!*" Not knowing that he heard me, I put my head down and again began inching my way toward the torch.

As I crawled forward, though, the ground-shaking grew in intensity, the smell got worse, and the screeching became almost unbearable. More rocks falling, more obstacles in the way of my escape. And then one, two, three, rocks came rocketing down from the ceiling of the cave, pinning me down. I looked up to search for Keith but only saw the flicker of light from the torch. It was flashing brighter and more intensely now. No longer was it beckoning me; it was commanding me! But how? I was broken. I was tired and hungry. I'd lost everyone that mattered. My legs were trapped.

So, I stopped. I just stopped, resolute that this was the end. The Offspring were here, and I was finished.

TORCH

THE OFFSPRING

"Oh no, you don't!" Keith was yelling in my ear. *"You don't give up now, Milky White! You don't give up!"*

I realized that Keith was frantically removing the fallen rocks from my legs, digging, lifting, grunting. His breathing was labored and heavy, but his movements were light and swift. I began to feel my legs again, but they were of no use. Crushed in the collapse.

Realizing that I couldn't move on my own, Keith scooped me up and threw me over his shoulder. And then he stood there for a split second, trying to find the best route of escape. That was when the Offspring made their move.

Like the beginnings of a violent thunderstorm, they came in like a tiny sprinkle, an evil sprinkle, one here, one there, one here, one there. But soon, the cave ceiling opened up, crashed down, and they were swarming in by the dozens. No, hundreds.

With me over his shoulder, Keith made his move. Bounding this way and that way, he was scaling fallen boulders and dodging falling ones. The problem was that I was weighing him down and thus slowing him down.

Leaping, shifting, sliding. I have to say: I didn't know good ole Keith had it in him. At this point, we were getting closer and closer to the wall with the torch. But the Offspring were getting closer and closer to us.

I was beginning to feel the warmth of the torch when the first of the Offspring landed on Keith's back. The molve almost tripped. When the second and third ones landed on him, he did trip, tumbling and stumbling and yet at the same time thrusting/throwing me in the direction of the torch.

"Go! Rescue them all!" Keith yelled.

Sliding to a stop a few feet away from the cave wall that held the torch, I heard Keith screaming agonizing screams. Screams of a dying animal. I tried not to think about the screams from Keith or the screeches from the Offspring. I focused fully on the torch, and it focused fully on me. With my legs useless, I used my arms to pull me closer and closer to the torch. Once again, the closer I got to the torch, the more I felt my body healing. The crushed bones were no longer crushed. My muscles began to fire again. My mind was sharpening. My resolve was strengthening. "Go! Rescue them all!" kept going through my mind as I was so close to grabbing the torch. In spite of the cave filling with the Offspring and Keith being overrun by them, I wasn't sure why but I just knew that if I could grab the torch in my hands, I would be okay.

When I reached the wall, I stood up as quickly as my body would allow me. The torch was right in front of my face. Reaching up to grab the torch, I was interrupted by the searing pain on the back of my neck. Claws or teeth, it didn't matter. I was in immediate pain, and my world began to spin. I felt the creature latch onto my back, digging its claws into my back and sides! Fearing I was going to pass out because of the pain, I heard, not in my head but with my ears, Keith yelling once more, *"Go! Rescue them all!"*

With the weight of the creature and the pain I was in, I willed myself to fall forward, toward the torch. Falling as if in slow motion, I reached out my hand, the one that still had the bloody rag wrapped around it, and stretched out my fingers as far as I could. Grabbing the handle, I felt power begin surging through me. But I didn't have a firm grip, and the handle of the torch was slipping! Not wanting to go down to the ground without it, I used the tips of my fingers to hit the handle of the torch, but it was no use. The torch was still in place, rocking from side to side, on the wall.

We crashed to the ground violently, momentarily knocking my assailant off my back, both dazed. I tried to get up and run, but the creature was on top of me before I could get to my feet. Now, in the torchlight, I could see this hideous creature, fangs, and claws like its evil master. It wasn't there to take me to the mines; it was there to kill me. My back against the dirt floor of the cave, my arms pinned down by powerful claws, bared teeth zeroing in on my neck. I looked up at the torch, hoping, praying for a miracle.

Sometimes miracles come from unexpected places. This one came from a second Offspring; in a hurry to help with the kill (me), it ran headfirst into the cave wall just below the torch. It landed on my face and momentarily caused its accomplice to ease its grip on my arm. Suddenly, the direction of the light changed as I saw the torch sliding down the wall and landing by my hand. The two creatures, in a burst of anger with each other, briefly lost focus. I gained it and the torch, and stretching out my hand, I felt the torch handle. This was about to get fun.

TORCH

YOU'RE IT

Gripping the handle of the torch, I once again felt a surge of power, a power that I've never felt before. First things first: get up. Harnessing my newfound strength, I threw both creatures simultaneously off me and jumped to my feet in one smooth motion. I've never been accused of being smooth until this moment. The first creature righted itself and was angrier than before. With a full head of steam, it charged me, using its oversized wings to hurl itself at my head, fangs, claws, and stench cutting through the air. Reacting to the prompting of the torch, I wound up, smashed it with the torch, and sent the creature tumbling directly into the path of its partner. Realizing that they were only stunned, I steadied myself for another attack. Regrouping, this time, they came at me from two different sides. Once again, I knocked the first one out of the air, but it caused me to turn my back to the second one, where it seized the opportunity to jump on me. With its claws digging into the sinew of my back, I instinctively took a few powerful steps backward, ramming the creature into the wall behind me and causing it to release its grip. I whirled around; with too little space to swing the torch, I thrust the flame into its hairy gut, claws, and fangs trying to tear at my arms and face. I would say it smelled like burning flesh. Even worse. The smell of death dying. That was the smell. Its face was contorting, writhing, wriggling, struggling. I was unmoved. It was losing, expiring, giving up. You could see a slight green vapor oozing out of its pores: noxious vapor, one last attempt to kill its victim. My eyes watered like when someone cuts open an onion. I began to cough as if I'd inhaled a spoon full of black pepper. Coughing and tearing up. And then the creature went limp, and now I could clearly tell that this Offspring resembled a man. Like the Chaos that Keith had described, just a different kind of creature. One that had taken over this person. I had killed it. It was my first. It wouldn't be my last.

The screeching behind me woke me out of my brief revelry. I spun around to see the first creature coming back again, this time going for my legs to avoid the torch. In one motion, I jumped up in the air, higher than humanly possible. I was rising above the creature when it went for my feet. Too late. I was swinging the torch straight down with the entire force of my body, crushing the Offspring's head. We hit the ground at the same time. Struggling to get up, the creature rose for one last attack. Its mistake. Knocking it into the sea of creatures that were mauling Keith, now that was *my* mistake.

Suddenly, instead of just two of the Offspring to deal with, now the entire herd turned their focus on me—hundreds, no thousands of Offspring. I knew I had to get out of there quickly. My last remembrance of this cave room was looking back to see scores of creatures trampling over Keith's mangled body. Impossible as it sounds, Keith was looking straight at me as if to say, *"Go! Rescue them all!"*

I didn't know where to go. I just ran. And fast. Fact one: you run fast to impress a girl. Fact two: you run faster when a herd of creatures from the pit of hell is chasing you, and you have a power-giving torch in your hands that helps you run superhumanly fast. The chase was on.

When I darted down the first tunnel I saw, the Offspring were hot on my heels. Screeching and clawing, they made sounds that reverberated off the walls of the cave, making them louder than they already were! Running faster and faster, not knowing if there was a top speed with my newfound agility, I sprinted through the tunnel ablaze, torch in hand, only seeing a few feet in front of me. Coming to a fork in the tunnel, I took a hard right to see if I could lose part of the herd. It seemed to work; the noise had subsided slightly. No turning back to look, though.

Kicking into another gear, I continued down the tunnel, twisting and turning every few feet; the Offspring weren't giving up. Another fork just up ahead, I slowed to make a more calculated turn. This allowed the Offspring to close the gap. The noise and stench were getting louder; this time, I turned left, where to my shock, I was heading straight toward the herd that I thought I'd lost. Offspring behind me. Offspring in front of me. The tunnel suddenly seemed very small.

Still running at top speed, I had but seconds to figure out my strategy. The torch took on a new glow. Sounding like the roaring furnace of a blacksmith's kiln, it was alive. I was alive. In the darkest place surrounded by the darkest creatures, I was alive. Any fear was replaced with confidence and boldness. And like that, the torch and I rushed to meet the evil before us.

Wings, fangs, and teeth were hurling themselves at me in a furious rage. I was smashing skulls and sending creatures into oblivion, one, two, three at a time. The air was pungent with the smell of death and green haze from every dying creature. My eyes and nose stung from the smell, and my progress was slowed, allowing the herd that was behind me to catch up. Knowing I couldn't defend my front and back, I instinctively trusted my gut and did something unbelievable: I ran up the wall and onto the ceiling of the cave just above the Offspring. Trying not to freak out (I had never run upside down on a ceiling before), I caught the herd off guard. I sprinted past them on the ceiling, all the while swinging the torch and clearing out the herd that had been in front of me. Once past them, I ran back down the wall and onto the cave floor. This seemed to work. I glanced behind me. The rear herd was having trouble getting through the carnage that I had just wreaked. No time to stop now. "*Go! Rescue them all!*" kept going through my mind. I turned to run, still not sure where I was going. I was just running. The screeches and clawing seemed to be growing more distant, but the creatures weren't giving up. The Offspring had a mission: to kill me. And nothing was going to stand in their way. I ran on.

Having no idea how long I'd been running, from what I could tell, the distance between myself and the Offspring had to be substantial.

It sounded as if they had spread out to search every nook and cranny. I had kept switching up my route—a right turn here, a left there—to throw them off, finally slowing down to a walk when it sounded like I had lost them. I slowed down to walk, not because I needed to, but because I *needed to*. Ever since I picked up the torch, I was reacting and going on instinct, but now, now I needed to think…for myself. I came across a little nook behind a boulder that was hidden from the tunnel. Retreating behind the boulder, I placed the torch against a rock on the ground. Then, I went around to the tunnel side to see if the flame was visible from the tunnel in case any of the Offspring came that way. It wasn't. I went back around the boulder where the torch was lying against the rock and sat down to think. This would be solo thinking. No torch in my hand. Just me and my noggin trying to figure things out.

TORCH

FREE-FALLING

(Ya, I'm Free-Fallin')

A plan. That's it. I had to come up with a plan.

1) Get out of the cave and not die at the hands of the Offspring, or just not die at all.
2) Find out where the Veiled City is located, where the mines are, and where my mom is being kept.
3) Figure out what happened to my sister, which was still a murky fog.
4) Get something to eat.
5) Take a bath.

Now, in order of importance, number one is definitely a top priority. The last four are a toss-up in order of importance. Finding and rescuing my mom has gotta happen, but I can't rescue people on an empty stomach. And the way I smell right now? I won't be sneaking up on anyone with the way I smell. It is a dead (literally) giveaway.

Now, back to number one: getting out of the tunnel and not dying in the process. When I ran out of Keith's area of the cave, I ran back and forth in a zigzag pattern, jumping from one tunnel to another. Although I have been going forward, I have been going from side to side in the tunnels as opposed to going straight ahead in one direction. So, I will go straight down the tunnel I was just on, see it to the end, and if it's a dead end, turn around, and try another. That sounded like a good plan to me. A straightforward plan. Literally.

Rising to my feet, I picked up the torch, or rather, I tried to pick up the torch. Strangely, it was heavy. Too heavy. My arm was in the proper torch-holding position, but I couldn't move it or my arm. Perplexed, I stood there until I heard what the torch had already known. A small group of Offspring was coming down the tunnel. I couldn't see them from my position behind the boulder, but I could hear and smell them. I didn't think these creatures could be quiet, but these were, and if not for the torch, they would have ambushed me. Slowly slinking back further behind the boulder, I stood there listening and plotting. How many were there? Where exactly were they? And then it was quiet. Too quiet. I wanted to peek around the boulder to assess the situation, but that meant leaving the torch. So I waited. And waited. Every so often, I would tug on the torch to see if it was ready to move, and over and over again, it wasn't. It was like a stubborn dog you're trying to walk, the kind that just wants to sit down and take a nap in the middle of the road. So, I sat down and surveyed the handle of the tempestuous torch, looking for a reason why it wouldn't move. I couldn't figure it out for the life of me. It was in this surveying, though, that I realized that I was still clutching the bloody rag. I had wrapped it around my hand, and, in the midst of the action, I had forgotten about it. In fact, I'd been clutching it so tightly that when I unwound it from around my hand, my hand ached. I spread out my fingers, trying to loosen the joints in my hand, and felt the blood return back to it. I opened up the rag and laid it across my lap. The side facing up was covered with bloodstains. Keith's bloodstains. So much blood. A brief flash of Keith the molve on the floor of the cave bolted through my thoughts. I instinctively flipped the rag over. This side, too, had bloodstains, but to my astonishment, there appeared to be something written on the rag. I held the rag up closer to the torchlight and, as my eyes began to focus, the word "*Sabre*" became evident. The lettering was red-colored, written in what I can only assume was blood. *What?* What does that even mean? The word "*Sabre*" written in blood on a bloody rag given to me by an oversized rodent, supposedly belonging to a guy named Keith, whose name the oversized mole took for his own? And then the torch, as if waiting for me to catch up with it in the mental department, as if it were a little ticked off that I wanted to think for myself, roared a whole new roar. The torch was ready. It was time to go.

Wrapping the blood-soaked rag around my hand, I reached down to pick up the torch, half expecting it to not budge. This time, though, there was no resistance. I left the safety of the boulder and headed down the tunnel, deciding to walk for a time instead of running. The Offspring coming up behind me had a different idea. There were only three of them, but I wanted to avoid these creatures. As much as I could fight them and most likely win, I didn't want to take that chance. So, I ran (again). Heading down the tunnel, I picked up speed. One of the Offspring, the fastest of the three, was gaining on me. I could hear its claws, smell its stench. These three seemed to be different from the other Offspring that I'd faced. They seemed smarter, faster, more cunning. As the first one ran to catch up to me, the other two also gained momentum and were suddenly flanking me on either side of the cave. And then, as if on cue, the two creatures by the walls ran directly into my pathway, causing the three of us to go hurtling down the tunnel in one big ball of wings, claws, fangs, and fire. We tumbled and tumbled. We were on some sort of decline and seemed to be building momentum. Faster and faster we went. Me and my flame. Them and their fangs. Neither able to parry or land blows…the cave was doing that for us and to us. Finally, the ground started to level out, and when the three of us came to a stop, it was clear that the two creatures had suffered the most. Laying there sprawled out but alive, the creatures rose to resume the fight. One I smashed in the head before it knew what was coming. It was gone in a green cloud of death. The other came at me over and over again. Teeth bared, fangs exposed, claws glistening in the light of the torch. This was a worthy adversary. Jumping, dodging, sliding, shifting, lunging. The creature seemed relentless. Up and down the cave walls, we dueled. Offspring and human blood splattering. A blow to my mouth, a scorched wing. A claw grazing my back, the torch shattering a leg. Round after round.

Neither giving an inch. Neither giving up. We may have still been there fighting had it not been for the third Offspring who came into the fight like a bolt of lightning. Seeing it out of the corner of my eye, at the last second, I grabbed my worthy adversary and jumped up in the air straight toward the ceiling and then let go just as its partner came flying in, sending them both careening down the tunnel. I immediately smelled death. One or both were dead, and they lay in a heap, wings and claws splayed out and entangled at the same time. My brief jubilation at my victory was shortened by the realization that the entangled Offspring lay directly in my path. Only one thing to do, "*Go! Rescue them all!*"

Moving down the tunnel as quietly as possible, I let my eyes scan the carnage, my pulse quickening as I got closer to the two downed creatures. A few body parts were strewn about. A few body parts that I had to step over to avoid crunching on. A part of a wing, a claw, something resembling a hand. I was almost on top of them now. Pulse increasing, sweat forming on my forehead—it was all I could do to not stare as if staring or not staring would wake them up from their dead slumber. This end of the tunnel was definitely different from the rest of the tunnels. Dirt gave way to mud, and even puddles of water marked the floor. The two creatures were lying in such a puddle. No movement came from the pile. It appeared I had, indeed, won.

Passing by slowly in the ankle-deep water, I saw it for the first time. So transfixed on fighting for my life, I had failed to recognize it. The "it" was the out, as in "a way out." Light was flooding in through the end of the tunnel about a hundred yards away. I could see it. I could smell it. I could feel it. The fresh air. The breeze. The…foot tripping over an outstretched arm of one of the creatures. Feet splashing and stumbling as I tried to keep my balance, immediately on high alert, waiting for one of the Offspring to attack. My eyes were darting here and there, scanning the creatures for any more movement. Taking a deep breath, I turned away to make a final sprint out of the cave. Two steps into my sprint, I heard the screech. As loud as ever, one of the Offspring exploded into life and was in hot pursuit! Trying to gain momentum, I pressed harder, willing my legs to move faster than ever before. The nearer I got to the entrance of the cave, the faster I ran. At breakneck speed. I was putting distance between myself and my pursuer. The screeches, however, were louder than ever. Now, they even sounded like a roar. A low rumbling mixed with high-pitched screams. It was almost deafening and quite unnerving, especially when you are running faster than you ever imagined possible.

Almost there. Almost there. Taking one last look behind me to see the gap between us, I turned back around to see a waterfall with a sheer drop-off directly in front of me. This "exit" was a cascading waterfall on the side of a cliff. *Stop! Stop! Stop!* I was trying to command my legs to obey, but I was going so fast. A mix of gravel, sand, and mud was making it impossible to stop. My feet were sliding; my legs were burning. Just moments before, I had willed them to go faster; now, I was trying to get them to stop. Normally, the cool mist of a waterfall would be welcomed, that is, unless it's accompanied by certain death or an evil creature chasing you and ready to devour you. Slowing down now, I was considering my options: (1) turn and face my foe; (2) leap to my death; (3) curl up in a corner and cry. This was a decision I wouldn't be making on my own...

Feet trying to stop, slipping, and sliding on the wet gravel. The Offspring didn't slow down. It took full advantage of the situation and ran into me at full speed, grabbing onto my back, claws digging in, hairy legs wrapping around my waist, the creature's teeth repeatedly trying to bite my neck. We went straight through the waterfall and were now free-falling, twisting, and turning in midair.

A kid flying through the air is completely unnatural. A kid flying through the air with a hideous creature from the pit of hell on its back is completely, completely un...It's just plain comical. Unless it's you. Then it's completely terrifying.

My hand, wet from the waterfall, lost grip of the torch, and I immediately and frantically stretched and wriggled my fingers to grab it, but I kept batting it around in midair. My fingertips kept nicking it over and over again. Not holding the torch in my hands brought out every painful bump, bruise, and scratch that I had endured during my time in the cave. Now, careening down toward the ground, torch just out of reach, the demon torturing my back and neck, was almost too much to bear. Turning over and over, I felt my head getting lighter and lighter. I caught glimpses of the ground that was rapidly approaching. As if I wasn't before, now I was desperate to grab the torch! With every turn, I was waving my hands, trying to grab it. By just feeling it in my hands, I knew I would be okay.

We kept falling and falling and falling. On one of the somersaults, I caught a split-second glimpse of something below us that gave me some hope…water. If I couldn't grab the torch, maybe I wouldn't be killed by the fall. Of course, as fast and far as we were falling, even the perfect landing would surely break every bone in my body. And the closer we got, the faster we got, and the tighter was the grip of the Offspring.

Focus. Focus. I was trying to will myself to concentrate through the pain. "Come on, T! Focus!" I yelled out loud, the wind whipping by so fast that I could barely hear myself. Glimpses of my childhood flashed through my mind. My dad was there. He was demonstrating how to jump off a cliff at a lake near my house: "The higher up you jump from, the stiffer you must make your body as you hit the water." And then he demonstrated it for me, jumping from the top of a high cliff, a cliff that was not nearly as high as the one I was falling from. Just before he hit the water, he brought his arms up above his head and straightened out his legs completely, keeping them together. His body cut right through the water like a knife. I remembered waiting and waiting for him to emerge from the water. "Daddy! Daddy! Daddy!" I kept yelling for what seemed like an eternity, my eyes fixed on the water below, looking for any sign of life. And, out of nowhere, my dad snuck up and grabbed me in a big hug while at the same time yelling, "Got you, T!" I was so mad at him that I refused to jump. I never had an opportunity to show him I could do it. Maybe now, this jump could be some sorta redemption. He might not have been here to witness it, but I would know that I did it.

The water was getting closer. The air was getting cooler. The mist was picking up. We were going so fast now that we were making a high-pitched whistle that quickly grew into a bloodcurdling scream.

"Stiffen your body, T," I began to tell myself, taking every ounce of strength to say this, let alone do this. I started with my legs. My left leg straightening. Now my right leg. This began to slow our tumble but not our speed. Now, bringing my legs together. Slowly, painfully I was able to bring them together. And now that we were more erect and more aerodynamic, more speed followed. There was no way I'd be able to straighten my arms above my head with the creature on my back, so my legs would have to suffice.

Closer now. Closer. I could feel my body instinctively bracing for impact. Muscles stiffening. Brain processing. We were going to hit the surface any second. The creature on my back seemed to be oblivious. It was still focused on the task of killing me. Little did it know that it wouldn't have to because in three...two...one...

TORCH

GRAVE ENDING

My muscles braced for the impact with my legs cutting through the water first. Hitting the water at such a high rate of speed, I momentarily blacked out but somehow knew we were still descending rapidly. The creature didn't seem to be moved at all by the impact or our rapid descent as its claws were still fully digging into my back. This didn't feel like ordinary water. It seemed somewhat thicker. Water, yes, but heavier. And then I realized something…We weren't descending because of our momentum from falling from such a great height. No, we were now being pulled down, further and further under the surface of the water. As if we were free-falling in midair, now we were free-falling underwater, flipping and twisting, over and over again. Picking up momentum, we were being pulled further and further down into an abyss of total darkness. Trying as hard as I could, I strained to stop spinning and sinking, but it was no use. We were building up speed, and had we not hit the bottom, we would still be tumbling. Crashing into the bottom at that rate of speed, we found ourselves rocketed into an underwater thicket, scratching and scraping us as we fell deeper into it. Still, my pursuer was attached, trying to carry out its mission.

It was completely dark. I had a creature on my back trying to kill me. Every part of my body hurt. I was trapped under a thicket pile, and I was running out of air. *I guess this is it*, I thought to myself once again. *This is the way I'm going to go out. Well, if so, this is a pretty epic way to go out.* I guess at moments like this, you're supposed to remember the good ole days. Back when life was kind and fun, and everybody you loved was still alive. You're supposed to remember faces and sweet sayings and the smell of your favorite home-cooked meal. Oh, and the light. You're supposed to go toward the light, which I desperately wanted to do but, since I was stuck, I guess I had to hope the light would come toward me. And…wait a minute. I saw it. In the pitch blackness, I saw it. The light. *I'll be with you in no time, Grammy and Grampy.* The light was slowly getting closer, illuminating the water around me. What the…

As the light got closer, it began to expose the thorns that had trapped me for what they really were…bones. All around me, I could see that I was surrounded by thousands of bones that seemed to go on infinitely. *I must be in between two worlds,* I thought. Some sort of transition between this life and the next. The light was so close now; it wouldn't be long. I'm ready.

Wait! What was that? Something moved behind the light. This isn't how it's supposed to be when you die. No one and nothing is supposed to get in the way of the light. Whatever it was, it made a dive right for us into the pile of bones. Sharp teeth on an oversized "fish" came crashing through the first few layers of bones, but the bones didn't stop it. It backed up and charged again and again and again, sending layer after layer of bones flying every which way. Still, the creature on my back clung tightly. My newest assailant, besides gigantically sharp teeth, had long fins that protruded out so long that it used them like hands and began using these fins to clear away the bones directly over us. Still trapped by the weight of the bones pressing down on me, I was helpless. I was going to witness my death. May it be swift.

Only a few more layers and the creature above me would be able to do what the creature below me could not. By now, this beast was enraged by how hard having to work for its supper was. With renewed urgency, it viciously attacked the pile. The floor beneath me began to shake from its fury. On the bright side, my sheer terror helped me forget about that all-important bodily function called breathing. Be it from fear or lack of oxygen, my mind was spinning.

Spinning. Spinning. The creature was getting closer. Spinning. Spinning. The creature was almost on top of me now. Spinning. Spinning. I could hear its teeth clamping down over and over again in anticipation of dinner. Spinning. Spinning. The claws still dug into my back. Spinning. Spinning. My mind was spinning. Or was it?

Spinning was quickly giving way to clarity. Darkness was slowly giving way to light. *But how? I should be dead, or I'm about to die*, I thought. But that's when I saw it. Getting closer, like in the cave, the torch was the source of light, and the closer it got to me, the sharper my mind became. I watched it slowly alight on the bottom of the lake floor, just outside of my grip. With the creature's weight bearing down on me, it was impossible to move, reach over, and get it. I strained as the creature strained. I groaned as the creature neared. Only one layer more, and that would be it. Think, think, think. I had only one shot, and I had no idea if it would work, but it was my only chance. *Wait for it*, I told myself. *Easy...Not yet...*

Now! I commanded my body. The creature had broken through the last layer of bones, and the pressure on top of me eased just slightly. I extended my hand as far as possible and felt the familiar handle of the torch. Immediately, power began to surge through my body. Warmth flooded my cells. My mind was ready. My body nearly ready. With the teeth of the creature ready to demolish me, I felt the water around me begin to swirl and swirl. I have no idea how it happened but the swirls, like that of a tornado, put a barricade between myself and the sharp teeth. The teeth were still chomping, trying to get to me, but couldn't touch me, further infuriating the creature. It was time to leave this creature and its graveyard.

Ready to fight against the force that pulled us down to the bottom of the lake, I held the torch straight up and pushed off the bottom with all my might. And like that, we began to rise faster and faster, leaving the lake creature frustrated as it fruitlessly chomped at my heels. As fast as we had free-fallen from the mouth of the cave was as fast, no, faster, as we were ascending. Faster and faster, I rose the torch ablaze in my hand, leading the way upward through the thick water. We were gaining speed even as we broke through the surface of the water and into the cold night air, our momentum propelling us not only out of the water but high into the air in an arc. Water and light mingled, making it look like a geyser shooting out a comet. What a sight I must have been, careening through the air with a torch ablaze in my hand and a creature on my back after shooting out of the water. Tumbling out of the sky toward the shore on one side of the lake, we came down very hard and very ungracefully. (Degree of difficulty points were off the charts. Style points were not.)

Crashing down into the mud, the last thing I remembered was that I could breathe and that I was alive. And with that, my mind faded off in the coolness of the dark night air.

TORCH

ROAR

As dawn broke, I found myself face down in the mud on the shore beside the lake. I saw the torch a few feet away, and after painfully extricating myself from the mud, I got up to retrieve it. Grabbing the handle, I felt an immediate warmth come over my body. I sat back down on the ground a little way from where I had landed, stuck the end of the torch in the mud, and then huddled up to it like a campfire. My clothes began to dry almost immediately, and I began to allow myself the luxury of processing all that had taken place in the recent history of my life. From getting chased in the woods and seeing my mom dragged off to the mines by the Chaos to my time with the oversized rat, Keith, to getting chased through the tunnels by the Offspring, to seeing Keith get mauled by the Offspring, to fighting the Offspring and finally, my latest challenge at the bottom of the lake. Once again, I was lost deep in thought, trying to figure it out. In front of me, the torch also seemed deep in thought as it lay on the ground, slowly pulsating. It would let out the occasional crackle as if letting me know it was there. I sat there for some time thinking, remembering, blaming, justifying. I felt tears well up in the corner of my eyes…

My thoughts were interrupted, however, by the faint sound of a twig being broken in the distance. My ears were on full alert. I sat there still, preening my ears to figure out what or who was approaching. More twigs breaking. The shuffling of feet. It getting closer, I heard a loud crack as a large branch broke under someone or something's weight. I jumped when I heard it. They/it were/was too close for me to run now. I quietly laid down and pretended to be dead.

Whispers came from the direction of the breaking limbs.

"Shhhhhhh...Watch where you're walking!" came the first voice. It sounded like an older man, maybe my dad's age but with a raspy voice that bordered on a low growl.

"I didn't mean to," came a not so whispered response. This sounded like a boy about my age, also with a raspy voice but not nearly as low.

"Where did you say you saw the flying torch creature?" came the older first voice again.

I was laying on the shore of the lake, down a slight incline that was made through erosion of the lake water. That being the case, I couldn't be seen unless you got almost all the way down to the water's edge.

"Up there, by the water," came the younger, again not so whispered, response.

Laying even more still than before, I tried to mask my breathing, which, in turn, caused my breathing to be more labored. I was about to meet the whispering duo, whether I liked it or not.

The ground shook slightly as the pair made their way down the shore where I laid.

The duo stopped to investigate something in the tall grass. I couldn't see them from my vantage point and only knew that because of their conversation.

"What is it?" the younger voice asked.

"It's what they call an Offspring," came the reply.

"Not that. I know what *that* is. Everyone knows what that is. But what is wrong with it? It looks dead," came the perplexed younger voice.

"Indeed, it does. Indeed, it does," said the older voice thoughtfully.

"I...I...I've never seen a dead one before. I didn't even know they could die," came the excited and trembling reply.

"Well, it seems as though you were wrong. We were both wrong. They can die. That is a good thing," a somewhat terse tone came from the other voice.

The duo was so enraptured by a dead Offspring that it took them a minute to notice me. After thoroughly looking over the dead carcass of the Offspring, making doubly and triply sure that it was, in fact, dead, they finally realized that I was lying there.

"There…" said the younger voice, "the flying torch creature I told you I saw!" no longer whispering.

I could feel them coming toward me. Slight vibrations on the ground. They smelled like an unusual mix of grass, dew, and power. If power had a smell, this was it. Confidence was coming toward me. I kept my eyes closed as they inspected me. Not sure what they were, I felt something poking me in my rib cage. Like a finger. A human finger. They sounded human enough. Maybe they would be friendly and might be able to help me find my mom.

"I think it's breathing," said a cautious younger voice. "Hey, are you alive?" it asked, poking me much harder in the rib cage with a powerful finger.

I just laid there motionless, not sure if I was about to be somebody else's breakfast or not.

"I asked, '*Are you alive?*'" the somebody asked, with a slight roar in its throat that was loud enough to shake the ground.

This time there was a much harder jab in my rib cage. Like a fist. A human fist. It hurt. Like cracking my ribs kinda hurt.

"*Hey! Hey! Hey!*" came a roar. Its face was next to my head, and its hair was tickling my face. The rumbling and tickling caused me to slightly crack my eyes.

"Ha, I knew it. I knew you were alive!" came the excited response of the younger creature. "Can I eat him?" the younger voice asked his partner.

With that, I was done playing dead. I sat straight up and reached for the torch. No sooner had I sat up than a powerful hand pinned down my arm. And then another powerful hand pinned down my other arm. This was no human. At least not all of it.

On top of me was a very strong creature with the upper body, chest, arms, and abs of a human. A human possibly my age. But that is where the similarities stopped. At its neck and waist, this creature transitioned smoothly from being human to looking like a lion. Around its face was a majestic/messy mane of hair which was dark brown. Its face was lightly covered with tan fur. It was so light-colored that it could almost pass for being fur-free with slightly human features. Its mouth tried, in vain, to hide sharp white teeth (why do they always have sharp teeth?) ready to devour me. The ears were on top of its head, again lionlike. The hands that gripped my arms were strong. Like human hands, just much, much more powerful. The knuckles on each hand were calloused as well from who knows what. The legs were not human; they were lionlike all the way. And then, there was the tail. I caught glimpses of it swaying from side to side on either side of the creature. It mostly sounded like a perfect mix of lion and human when it talked, not that I've talked to a lion before.

Now he just stood over me, pinning me to the ground and checking me out. He was just waiting on his partner's cue.

"*Whoa*!" roared his partner, chuckling. "Let's not eat him yet."

This lionesque creature was clearly older than the one on top of me. His face looked more like a man than a boy, and he had a beard of light tan fur masterfully trimmed on his taught face. His arms and chest radiated power. Every muscle was perfectly etched on his upper body. But more than the muscles and facial hair, the most outstanding feature of his was craftily camouflaged on his back...*wings*. Long graceful wings, which started just below his shoulders and flowed down his back and stopped around his tail. They seemed to have a mind of their own, too. A power, like it was all this creature could do to keep them under control. They were meant for flight. They were anxious to soar.

My eyes were big, and my heart was about to burst through my chest. Struggling was not an option.

"Easy there, fella," the older one continued. I couldn't tell if that was for the beast on top of me or me. "We aren't going to eat you."

"Ya, relax," chimed the younger one on top of me. "We're not going to hurt you. Now, I'm going to take my paws off of you, but please don't run," he pleaded with me.

As soon as he released his grip, I quickly sat up and pushed away from the beast. This gave me a better view of them both. One was clearly bigger than the other. They were the most breathtaking creatures I'd ever encountered. They exuded confidence. Their countenance was regal. They were both ferocious and kind. Safe and dangerous. I took a deep breath.

"Milky white. Man, are you a milky white?" said the smaller one. "What is your name?" he asked.

"You can call me that for now. Milky White," I replied with a tone of cautiousness.

"Ah, I see. A cover name," said the smaller one with a slight chuckle/roar. "My name is Judah, not a cover name, and that is my dad. I call him Dad, but you can call him Roaring Lion," he said with a roaring laugh as he emphasized, "Roaring Lion."

"Don't listen to him, Milky White. My name is Sampson. Not a cover name. Just Sampson," the older one said.

"How did you get here? How did you kill that Offspring? Where are you going? Are you the One?" asked Judah.

"The One?" I asked, confused.

And before I knew it, Sampson had grabbed Judah in one of his large hands and marched him a little way from me so I'd be out of earshot, which would have been the case if not for the randomly raised excitement in their voices.

Whisper, whisper, whisper. Paw movements. More whispering. More paw movements. Traces of snarls and growls mixed with whispers. I found myself briefly enjoying the scene. A few hours ago, I was fighting for my life. Now, I was witnessing a father and son, hybrid human-lion flying creatures, having a "private" discussion, not unlike some I'd had with my own father. Life is strange.

"But what if…" I heard Judah say, trying to conceal his excitement.

Sampson kept shaking his maned head and speaking softly enough that I couldn't hear him, but his expressions, however, spoke volumes. Even now, while whispering, the hushed tones rumbled out of Sampson's mouth, causing the ground beneath me to shake slightly each time he spoke. The only thing I clearly heard him say was the word *ligo* when referring to Judah. It came across as a nickname or a term of lion-man endearment.

"Just think what this could mean…" Judah was pleading. "Just imagine."

After a minute more of private discussion, Sampson and Judah made their way back to where I was sitting.

"We have some more questions for you," Sampson started.

"A lot more questions," Judah interrupted with a slight snarl, pointing a finger at me. Sampson shot him a look, and Judah quickly put his hand down and looked away sheepishly.

"Yes, a lot more questions," Sampson continued, "but you are not safe here. We are not safe here. We took a chance coming down here this morning. The sun will be up soon, so we must leave right away." Sampson said this with urgency in his voice, the ground shaking. This time when he spoke, it appeared as if I could see the air moving as a wall of vibrations rattled my ears.

I had only just met these two, so I was a bit wary of them. How to know if I could trust them? I leaned over and picked up the torch. This would help me think. The sun was quickly breaking through the dawn haze, and as it normally does, it went from dawn to daylight in the blink of an eye. I looked at the father-and-son duo who I just met. How do I know if I can trust them?

As Sampson paced back and forth in front of me, he was getting more and more anxious, staring up at the sky. Whatever it was that scared this mighty creature, it must be something very nasty.

"We need to go now!" Sampson roared at me. I noticed that Judah was looking around intently, too, and now appeared to be shaking.

"Now!" roared Sampson. His voice was completely shaking the ground now.

It wasn't the only thing shaking the ground.

TORCH

TO THE SKY

The rumbling grew in an instant, and without warning, a swarm came up from the belly of the lake. I turned my head toward the sound, and what I saw was the thing of nightmares. No. Worse than nightmares. It was like a volcano spewing lava, but instead of lava, it was a swarm of what appeared to be spiders with wings and large stingers. The sun was up, and these creatures were hungry.

"Judah, get them to chase you to buy us some time and then head for the woods," Sampson roared to his son. With that, Judah sprinted away in the direction of the woods but along the shore of the lake to our left.

"*Now!*" roared Sampson again.

With the swarm coming toward us, Sampson sprinted to where I stood, grabbed me, and in one fluid motion, threw me on his back. He was moving even before I grabbed onto his massive mane. We were off, and once again, the chase was on.

It didn't take us long to catch up with Judah, but neither did it take the swarm. By now, their buzzing was deafening. Swooping down from the sky, they were right on our tail, literally. Judah was still off to our left but now running in our direction away from the shore of the lake with the main swarm following him.

Sampson and I were closing in on a thick grove of trees, so thick it looked like a wall of darkness. Where the trees started, the light ended. We were about to enter the woods when we both heard it at the same time. A roar/scream coming from behind us. It was the roar of a wounded animal mixed with the cry of a boy. Judah. Turning and sliding to a stop in one lightning-fast motion, Sampson turned around, and we both saw Judah batting a creature off his back with one of his powerful hands. The damage had been done, however, as a large stinger was lodged in his back near his tail. He began to stumble toward us, with more of the spiders closing in on him.

"*Noooooooo!*" roared Sampson. He raised up on his hind legs and threw me off. Turning to me, Sampson yelled, "*Run to the woods!*"

Everything was happening so fast now. Just a minute ago, we were sitting on the shore of the lake, exchanging pleasantries; now, we were fighting for our lives. I landed on my bum, and before I could jump to my feet, I saw Sampson do what I can imagine only fathers would do when their child's life is on the line: he bounded faster and faster down the shore toward his impaled son as the spiderlike creatures closed in for the kill. Sampson shot through them with a mighty roar. He first ran through them and then took to the sky in a powerful, breathtaking arc. The spiders were in pursuit, their attention now fully on Sampson. Streaking upward, he was flying so fast now that he appeared to be glowing. The air trailing him was on fire. Further and further away he flew, the swarm of spiders still following. He was nearing the waterfall, and suddenly, he turned abruptly and headed straight for the swarm.

"*Run!*" he roared at me so loudly you'd thought he was standing right beside me.

Turning to run, I heard a whimper from behind me. For a brief moment, I had forgotten about Judah. He was trying to move but couldn't. He was dying. There was froth forming around his mouth, and his face was beginning to darken. With the sound of Sampson's voice still reverberating in my ears, I turned my head back and forth from Judah to the safety of the forest. I could make it to the woods easily before the swarm got to me but...

In an instant, I found myself at Judah's side. His whimpering had turned into a dull moaning roar. I noticed the stinger had changed the color of his skin to a dark purple and gray all around the entry point. It was still releasing poison. I had to get it out of him. I grabbed hold of it with both hands, the spikes of the stinger digging into my hands. I pulled up as hard as I possibly could. No use. I tried again. No use. Again and again, the spikes rip my hands to shreds. No use. I knelt down beside this boy-cub. His breathing was now laboring under the effects of the poison that was coursing through his body. I felt helpless. I felt tears. I felt the handle of the torch. *When will I learn?* I asked myself. My hands suddenly felt perfectly normal. In fact, they felt powerful. Once again, I reached for the stinger but with one hand this time. The other hand held onto the torch. Gripping the end of the stinger, I pulled straight up, and the stinger came out slowly, grabbing tiny pieces of flesh. Judah gave an extra moan as the tip slid out of his skin. I threw the stinger off to the side and listened. Judah wasn't breathing. He wasn't breathing. I was too late. He risked his life for me. He died for me. My head dropped along with my heart for a brief moment.

I don't know which I heard first, the buzzing of the swarm or Judah taking a breath. One was terrifying; the other was comforting. Judah was alive! Barely. But he was alive, and so was the swarm chasing Sampson.

"*Run!*" came the panicked roar from the sky.

Torch in one hand, I bent down and grabbed one of Judah's arms. I don't know how I did it, but I leaned my shoulder down toward the ground and bent my knees. In an instant, I had this boy-cub draped over my shoulders, and we were sprinting toward the darkness. Sampson was closing in on us from just overhead. His velocity was so great that the air ahead of him was driving so fast that Judah and I were being pushed along even faster. It was as if we were running on air. I'd never experienced this sensation.

We were on top of the woods now, and the darkness stood before like a thick, pitch-black curtain. And, as if on cue, we hit the darkness and lost our footing. Tumbling in the darkness at a high rate of speed, I lost my grip on Judah. He rolled on the ground ahead of me like a rag doll, limbs flipping and flopping over and over again. We tossed and turned what seemed like forever, finally stopping not too far from one another. We landed far from the light of the lake. We landed in complete darkness, save the light from my torch.

TORCH

JUNGLE FEVER

Catching my breath, I sat in the darkness, trying to collect my thoughts. In other words, I was trying to figure out my next move. Here I was, in a pitch-black forest just feet away from a lion-boy hybrid creature that may very well be dead. I wasn't sure what happened to Sampson. I was hoping he made it to the trees before the swarm, but right now, there was no sign of him. In the torchlight, I could see Judah's body lying there, still, unmoving. Or was it?

I got up and made my way over to investigate. Yes, he was breathing, but it was very shallow. He was sweating. He radiated heat. The poison wasn't done with him yet. He had a fever that would've killed most people, but Judah was fighting it. Not sure if he was conscious or not and not knowing what creatures might be lurking in these woods, I whispered to him.

"Judah, I'm here right beside you. It's going to be okay. You're going to be okay. Just rest and try to relax," I said to him, mostly for my sake rather than his. I wondered if he could hear the doubt in my voice. I wasn't sure that it was going to be okay. I wasn't sure of anything right now. I sat down, torch in hand, and just waited. I don't know what I was waiting for, but I didn't know what else to do. Waiting and waiting. Watching and waiting. I felt my eyes get heavier and heavier. I didn't realize how tired I was until this moment. It was like I was being lulled to sleep. I stuck the torch in the ground beside me and allowed myself to close my eyes for a few minutes. *Just a few minutes*, I told myself. *That will help me think of my next move.* Darkness. Sleep.

I don't know how long I was asleep. What I did know was that I had dreams. Broken flashes of memories of a not too distant past. Faces that I remembered like my mom's and dad's. Faces that I tried to remember, like my older brother's and my little sister's, but couldn't. Trying to bring their faces into clarity, all I saw was a void, no facial features, just a haze. It was like my brain willfully blurred out their faces. I tried to recall their voices or stories we shared. All I remembered was my brother's back as he left our house a few months before the raid. My mom seemed so proud. "He's going to fight," she would say in an almost reverent tone. That was all I could remember. So now, my dreams were more frustrating than fruitful. They begged more questions than answers. More confusion than clarity.

A low-moaning rumble woke me. My brain slowly began to process the sound, which woke me from my slumber. It was Judah. He was saying something, but I couldn't understand him. He was still hot, but he was no longer sweating. His breathing also appeared to be less labored. He needed something. He roared and moaned again. I got closer to listen.

"Waaaer," he mumbled. "Waaaer."

Water? That must be it. The poison and the fever combined to make him extremely parched.

"Judah," I said, "I'll be right back. I'm going to get you some water," not sure where on earth I would find water in this dense forest.

I picked up the torch and, with a glance back at the sprawled-out lion-boy, began my search, knowing that his life depended on it. I let the torch lead the way. The forest may have been thick and dark, but when my eyes adjusted, I could see that this forest was actually filled with all kinds of wonders. The trees themselves were bigger than any I'd ever seen. Wider than a house and so tall you couldn't even think about seeing the tops. Each tree was covered with a bark that seemed almost velvety, and each was a slightly different shade of dark brown. The branches were high up as well, and the only thing on the forest floor that I had to navigate around were the trunks of the trees and the roots that fanned out in all directions. I also saw an occasional creature scurrying along the ground. These creatures were quite curious to look at and not in the least bit interested in me. Some had funny round-shaped bodies with oversized eyes and thousands of little legs whisking them here and there in an erratic path. Some were brown, sticklike insects with comical-looking eyebrows highlighting squinty eyes and long arms and legs that made them appear to glide across the ground. Others appeared to be more reptilelike: frog-snake-looking hybrid creatures that intermittently slid and hopped. These creatures were different shades of dark blue. It seemed as if this forest that had appeared dead was actually full of life. Strange and wonderful-looking life, but life, nonetheless.

The torch and I trekked through trees, around the massive trunks, and over gigantic roots. I was still trusting the instincts of the torch to guide me, but I was so concerned with looking down that I had failed to look up. I was so intent on not losing my footing as well as looking at these new fascinating creatures that I was oblivious to the wonder all around me.

Climbing over an especially large root, I slipped, and my feet came out from under me, causing me to fall down hard. I was flat on my back when I saw the "up wonder" for the first time. One here, one there. My eyes began to focus. Another one. And another. And another. Hundreds, no, thousands. All around me, tiny lights were appearing. Flying lights. As I focused, I realized that these creatures were kinda like light bugs, but with tiny little flames coming off them. They weren't flickering randomly as light bugs do, but their embers were purposefully glowing. They reminded me of the fairies that my mother used to tell me about at bedtime. Tiny wings fluttering, they were all dancing in the air around me, filling the darkness with a beautiful warm glow. As I stood to my feet, I held out my hand to the nearest one, and it floated into my open palm. It was warm, but it did not burn me. It simply danced, and as it danced, it acted like a toddler trying desperately to communicate something to me but unable to articulate it. I just stared, mesmerized. *What was it trying to tell me?* I thought. Looking back up, I saw the other flames coming together. They were dancing in unison, thousands of them stretching out before me like they were beckoning me to follow them. I glanced at the torch. It was gleefully dancing as well as if it had met its long-lost relatives. Rhythmically pulsating, the fire fairies lead me down a pathway that glowed with light. Following the lights around more trunks and over more roots, we trekked deeper still into the forest. And then the trees gave way to ground cover and low-lying bushes. The air held the smell of rain, of water. The ground had changed from being dirt to mud. Water must be nearby. And it was.

The terrain began to slope slightly downhill as the fire fairies parted. They had led me to a stream. A beautiful stream with cool, clear water flowing in it. It was illuminated by a warm white incandescent glow. It was both dreamlike and magical. The bank along the stream housed fantastic otherworldly flowers along with other aquatic plant life. A group of about a dozen or so flowers that stood about knee height looked like dandelions. They also looked like they were singing in unison, and a faint sound like a high-pitched choir was coming from their direction. They bobbed and swayed from side to side and up and down as they sang. Lily pads were floating on top of the water near a group of extremely tall cattails, twice as tall as me. The lily pads were a typical color green, but each had a face and a purple lily flower just off the center of the face at the top of the pad. It was as if the flower had been placed in its "hair" even though it didn't have any hair. Dotting the bank on both sides of the stream were flowers of different heights, each with distinctive features. Some had skinny stems and oversized petals. Some had thick stems and petals so small you could barely tell they had any. All were colored in dazzling tints and hues.

And there were unusual creatures there too. On the banks, in the overhanging tree branches, and even in the water. The first creature that caught my eye, though, took my breath away. It was a regal-looking stag with the most luxurious-looking white coat of hair. Set atop its head was a beautiful pair of antlers that were a brilliant metallic silver, and, on its back, flowing like a robe, were feathery white wings. Beside it was an almost identical smaller stag. A momma and her baby stag. Both were drinking from the stream when I approached its edge. Both looked up when they saw me, and to my surprise, it looked like they bowed toward me, with the momma directing the baby to bow. There were other creatures as well along the bank enjoying the cool, clear water. A bright yellow monkey with a bulbous nose and the feet of a kangaroo was talking to its reflection and making faces. A family of beaver-duck hybrids floated down the stream excitedly, enjoying a family outing. They had the upper bodies of beavers but the legs and tails of a duck. Each member of this family was distinctly colored: one red, one green, one blue, one purple, one pink. And as they talked/quacked, they all changed color, with no one being the same color as the others at the same time. It was positively gorgeous. Yes, I just said that a family of beaver-duck hybrids that change colors are gorgeous. On a tree limb that hung out over the stream laid a creature that was part cat and part skunk. The head and torso were like a cat, and the limbs and tail were like a skunk. It was mostly white with a black streak running down its back and tail. All four legs were also black. It was lying on the branch facedown, with its legs dangling from both sides of the branch. Clearly, it was taking a nap and a good one, based on the sonorousness of its purring. Looking into the water, I saw even more creatures. Multicolored fish with arms and hands that waved in my direction as they swam past (instinctively, I waved back). Fat round white fish with polka dots of every color bobbed up and down and appeared to smile at me when they passed by. I guess they had eyes, but it was hard to tell because of both their roundness and their polka dots. It was so mesmerizing I could stay here all day! In fact, I felt like I was in a trance. Like a fever had come over me. Creatures bowing and waving and smiling at me! It was like they had put a spell on me. Or was it just my imagination?

A tiny flame suddenly started to dance in front of my face. It seemed to come out of nowhere. I tried to look past it until I realized this little fire fairy meant business, and by business, I mean that it danced its way through the air and right into my unkempt bangs on my forehead. It took a second before I realized what was happening. Yes, my hair was on fire! Not a towering inferno, but on fire nonetheless. I quickly smacked myself in the forehead repeatedly until the burning sensation stopped. That's enough to wake you out of a trance. The little fire fairy danced back in front of my face and did some little cocky move as if to say, "Got him!"

My bangs were still smoldering when I heard the cry. Faint, low, rumbling. A cry of distress. *Judah!* I chastised myself, suddenly remembering the sick lion-boy and why I was at the stream in the first place…*water!*

Looking around in a panic, I suddenly realized that I didn't have anything to carry water in. How was I supposed to take water back to him? "Think!" I berated myself. What to do? No shells. No rocks with indentations deep enough to carry water in. I had my torch in my hand, but what good would that do in getting water? I decided to stick it in the ground for a moment while I searched for something to carry water in. With the torch firmly in the ground, I turned toward the water and allowed my right hand to swing freely. As I took a step toward the water, I felt something fall at my feet. The bloody rag! I had it wrapped around the handle of the torch, and it became stuck to my hand, but I didn't even realize it was still there. What if I could carry water in it? Could it hold? Only one way to find out.

I walked over to the water's edge, and, with quite a crowd of onlookers, I rinsed the rag as best as I could. This only removed a little dirt. The bloodstains were still there, along with the name, *Sabre*. For some reason now, when I saw this name, I got a slight chill. The hair on the back of my neck stood up. That didn't matter right now, though. What did matter was whether or not this rag could hold water. I folded it in half and made a little trough out of the fabric. I plunged it under the water. A round white polka-dotted fish scattered while the other creatures around the river's edge appeared to be looking on curiously. I brought it up, and it seemed to work. I held it there for a moment to see if it would hold…It did. I dunked it under once again to make sure I could get the most water possible and then made a crude knot with the remaining fabric. Now, to get back to Judah.

I turned around quickly and grabbed the torch. The dancing fire fairies fanned out before me, making a pathway for me to follow. They were leading me back to Judah. I ran at breakneck speed, wondering why I hadn't paid attention to them the *whole* way down to the stream. Never mind. Right now, I had to get back to Judah. "Alright, torch, let's see what you got!" And like a comet streaking across the night sky, we took off through the dark woods. Hopefully, Judah was still alive.

TORCH

LIKE A BOSS

As I ran, I heard more groaning roars coming from Judah. With each step, these groans grew louder and more frequent. The rumbling began to shake the ground. I had no idea where I was, but the dancing fire fairies seemed to be leading me right back to Judah. Running now as fast as my feet would move, I moved in concert with the torch, weaving my way, once again, around massive tree trunks and over their equally massive roots. Every few steps, I was reminded of the precious cargo I was carrying as the water in the bloody rag would slosh, and a trickle of water would run down my hand. I had to be getting closer.

The roaring increased. My speed remained steady. Over, around, up, down, moving, jumping. The dancing flames were still leading the way. Further and further from the white incandescent light of the stream, it was now very dark but for my torch and the dancing flames. More roaring and moaning. More ground shaking. I was almost there.

Running at top speed, water in one hand, torch in the other, I rounded the trunk of one of the massive trees and stopped in my tracks. Ahead of me, I saw Judah's body right where I'd left him, but he wasn't alone. The dancing flames began to surround Judah and the other creature with light. Another roar broke my momentary trance and shook the ground so violently it caused my knees to buckle. I steadied myself and waited for another roar. The next roar did knock me down. Trying to stand to my feet, I looked in the direction of the beast. My heart skipped a beat. It was Sampson.

The fire fairies flooded the surrounding area where Judah still lay. Cautiously, I approached him, anticipating yet another ground-shaking roar. It didn't happen. Judah's eyes were open. He appeared to be breathing. He wasn't sweating. Sampson stood over him, watching him and keeping an eye out for any would-be enemies. Momentarily, this included me. The flames dancing around him made Sampson look even more intimidating, more ferocious, and more regal now. It was like he was glowing red-hot with his hulking mane being silhouetted in the fire's light. Whereas Judah's breathing was calm, Sampson's was heavy but not from physical exertion. No, his breathing came from a place where emotion intersects with thoughts. A place deep down in the depths of the soul. I watched him breathing in and out, his muscles in his chest and arms flexing, veins bulging through his skin. *I don't want to be on Sampson's bad side, ever*, I thought to myself.

And then our eyes locked. Sampson, blinded by his emotions, hadn't noticed me standing there until now. He looked like he wasn't sure how to react to my presence. He began to shake. His mighty fists balled up. He looked at me and then at Judah. And finally, he spoke.

"*Why?*" he roared at me, trying to keep his composure. "*Why did you save my boy, my ligo?*" Sampson was still flexing, and his breathing was still labored. "*I told you to run, and yet you stopped to save him!*" he roared. Both the ground and my knees were shaking even though I was trying to be brave, trying to be confident. It wasn't working. I couldn't look Sampson in the eyes at that moment. They were too fierce. He continued, "*You...*" he stammered, "you...you risked your life to save him. You could have been killed. You should have been killed. You both should have. And yet..." Sampson's voice trailed off as he looked down at his son. And the mighty warrior standing in front of me wept as viciously as he fought. Muscles relaxing, body convulsing. Sniffles mixed with the low rumbling of a roar. This was coming from a place that only a parent can know or understand. To fear your child is dead. To see it happen in front of your eyes. To know that you were the one who put him in that position, in harm's way. And then to discover he is alive! That is the emotion of heaven. It is otherworldly.

I moved slowly toward the father and son. As I approached them, Sampson fell to his knees and picked up Judah's head in his powerful hands. He began repeating softly, tenderly, "My *ligo liontári*. My *ligo liontári*."

Judah looked up at his dad. They shared a moment. They shared a smile.

What do you say in a moment like this? You don't say anything. At least I didn't. I couldn't. I just stood there, reverently, still holding the torch and the water. The flames continued their dance. Father and son just sat in silence.

It was Judah that broke the silence and welcomed me into the "moment."

"Water?" he asked, his voice scratchy from being parched. "Milky White, did you get the water?"

Sampson snapped his head up in anticipation of my response.

Stepping forward, I held up the bag of water. "Yes," I said, barely above a whisper. "It's right here," I finished, feeling overcome with emotion myself now. I brought the water over and, with Sampson holding Judah's head, I poured the water into the boy-cub's mouth.

I took a step back after Judah had finished drinking the water to look him over to see if there were any visible signs of the poison. The entry wound was mostly healed. His skin color had almost returned to normal. His tail was moving every so often as cats do without even thinking about it. It appeared that the worst was over.

"What now?" I asked Sampson.

"Now, we need to get moving," he replied, still holding his son's head in his hands. "We've been very fortunate that we haven't had any more trouble, but we are not safe here, and the longer we're here, the more dangerous it becomes. Those creatures that attacked us are called Arachne. They tend to patrol when it is daylight, and the Offspring tend to patrol at night. They both report to the Chaos, and the Chaos reports to Antioch. Their sole duty is to seek and destroy and report back their findings. The Arachne and Offspring have been increasing in both their numbers and in their patrols. But they are just the first wave. There are more, far worse creatures that Antioch is sending our way."

"But where will we go?" I asked.

Looking down at Judah, Sampson responded, "There are some people that we know that will take you in. They have a safe house about a day's journey from here. Judah can recover there, and you can get some food and rest, but we must leave now."

"Can Judah make the journey?" I asked as I looked down on this lion-boy.

"I will carry him on my back. In fact, I will carry you both on my back," Sampson said with a wry smile. "How are you with heights?" he emphasized with a full, toothy grin.

TORCH

HEARING IN COLOR

I carefully laid Judah across Sampson's muscular shoulders. It was then that I noticed the deep scars on Sampson's back, no doubt from his most recent run-ins with the spider-wasps. Looking a little closer, though, I could see other scars peppered all over Sampson's body. These were older scars. Scars that told stories. Scabs, scrapes, and bruises that gave him character. Wounds that defined this magnificent creature, a warrior.

"Hop on!" Sampson roared. "We've got a journey ahead of us!"

Gripping the torch in my right hand, I flipped my left leg over Sampson about halfway down his back but just below his wings. I scooched forward on my bottom just a bit so that my knees rested just below his wings. I squeezed my legs as tightly as I could and braced my entire body for the takeoff. And take off we did! We took off so fast I wasn't as ready as I thought. I began to slide off to the torch-hand side of Sampson's back. Bouncing, bouncing, bouncing. I was leaning over one side and frantically trying to right myself. I could hear him laughing/roaring, knowing that he about knocked me off. I was able to quickly recover, and in no time, I settled in, my knees bracing extra hard now. I was ready for this journey...So I thought.

Running in the direction of the stream, we zigged our way around the massive tree trunks and over the equally massive roots. Surprisingly, Sampson's gait was smooth. It was like his body was one with the ground. I could imagine him running in the air. The fire fairies were once again leading the way, though I don't think that Sampson needed them. They acted more like a tunnel, lining either side of our pathway, cheering us on. Like when a bride and groom leave a wedding through a sea of well-wishers.

We slowed down to a stop as we got to the edge of the stream. Suddenly, as if out of thin air, all of the creatures that I had seen before at the stream had multiplied. There were two to three times as many of each. *And* other creatures I had not seen before. Magnificent creatures. Colors and claws. Polka dots and stripes. Wings, feathers, and fur. Chirps, screeches, croaks, meows, barks, moos, and neighs had changed the quiet stream that I had visited into a cacophony of sounds. Excitement charged the air. Some creatures were pawing at the ground, some were splashing the water, some were hitting rocks together, and some, with human hands, were clapping loudly. Vast combinations of creatures, all animal hybrids, were brilliantly displayed before me. Well, not before me. Before Sampson. And as if on cue, the noise stopped. The creatures bowed. They were in the presence of greatness.

Sampson had perched himself on top of a rock. There was a slight breeze blowing his mane, and in the ambient white light that flooded the area, he truly looked as if he were glowing. Sitting upright on his back, I wasn't sure whether or not to bow too. And then he spoke.

"Friends," he began, "the evil is growing stronger, and the Chaos is getting closer. You must be on your guard. Be aware of possible infiltrators that might be cloaked in your midst." A collective gasp came from the gathering of magnificent creatures. "If anything should happen, I want you to seek refuge in the Three Sisters mountain, a day's journey beyond the tree line to the north. There you will find refuge. I have urgent matters to attend to, and I must leave you for a time, but do not lose heart. The One is coming and is now here. This is the One that will defeat Antioch once and for all. The darkness will be defeated, and the light will triumph!"

With that, Sampson let out one of his signature roars, which sent the creatures back into their frenzied state of noise. We took off. No, we really took off.

One powerful step, two powerful steps, three powerful steps, and *wabam*! In an instant, Sampson's glorious wings unfurled like majestic sails, and we were no longer running on the ground; we were airborne!

We started following the stream, hovering just above the water. The coolness of the stream, though, gradually changed to the coolness of the sky as we began to rise higher and higher into the air. The stream got smaller, and the tops of the giant trees were now visible. We were really moving now with Sampson's powerful wings pushing against the wind and the three of us cutting through the air like a knife. As we crested the trees, I had to catch my breath. Ahead of us were mountains, majestic, towering mountains. The kind that you only dream about! Some had rounded tops, and some had craggily tops. Some had perfectly formed holes in the middle that went clear through to the other side. Some had snowy peaks; some were covered with color: red on one, yellow on another, and purple on others. There appeared to be creatures on them too! From our vantage point, we were too high up to make out features of any sort, but it looked like little towns and villages were dotted on throughout the various mountains. And up ahead, I saw a mountain with not one but three distinct female faces. The Three Sisters Sampson told the creatures about. Besides the facial features of the three sisters, there weren't any others noticeable about the mountain. The mountain was dark gray, and the stone looked like slate. I didn't see any movement on Three Sisters. No towns. Nothing. It looked quite dead compared to the surrounding mountains.

Up to this point, Sampson and I hadn't said a word to one another, not that you can talk with the wind whipping in your face and your cheeks suctioned tightly to your face. The wind was stinging my skin. My eyes were squinting and tearing up as the cold air whipped into my corneas. We were high up now, higher than the tops of the massive mountain structures. From our forward trajectory, we began to bank slightly. This turned our flight path directly toward Three Sisters. A large flock of strange-looking birdlike creatures flew just below us, and it sounded as if they were squawking encouragement to Sampson. They were long and skinny like a wiener dog and furry, like a lamb but with perfectly formed wings of a goose. White in color, they had the faces of ducks with startling blue eyes. Sampson gave them an acknowledging nod.

"*Hold on!*" Sampson said. Or did he? Did I just imagine he said it?

"Yes, you heard me say it," came Sampson's reply. "Now, *hold on!*"

My knees squeezed tighter on Sampson's midsection, and my hand squeezed the handle of the torch that much harder. And then, Sampson began to dive straight toward the Three Sisters mountain. We were flying faster than we had before, a combination of gravity and Sampson's power. With us picking up speed, I could no longer open my eyes for the rushing wind. I had to take short breaths through my nose. My nose and forehead felt like they were about to break off with the icy cold air pummeling us.

Eyes closed, I felt myself losing consciousness. Lack of oxygen mixed with hypothermia will do that to you. And then Sampson roared to me, his words cutting effortlessly through the wind. It was almost as if we were sitting next to each other at a park with no one else around.

"*Hold on! Don't force it. Don't fight it. Just hold on!*" Sampson's voice reverberated. "*Stop trying to see things with your eyes, the ones in your head, because you're only seeing an ounce of what's right in front of you!*"

Concentrating on Sampson's words, I began to listen. I strained my ears to hear through the whistling wind. *Concentrate!* I berated myself. And suddenly, as if lighting a match, I began to hear and see beyond the whistling wind and the darkness of my clenched eyes. *What? Blue. Blue everywhere.* I could hear it. I could hear the color blue. It was mimicking the cold air that surrounded us. It was a brilliant blue. One that sounded like a crisp cold clear day. I could taste it too. Water and ice, like eating snow, fresh, pure snow. The blues undulated, moving slightly from one hue to another. As the hues undulated, so did their sounds. A whistling, like a flute, moved into something that sounded lower pitched and more earthy but still beautiful. The taste also changed, going from the taste of fresh snow to the taste of raindrops on a spring day. It was incredible. I was flying at a high rate of speed on the back of a flying lion-man and listening and tasting colors. Wow! If my mouth wasn't closed tight by the pressure of the wind, I would've let out a yell.

"I know how you feel," came Sampson's voice, "I remember the first time that I experienced that. You will never *ever* see things the same again," with an emphasis on the word "ever."

Suddenly, without warning, the blues turned bloodred. The taste went from spring rain to sulfur. The sound went from whistling to shrieking.

"*Arachne!*" Sampson roared. I could tell by the air hitting my skin that we were getting closer to the ground, and my new vision told me that the sun was setting. If my sense of direction hadn't failed me, we were almost at Three Sisters.

"Not much further now," Sampson reassured me. Judah moaned, reminding me of the urgency of getting to Three Sisters. It also made me wonder if Judah could hear and taste in color too? And if so, was he aware of the Arachne? Did he know where we were going? These questions would have to wait. Back to the business of holding on for dear life.

My eyes were still closed because of the rushing wind still pounding my face, but my new vision had fully taken over. The bloodred I could hear was mixed with the grays of the slate mountain ahead of us. The smell of sulfur was now mixed with dirt and stone. I could taste it all at the same time. With us getting closer to Three Sisters, the grays and dirt seemed to be breaking through. Sampson appeared to be kicking into another gear as we surged downward. Reds and grays swirling in my head. The Arachne must not have been gaining on us, but neither were we losing them.

I could smell the reds and the grays, but the grays suddenly started turning darker and darker.

A demonic chorus roar rose up from the valley floor below us. It was a legion of the Chaos on the ground, destroying everything in their path and directing the action in the sky.

Instantly the sound of gray was exchanged for the sound of blackness. The taste of dirt for the taste of rotten meat.

"*Offspring!*" Sampson roared.

TORCH

SEEING IN COLOR

The wind pounding against my face finally eased enough for me to open my eyes. I should've kept them closed. It was twilight now. The perfect time of day for both the Offspring and Arachne to be looking for prey. Right now, we were the prey.

There was no place to go. Above us, the two sets of evil creatures came together to form a canopy over us. In front, the Offspring. Behind, the Arachne. Below us, the Offspring were swirling, and on either side of us, the Arachne were closing in. It was like we were caught in a net, and the evil was swallowing us up. The air was black and red. It smelled of sulfur and rotting flesh. My eyes and my lungs burned from the rancid smell. Once again, I was nauseous. Sampson, though, had not altered his course. We were still careening at a high rate of speed in what I believed to be the direction of Three Sisters.

Suddenly it was dark. Not because the sun had fully set, but because the air was thick with evil…evil creatures to be precise. Not sure from which direction it would come from, I was sure that a collision was imminent. A collision with the Offspring, the Arachne, the Three Sisters mountain, or all three simultaneously.

Initially, the evil appeared as one big mass, but now, as it pressed in around us, I could make out individual creature's features even in the darkness. The screeches were getting louder as if they were getting more excited to finally devour their prey. I was still trying not to pass out from it all: the smells, the sights, the sounds. And if I vomited in midair, going as fast as we were going, it would surely get all over me: my face, hair, body. I had no idea how we were going to get out of this.

Sampson, on the other hand, seemed as confident as ever, his massive wings pushing against the wretched air. I could also feel his muscles were tightening. He was bracing for impact. And he began to speak again.

"You are our only hope in getting out of this," he snarled. "You must do exactly what I tell you, and you must do it immediately, or we all die!" he snapped.

"I am ready; tell me what I need to do." However, I was not sure I was really ready.

"I'm going to dive down through the creatures, and as soon as I begin to dive, you *will* stand up on my back and hold your torch high. We will cut through the line using your torch. This is the only way we will survive!" he roared.

Wha, What? I thought. That escalated quickly.

"Don't think, trust! Your whole life has been lived on doing things that you can taste, touch, see, and feel. Now, you need to learn what faith really is. Get ready to stand up!" Sampson implored.

No sooner had he said it than he dove. Not straight down but angled sharply and heading toward the Offspring directly in front of the mountain.

It was enough for me not to fall off by simply sitting on Sampson's back. Stand up? No way! With our downward trajectory, the wind was cutting across us from both sides. Even Sampson's powerful wings were struggling to cut through the cross breeze. His whole body was shaking. And then, I saw the first line of the Offspring directly in front of us. As we sped toward them, they began to close in on all sides. Any second now, and they would overtake us.

"*Stand up, now!*" came the roar.

Stand? Stand up? What else did I have to lose? I pondered, *If I stand up, maybe, as Sampson said, maybe we have a chance to survive. Or I stay seated and watch my own death horribly, painfully play out before my own eyes.* Nobody ever achieved greatness by sitting around or playing it safe.

It was time to act. And as if on cue, I felt a surge go through my body. It was the torch prompting me to stand.

My knees were still pressed tight to Sampson's back. Putting my left hand on his back, I brought my right leg up. I was trembling. I leaned forward slightly and brought my left leg up. It was all I could do to steady myself to keep from somersaulting off Sampson's back. I was on my knees now, still shaking. My left hand was on Sampson's back, trying to both steady the rest of my body and make sure I didn't fly off. My right hand still held the torch. This would be much "easier" (not that anything would make it easier to stand up on the back of a flying lion-man hybrid in a downward trajectory with evil creatures about to eat you) if I didn't have to worry about the torch. But the reality was, I couldn't do this without the torch.

Tentatively, I put my left foot down. *Steady, steady*, I told myself.

"Stop thinking and trust!" Sampson roared.

Right foot now. *Steady, steady*, I told myself. I was squatting now.

"Overthinking this is going to be the death of us. Believe!" came the roar.

Closing my eyes, I took a deep breath. *You can do this, T!* I willed myself to believe.

Now! I screamed to myself. I shot up onto my feet, my left foot slightly in front of my right foot, my knees bent slightly. From this position, the crosswinds were even more severe. The wind, though, was the least of my problems, for we had reached the front lines of the Offspring.

"A little help here," Sampson snarled. On either side of his wings, a half dozen or more Offspring were zeroing in. Still trying to get my legs, I swung the torch toward the end of one wing and then the other. It did no good. The Offspring grabbed onto both of Sampson's wings. I heard a roar of pain come from the lion-man. It sent shivers down my spine to hear this warrior in agony. A half dozen creatures viciously attacked each wing. We began to slow down and then plummet out of the sky as more and more Offspring joined in, some on Sampson's wings and some on his head. Some had even jumped on Judah and were attacking him. Sampson's wings, covered in Offspring, were useless. We began to plummet. And then, as if an alarm went off, they closed in on me. Teeth, fangs, and claws came at me over and over again. We were still plummeting, falling out of the sky as I blocked blow after blow. To my right and my left, they came. Bashing one and burning another. There were too many of them. I felt my knees buckle. Initially, I thought it was from exhaustion and despair, but the shooting pain in my back could only mean that an Offspring had landed on my back. And then another joined it. And another. And another. My knees gave way to the weight of the Offspring, and I was now facedown on my stomach, four Offspring on my back, ripping and clawing my back to shreds. Trying desperately to think, I felt darkness overcome my thoughts. My mind was giving up. Somewhere in the recesses of my mind, though, my mother's face appeared in full clarity. She was instantly there, the way I remembered her before she was taken. And just as quickly, the flashes of her being taken by the Chaos in the woods that night, screaming in pain. Another flash of memory: my last remembrance of Keith. "*Go! Rescue them all!*" Keith yelled. An emotion I don't ever recall began to immediately sweep over me. Revenge? No, something deeper. *Purpose.* Purpose mixed with righteous anger. More than confidence. More than rage. A wave of holy anger began to well up inside of me. The evil that I had witnessed. The evil that surrounded me, no, more. Wrongs needed to be righted. Hurts needed to be healed. Evil needed to be eliminated. It had to begin now.

Clutching the torch in my right hand, I gripped it tighter, and once again, a surge of power came over me. A surge more powerful than any time before. Warmth rocketed through my body. I felt as if I was on fire, but I wasn't burning up. No, I was not on fire, but the Offspring on my back were. The smell of burning Offspring was horrible and sweet at the same time. On fire and dying, they started to tumble off my back and into the sea of Offspring behind me. The fire was so intense, fueled by the wind that every creature they careened into immediately caught on fire. The sky was beginning to light up behind us with burning Offspring. However, other Offspring pressed in. Sampson's wings were still covered with Offspring, and Offspring were still attacking Judah. Jumping to my feet now, without a thought, I ran straight toward Sampson's left wing. With one blow, I took out half of the Offspring. With another blow, I took out the rest, flaming Offspring tumbling into their comrades. Off to the right wing. Two leaps and a swing of the torch freed this wing completely, with flaming Offspring once again tumbling into the ranks of their evil cohorts. Now, Sampson was free to fly. Though he was wounded, the mighty beast powered up his wings and almost immediately corrected our freefall. Judah was still being attacked as they were trying to rip apart his precious wings. That didn't last long. I grabbed the torch with both hands and wound up. I sent all three of them in a blazing arch into the nearest line of Offspring, who were instantaneously set ablaze. Judah was in bad shape. Worse than when we were in the woods. He needed help, fast.

We were still surrounded by the Offspring, but now, many of them were falling out of the sky to their deaths. Fireballs from the sky landing at the feet of the furious Chaos overlords on the ground.

We were almost at the mountain now when I realized, however, that the fight was not over. Offspring *never* give up. They never give in. That is the way evil is. It doesn't stop. It devours. It destroys. It won't stop until everything good is gone and everything right is wrong. And then it turns on itself. This is the point in the fight that the Arachne caught up. It took me a second to realize what was happening. The Arachne ranks were tearing through the rear ranks of the Offspring. Literally tearing through them. Offspring were being dismantled limb by limb in midair by their evil counterparts. Most didn't even know what hit them (or bit them). The Arachne, though, really didn't care about destroying the Offspring; the Offspring were simply in the way. No, the Arachne were after us.

TORCH

BREAKTHROUGH

The Arachne were gaining on us as they sliced through the rear flanks of the Offspring like butter. *We had to be close to the mountain,* I hoped and willed. Still ahead was a final line of Offspring waiting for us. From behind, I could see the first few Arachne, some of the fastest fliers, hot on Sampson's tail (literally). I jumped onto Sampson's back and charged straight at the Arachne, sending them tumbling toward their friends in a ball of fire. This slowed them down. I made my way to Sampson's shoulder blades, directly in between his wings. I held the torch high into the sky. I knew we couldn't punch our way through the line of Offspring ahead of us; it was too thick. We would have to fight. Strategically fight.

Yelling to Sampson, I told him to fly straight toward the right end of the Offspring line and, at the last minute, turn sharply to the left. He made a beeline toward the end of the line and turned on a dime. As we banked hard left, I reached down with my left hand and grabbed Sampson's left wing. I allowed the force of our momentum to swing my body out, away from Sampson. Holding on with my left hand, I reared back with my right hand. The torch began slicing the Offspring in half all the way down the flank. Offspring body parts, set on fire, were now falling onto the ground below and landing on the heads of the irate Chaos overlords. At the end of the line, we turned to witness a sea of bloodthirsty Arachne ascending on us.

"Climb!" I yelled to Sampson.

He shot up and above the Arachne. We soared higher and higher. The Arachne followed.

"Dive!" I commanded Sampson, and in one fluid motion, he turned and faced our attackers.

Diving straight into the fray, I crouched slightly, ready for the first wave. We reached the first of the spider-wasps, and my instincts took over. Sampson dove, and I swung. Smashing, slicing, blocking, swinging. We were blazing through the sky like a comet…a killer comet, destroying everything in our path. But they kept coming, and some had now circled behind us. Still diving, I realized that Sampson was killing his fair share of Arachne too. I also realized that I hadn't been simply standing on Sampson's back, no—now, the torch and I were one. I was jumping and dodging the attacks. And I was fighting fast, extremely fast. Punch, jab, stab, slash. Jump, weave, bob, duck. Faster and faster the fighting went. Hundreds of Arachne were falling from the sky, joining the dismantled Offspring. But there seemed to be no end to these creatures, though.

"We're going to the mountain," Sampson roared.

Though we were both destroying our fair share of Arachne, they were everywhere. In front of us and behind us. We needed a way out, and then I knew just what I had to do.

"*I'll catch up to you in a few!*" I yelled to Sampson.

My knees bent; I took a deep breath and pushed off of Sampson's back headfirst, the torch leading the way! I was flying, sort of. Maybe more like falling. Years later, someone would say that sometimes flying feels more like falling at first. Well, this looked and felt every bit like falling. Fortunately, my momentum rocketed me forward headfirst into the incoming Arachne. The torch was brighter than I had ever seen it. And though awkward, it felt comfortable to be flying/falling through the air, torch swinging against the black of the night, destroying evil spider-wasp creatures. I was able to punch a hole in the Arachne's lines giving Sampson some breathing room. He was still careening in a downward angle toward Three Sisters. I spotted him, and not knowing what else to do, I pointed the torch in Sampson's direction. Honestly, at this point (and maybe a few points prior), I had *no* idea what I was doing. "Torch, dive!" I commanded, and we flew straight down toward Sampson. Closing in on Sampson's back, I glanced up just enough to realize that we were about at the face of the mountain. Which sister's face, I don't know, but we were both approaching at top speed. I was right over Sampson now. I glanced down at Sampson's back and then at the mountain. He must know something I didn't. I stretched out my hand as far as I possibly could and grabbed the very end of his powerful tail. As we hit the mountain wall, Sampson indeed knew something I didn't because at that precise moment, the mountain wall "opened" up. It was like going through a thick liquid doorway, and as soon as we were through, the wall closed. Still holding onto Sampson's tail, I could hear the thundering thuds of hundreds of Arachne slamming into the wall of the mountain to their deaths. I could imagine the scene behind me as the spider-wasps, fixated on our destruction, ran headfirst into the mountain and fell unceremoniously to their deaths. I could also imagine the enraged faces of the Chaos overlords when they realized that we had escaped. Thud, thud, thud reverberated behind me. And then silence.

Breaking through the mountain wall, we entered a tunnel. A very short tunnel but a tunnel, nonetheless. I had been concentrating on holding onto Sampson's tail so much that I hadn't realized that he was no longer flying in the air but was on the ground of the tunnel floor, simply trying to stop. I was still holding onto his tail and bouncing up and down along the tunnel floor. And then we stopped.

"You can let it go now," came a chuckled roar from Sampson.

We had stopped. Judah lay on the ground near his father while I was sprawled out on the ground behind Sampson. My left hand gripped Sampson's tail, my right hand the torch. Both hands ached. I released them both. Sampson's tail swung free, and the torch toppled onto the dirt tunnel floor. With the torch out of my hand, I began to realize how much damage both the Offspring and the Arachne had done to me. I hurt all over. Bloodstains were all over my shirt and pants. Sweat mixed with dirt covered my face. My breathing was slowing, but the emotion of what we just witnessed was taking its place. *How close did I...did we come to dying?* I thought to myself. A salty tear rolled down my cheek as if to accentuate the flood of emotions I was feeling.

"But you didn't. You didn't die," came a firm but gentle reply from Sampson. "You, we, we survived. Countless evil creatures died as a result of what you did. You made a dent, a significant dent in Antioch's empire. I don't know why you haven't died up to this point, but you haven't. You should have, but you haven't. What I do know is that there is a reason you have made it this far. There is a reason why you helped my son and why I helped you. There is a reason. There always is. Nothing happens by chance. You didn't stumble upon that torch in a cave. There is a reason that you met Keith. There is a reason. What else I know is that you were called for a higher purpose. Is that purpose to simply save your mother and others that are enslaved by Antioch? I don't know."

"But I'm a nobody. Nobody special. I can't do anything particularly well. I'm not smart. I'm not strong. I'm not brave or bold or confident. Unless I have the torch," I said to Sampson.

"Unless you have the torch?" Sampson asked rhetorically. "What does that have to do with your being brave? What does that have to do with being smart? You need that torch, but it needs you too! Without you, the torch is merely a flame on a stick. But in your hands, the torch is a powerful weapon. One that heals. One that destroys. One that can take down strongholds like you did today. One that gives you both the courage and ability to jump off the back of a flying lion-man! And if the legends are true, you've just scratched the surface of what you and the torch can do together. Again, maybe your purpose is to simply save your mother and others that are enslaved by Antioch. Or, if you are indeed the One, as Judah believes, you have a much greater purpose. I don't know. But there is a reason. There is a reason you made it here, to this place," Sampson said with a little drama in his voice. He moved out of the way and waved his hand to the view that was directly behind him. "Welcome to Three Sisters."

"Oh…" was all I could muster. My heart skipped a beat. I was in awe.

TORCH

DIRT

The entrance of the tunnel overlooked a breathtaking valley, one that was surrounded by majestic towering mountains. In fact, from where we were in the opening of the tunnel, we couldn't see the tops of the mountains. The valley floor was an idyllic-looking scene, like something from a painting. No, better than that. It was like a hidden paradise. Imagine the earth perfected: perfect grass and trees and temperature, mixed with heaven, that was what I was looking at. It was unbelievable.

A swift-moving stream meandered its way from one end of the valley floor to the other. There were trees lining different sections of the stream while meadows flanked the stream on either side with perfectly green grass. A sprinkling of wildflowers of various colors and varieties mixed in with the grass, making it look almost like a large comfy patchwork quilt. Of course, in a place this beautiful, this perfect, the word "wild-flower" seemed out of place. Their radiance made them glow as if they were lit up somehow. Instead of wildflowers, here, in this place, they should be called fireflowers for their brilliant glow. I could imagine the fire fairies at home in a place like this. My mind wandered back to the stream and the lush green grass. I wondered how many picnics took place here. It was that kind of scene. I didn't see much in the way of people or creatures, but I did see a couple of small structures toward the far end of the valley floor. *Houses?* I wondered. And at the very far end, there was a larger structure. It looked like a superfancy log cabin.

From where I was standing, I could make out a large porch, oversized windows, a green painted metal roof, and a chimney. I thought I could see a wisp of smoke rising from the top of it. The sky was perfectly blue; the air was perfectly temperate: neither hot nor cold but with a slight, refreshing breeze. *Is this paradise?* I thought to myself, still in disbelief.

"We need to get moving," came the firm command from Sampson. "Help me with Judah." I helped him put his injured son across his shoulders, and the three of us set out across the valley floor. I can't imagine what we looked like. The three of us were dirty and battle-scarred. Dried blood (and not yet dried blood) mixed with mud and the pungent stench of dead Offspring made us look like pitiful vagrants that got beat up and left for dead. My clothes were tattered. My heart was torn. But I was alive. Very alive.

"One more thing," Sampson said as we reached the beginning of the luxurious grass, "no matter what, no matter who we encounter, let me do the talking. If you couldn't tell, this is a special place. A sacred place." We walked on in silence, both lost in our own thoughts, both staying out of each other's way.

The valley floor was even more beautiful up close than it was from a distance. Everything smelled fresh and clean, like fresh laundry or a hint of perfume like the one that my mom would wear on special occasions. It was the smell of comfort. It was a pristine place. The water in the stream was crystal clear, as you'd expect in a place like this. Looking intently at the stream as we walked, I noticed a few stunningly dazzling and yet unfamiliar creatures swim lazily in the water. They were small, maybe a foot or two long, with the faces of the loveliest ladies I had ever seen and the tails of a fish. I had heard about this kind of creature, but I thought they were just a myth. Some referred to them as ladyfish, others as mermaids. They were much smaller than I imagined (not that I had imagined them much before) and yet more stunning. I went to the bank of the stream to get a closer look and possibly get a drink.

"I wouldn't do that if I were you," cautioned Sampson as if reading my mind. "This is pure water. You are not pure," he said matter-of-factly.

Not sure what he meant, I couldn't resist, though. It was as if these little ladies had me in a trance. Being fourteen years old, I was too young to know what love is (romantic love) but *not* too young to know what beauty looks like. I kneeled down to get a drink. I reached my hand in the water to get a drink but immediately, from out of nowhere, dozens of little ladies attacked my hand. "Attack" might be too strong a word. They didn't bite it or scratch it. They simply joined in force to remove my hand from the water. They were amazingly strong! Startled, I fell backward onto the muddy bank. I looked back at the lovely ladies, some of whom were laughing at me while others were shaming me. My heart sank. I guess I don't have a way with the ladies.

Not only were the little ladies laughing, but so was Sampson. *And* so was Judah. Laying across his dad's shoulders, I could hear the faintest chuckle coming from him.

"Don't say I didn't warn you, dirty boy. Or should I say, 'lover boy'?" came a chuckled growl from Sampson. "Let's go," he said, continuing to chuckle.

And so we moved on, following the edge of the stream. We were also next to the field of fireflowers, and up close, they were even more spectacular. They swayed rhythmically from side to side and sounded like they were singing a soothing lullaby. Sampson didn't seem to notice. Either he'd already seen these flowers before and was unimpressed, or he didn't see them now. He hadn't said where we were going or who we were meeting, but it seemed apparent that we were heading to the big cabin at the end of the valley. Again, except the lovely ladies in the stream, we saw no other creatures. We made our way past the smaller structures that I had noticed back in the cave. They looked like work sheds of some sort, but they appeared to be empty. Not necessarily in an abandoned, run-down way. They were just empty. The sheds were made of wood that was slightly gray in color, weathered-looking in a place with perfect weather. Each had large sliding doors on the front, and they were open to reveal a cavernous empty space. There were three of them, and they were identical except for the color of their roofs. One roof was black, one was white, and the other was gray. In any other place, you might get the shivers walking past such structures, but not here. Not too much further now was the big cabin.

The stream began meandering off to our left as we neared the large house. A pathway leading to the cabin was now in view, and we could clearly see the detail of the front of the cabin. Its size was even more immense than I had imagined it to be from the entrance of the cave. The first thing I noticed was the wide set of wooden steps leading to the porch. The steps were painted white, and they were flanked on either side by a green railing. It was an inviting set of stairs. It was as if they were welcoming you home. These steps led to an enormous porch that spanned the width of the cabin and appeared to disappear around the corner. My guess was that it wrapped its way around the whole of the cabin. The porch railing matched the color scheme of the steps. The balusters were white with intricate details carved in each one, not in a disconcerting pattern or randomly but in such a way that they almost appeared to be alive. The handrail on top of the balusters was painted the same green as the handrail for the steps. On the newel posts on either side of the steps were carved lions. Lions with wings. And the lions were holding something in their hands…a torch! They were not painted white or green but looked realistic as if they would come to life at any minute, their torches appearing to glow. On the porch, I could see a few rocking chairs, and on the left side of the porch, hanging from the ceiling of the porch, was a white bench swing with a few comfy pillows lining the swing, making the cabin all the more inviting.

I hadn't realized that we had stopped walking. No, I was standing there, not far from the base of the steps, gawking. Now, I was sure of one thing: if the outside was so warm and inviting, I couldn't wait to see what the inside of this cabin was like.

A throat cleared. Not mine and definitely not Sampson's or Judah's. I scanned the cabin to see what or who made the sound. To my dismay, on the second step of the stairway stood a little man looking directly at us. He was little and old, with the emphasis being on *little* and *old*. He just seemed to appear because he wasn't standing on the steps a few minutes ago when I was taking it all in. Unless I completely overlooked him, which was probably the case. Standing against the backdrop of the enormous cabin, this little old man couldn't have been more than four feet tall. He was slender but not skinny. He had snow-white hair and a face that had the creases and wrinkles of the aged. His eyebrows were bushy white, and his eyes were a dazzling bright blue with a hint of youthful curiosity. His nose was slightly pointed and his cheeks slightly pink, almost as if he were blushing. He stood perfectly erect, not a common posture for someone as old as he appeared to be, again, giving him quite a youthful disposition for someone his age. He was wearing dark gray trousers and a white, long-sleeve button-down shirt tucked neatly into his trousers with his sleeves slightly rolled up. To complete his look, he had on a bowtie. A red bowtie. His pants were a bit long and wide at the base, so it was hard to see his shoes or if he was even wearing any. You could say he looked like a grandpa. A very short and old grandpa but also a cool, youthful grampa. The kind that would take you on adventures or tell you amazingly fantastic stories about his adventures.

We continued closer to the porch.

And then he spoke.

"*Stop!*" came a firm command from a strong voice. There was no cracking, shaking, or frailty in his voice, the kind that one would associate with the elderly. No, there was confidence and authority that came from the little old man on the steps. He didn't have to say it twice. I froze in my tracks, feeling his bright blue eyes piercing my brain!

Sampson, on the other hand, didn't. He kept approaching.

"I said, *stop!*" the little old man said a little louder and firmer. He was looking directly at Sampson, who was midstep. The little old man raised his bushy eyebrows and grinned wryly at Sampson as if to say, "Take one more step and see what happens, son!"

Sampson retracted his step and took one more step back for good measure.

"Wallace, it's me, Sampson. You know me!" said Sampson, stammering and chuckling uneasily. I'd not witnessed this side of Sampson before.

"It doesn't matter whether I know your name or not. I know everyone's name," Wallace said to the now sheepish lion. "It's about whether or not you are clean. You are not clean. You cannot enter the house. You have the filth of battle and the sheen of darkness covering you. You are still cloaked in a dark garment of rage and anger and revenge. This is a place that is free of evil, free of darkness. It will be kept that way. You couldn't enter this place even if I wasn't standing here and you rushed up these steps. You are not ready. Yes, I know your name, but that is not enough to enter. To enter, first you, all three of you, must be clean. Go and follow the stream until you reach the large pool. The pool is surrounded by large bushes and shrubs. You will notice an opening in the foliage. Enter through the opening. There you will get into the pool of water. You must go under the water and count to seven. When you emerge, you will be clean. You can enter the house if you are ready." And with that, Wallace, the little old man, was gone. He was there one second and gone the next—in the time it takes you to blink. Fast enough to make you second guess whether or not you witnessed what you just witnessed. I saw something move on the front porch. The swinging chair was swinging ever so slightly. I caught a glimpse of a woman on the swing. I couldn't make out too much of her features except that she was smiling at me. She waved at me, and I gave her a shy wave back. Her wave turned into a point. That's when I noticed that Sampson had started off toward the stream. I guessed we were going swimming.

TORCH

BATH

I had to jog to catch up with Sampson and Judah. The stream hadn't changed in appearance, just in direction. We walked along its bank for about fifteen minutes before the stream abruptly stopped, giving way to a waterfall. The waterfall appeared to empty into a large pool. There were shrubs and bushes on either side of the waterfall with a small opening that the pathway led us to. Once through the opening, we found ourselves standing on the edge of the pool on the opposite side of where the waterfall cascaded. We were up high, though, still at the level of the stream and the head of the waterfall. We were on a cliff. Wallace didn't tell us we had to jump off a cliff to enter the pool. A little detail, and yet an important one. What else had the little old man left out?

I looked over at Sampson as if to get a cue. Not being very bright, I only then realized that of the three of us—me, Sampson, and Judah—I was the only one wearing clothes.

"Help me get Judah off my back," came the lion-man's order.

I put the torch down against a rock and helped Judah off his father's shoulders. Sampson took Judah into his powerful arms and began to walk with him to the edge of the cliff. *Judah is in no condition to swim!* I thought to myself. I started to say something to Sampson when he cut me off.

"This is the way it has to be. Remember when I challenged you to see with more than your eyes? This is one of those moments," he said, looking down at his beleaguered son. "Sometimes you have to trust, even when you cannot see the outcome. Any of the outcomes. That's called faith, confidence in what you hope for and certainty about what you don't see." Looking down at his son one more time, Sampson kissed him on the forehead and dropped him into the lake. I watched in disbelief as Judah tumbled through the air, finally splashing into the water below. Slowly, he sank beneath the surface of the water and out of sight. Turning back to me, Sampson simply said, "Believe." And then he jumped off the cliff with style, flipping and somersaulting in the air before knifing gracefully into the lake. If I hadn't before, I now fully appreciated the fact that Sampson was no ordinary cat. And then, he, too, slipped below the surface of the water and out of sight.

Standing there all by myself, I was suddenly lonely. The gentle breeze that I felt in the meadow lapped gently against my face. I felt my heart pounding in my chest. This seemed pretty silly to me. I knew it had been waaaaay toooo long since I had a bath and all, but jumping into a lake to be "cleansed" so I could go into some mysterious house? Weird. And what was the point? I stood there, my mind racing, scared to jump and confused as to why I needed to jump.

Suddenly, to my surprise, Sampson popped his head up out of the water and roared, "*Believe!*" which reverberated off the walls of the cliff.

What did I have to lose? I took off my filthy shirt (it was truly disgusting), kicked off my shoes, and picked up the torch. I neared the edge of the cliff and as if on cue, I heard the oversized rodent's voice in my head, "Go save them all!"

I jumped.

Not nearly as graceful as Sampson, in fact, not graceful at all, I tumbled through the air, thinking again about the fact that sometimes flying feels more like falling than flying and hit the water with a large splash. There was no flying, just falling. Like everything else in the world of Three Sisters, the water temperature was perfect. It was neither too hot nor too cold. It wasn't tepid either. It was just right. Sampson and Judah were nowhere in sight.

Neither was the torch! I frantically scanned the water, but it was nowhere to be seen. I suddenly found myself being gently pulled down. *Sampson*, I thought, *He must be up to something*. But I realized at the same time I was being pulled down that I began to feel exhausted. What did Wallace say to do? That's right, count to seven. So, as my head slipped below the surface of the water, I began to count: seven, six, five (I was sinking deeper with each number), four, three, two…

I don't know how it happened, but you *never* forget the smell of bacon! Nothing else smells like bacon except, well, bacon! And cinnamon rolls. Definitely the smell of cinnamon rolls! I found myself lying on the most comfortable bed I'd ever slept on. I was covered with a magnificently soft blanket that was multicolored, hand-stitched, and felt like an old friend—comfortable. It smelled freshly laundered, which, mixed with the smell of bacon and cinnamon rolls, was about as perfect a smell trifecta as you can get. It wasn't until I heard someone cheerfully humming that I remembered jumping into the lake in a dirty pair of pants. I took a quick peek under the blanket. Whew! I had clean clothes on. They weren't mine, though. Must have been loaner clothes. Mine were quite disgusting, and besides, I had left them at the rim of the lake. But wait, who put these on me? A brief moment of panic set in.

"I did," came a soothing voice from outside of my room. It reminded me of my mom's voice.

"No dear, I'm not your mother," came the soothing voice.

And then she was standing in the doorway, with a plate piled high with breakfast. "I'll bet you're starving," came the soothing voice as I was handed the plate of food: bacon, eggs, cinnamon rolls, and juice. In the dim light of the room, it was hard to make out any of her features, not that I was looking at her. I was looking at the food! It looked as good as it smelled. How long had it been since I last ate? Keith tried to feed me grubs just before we were attacked by the Offspring. No, the last thing I ate was a piece of stale bread that my mother pulled from her dress pocket while we were fleeing from the Chaos. Hunger overcame me, and I ate ravenously! The woman just stood there quietly, watching me. Observing me. I hardly noticed her until the last morsel of bacon entered my mouth and my plate was completely empty.

"Still hungry?" the woman said to me.

I wasn't. I was full.

Not waiting for me to respond verbally, she cheerfully said, "Good, we have a journey to take, and I don't want you to be hungry. We need to get moving. Take a minute to get your legs under you and put on some shoes. You'll need them."

For the first time, I looked, really looked at the woman in the room. And she stood there for a brief moment to let me observe. There wasn't anything particularly particular about her. She was of medium height, with medium beauty. She reminded me slightly of my own mother, but unlike my mother, who had fair skin, the lady in front of me was dark-skinned. Very dark-skinned. And her skin was flawless. I couldn't tell you how old she was. When you're fourteen, anyone over the age of thirty is old. Her hair was a magnificent white, metallic-looking and almost appeared to have a soft glow. Across the top of her head, flowing down behind her ears, was a scarf of some sort. It, too, was black. It matched the color of her skin, which stood in stark contrast to the color of her hair. Her eyes were a brilliant shade of blue similar to Wallace's eyes. Her eyes were piercing and comforting at the same time. She was wearing a simple white dress with little black flowers dotted on it. The dress went down to the floor and covered her feet. She wore a cooking apron that was a different hue of white and almost completely blended into her dress. Of course, there was not a speck of food preparation on her dress. It was most likely for show. I guess she was beautiful after all. Beautiful in a subtle, sneak-up-on-you kinda way. And compelling. She was definitely compelling, and she told me to get my shoes on. I couldn't get them on fast enough!

TORCH

FIRESIDE CHAT

My outfit was similar to my old one: a pair of jeans with a button-downed red flannel shirt and a white undershirt. My shoes were a simple pair of blue sneakers but seemed very well made and very comfortable. A pair of white socks and a new pair of undies completed the outfit.

After I dressed, I exited the simple room with the luxurious bed and entered the kitchen/living room/entryway. It was a single room used for all three purposes. If the bedroom was simple, the kitchen/living room/entryway was equally simple. Not in a boring way, mind you. They were simply simple. The room had everything you would need to be comfortable and nothing more. No trinkets, no wall art, no family photos. Just the barest of furniture, a couch, a stuffed leather oversized chair, a dining table, a stove/oven, a sink, and a few dishes. Against the opposite wall from the kitchen, in front of the couch and the stuffed oversized chair, was a simple fireplace. The fire burning in the fireplace added to the comfortable atmosphere in this small space.

The lady was sitting in the oversized chair. The chair faced the fireplace, so when I entered the room, her back was to me. She seemed to fit this place perfectly. There was nothing extraordinary about her, which, after all the amazing creatures I'd encountered, seemed both odd and comforting in itself. I stood there taking it all in—the simple room, the simple woman—both not so simple, both comforting. First impressions can be misleading.

"Come, sit," came the soothing voice; she was still not looking in my direction. I did as I was told and made my way to the couch, which was beside the oversized chair and slightly angled toward the fireplace. The lady sat straight upright and stared intently at the fire as if she was looking for something. Sitting down, I looked back and forth between the lady and fire. The fire. It was the first time since I landed in the water of the lake that I had remembered the torch.

As if reading my mind, she said, "Don't you worry about the torch." It was the kinda thing that my mother could do: know what I was thinking. "You don't need it. Not now. When the time is right, you'll get it back. For now, you and I are going on a journey." She turned her head toward me, finally breaking her gaze from the fire. Her stunningly blue eyes looked at me, at my soul, and she said, "This journey is not a cinnamon-roll-and-bacon kind of journey. No, where we are going, you've already been. A familiar place. A forgotten place." She stared intently at me. I wasn't sure what she meant, but the way she said it caused a chill to overtake me, even in this most comfortable of places.

"My name is Annis-Chuya," she introduced herself. "You can call me Anni. Yes, I was the one you saw on the porch of the cabin. I was waiting for you and Sampson and Judah to arrive. I take a journey with everyone who comes to Three Sisters. I help them with their transition. I know you have a flood of questions, but trust me, the answers will be revealed in time. Just know that this journey we're going on is part of the transition." She continued staring at me as if giving me permission to speak.

"Sampson and Judah. Where are they?" I managed to ask feebly.

"They are on their own journey," came Anni's reply.

"With you?" I questioned.

"Yes. With me," she said, her left eyebrow raising while she gave me time to process this. Before I could say anything else, she continued, "There are things that you don't understand, you won't understand. They are above your comprehension as they should be. If you, or any other of your kind, understood all the depths of the universe, of Jacob and Antioch, well, let's just say that the Offspring would be the least of your problems."

"What do you mean?" I asked, trying not to sound totally confused.

"The Offspring were not always evil. They were not always disgusting-looking creatures. They weren't and aren't a whole lot different than you. But they kept desiring to know more about that which they were unprepared and unworthy to know. They wanted to make little of the big and dumb down the amazing into bite-sized morsels of the common. They wanted to take Jacob and make him like them: dirty, filthy, and vile. Their passions for pleasure—money, sex, power—consumed them! Antioch seized on this and promised them knowledge and understanding and whatever other desires they longed for in return for service. They thought, though, that they had everything under control and that they could turn back at any time, that what they were craving wasn't so bad, but it overtook them in most cases slowly, over time. What Antioch referred to as 'service' was really slavery and a complete change of appearance and appetite." Her voice had changed now. Now, it was sad. I was sad hearing her, but I had so many questions.

"So, the Offspring are or were really men like me?"

Anni nodded.

"But they're hideous!" I exclaimed, my voice bursting with indignation.

Anni put a black finger up to rose-colored lips to hush me. "Child," she said soothingly, "that is what evil does to you. It changes you. Your appearance, your thoughts, your desires, the way you treat others. It takes over. Most don't realize it because it happens so slowly; they don't know who or what they are because they are completely unrecognizable. They wake up one day wondering how in the world their lives ended up in that condition. Most, though, don't ever wake up. They become slaves to Antioch and the Chaos. But that's not why we're here. You and I are going on a journey. Shall we begin?" she asked soothingly.

TORCH

FACING DEMONS

Anni stood up and made her way to the front door. As we exited the little house, I turned and looked back at it. It reminded me of one of the empty sheds we had passed on our way to the cabin, but my memory was extremely sketchy these days. I could only remember bits and pieces from my past, not much more than a spark of a faint memory but just enough to make me question whether or not it actually happened. A flash of memory here or there like my dreams. For instance, I remembered my mom and me running from the Chaos, but prior to that, there was a wall or maybe a veil of some sort blocking my memory. So, I didn't remember seeing a house like this when we had crossed the valley floor. Besides, it was dark outside now, with just the scantest moonlight silhouetting the landscape. From what little I could see, it did indeed look very familiar. And I heard what I thought was the flowing water of the creek. Like the valley floor of Three Sisters.

We walked a few minutes along a dirt pathway with low-lying grass flanking the path with a bright moon and Anni's glowing white hair, the only things illuminating the pathway.

So, this journey is more of a nature hike, I thought to myself.

Without warning, Anni stopped and turned to look directly at me. She grabbed my hands, looked me dead in the eye, and said, "Be strong and courageous. Don't be afraid to face it."

Instantly, we were flying through time. Or was time flying through us? Faster and faster, we went. Everything was a blur. Trees, people, faces, sights, sounds. This continued for what seemed like an hour or more. And as suddenly as we started, we stopped.

We were standing in a barren field, save for the remains of harvested wheat, which lay on top of the dirt like a crunchy rug. A smiling scarecrow stood at its post, not realizing that its duty was over. The sun was high in the air, and there was a gentle breeze but, even with the breeze, the heat of the sun caused me to start sweating. If this was some sort of trancelike dream that Anni was causing, it was extremely realistic! A short way across the field was a small timber-framed house. It was a simple house, flecked with remnants of weathered white paint. The red roof was pitched and, like the siding of the house, was weathered. A stump of a chimney barely peaked up above the roofline. No inviting smoke floated from it. Like the rest of the scene, it was dead, giving the appearance of being scorched. That's it! The picture in front of me appeared dirty: the field, the scarecrow, and the timber-framed house. Everything had what looked like soot covering it. Not from the chimney. No, it was something much more ominous! Up a few rickety-looking wooden steps was a screen door, the entry to the home. The screen door was closed, but the front door itself was open. Like the chimney, the front door wasn't inviting either. Undersized windows flanked either side of the front door. To the right of the simple house was a clothesline with a few items draped over it, fluttering in the gentle breeze. These, too, were covered with a thin layer of soot, and in the breeze, some of the soot was gently wafting into the air. Except for the soot, the scene seemed ordinary. Maybe, some would say, even plainly picturesque in a depressing, lifeless kinda way.

"Where are we?" asked Anni, still holding my hand but looking straight ahead at the house.

"I'm not sure," I replied. It seemed familiar, but I couldn't put my finger on it.

Turning to look me in the eye, Anni asked again, more firmly this time, "Where are we?"

"I…I…don't know," I stammered, my mind trying desperately to recall this place.

In a blink, we were standing in front of the steps leading to the screen door.

"Be strong and courageous. Don't be afraid to face it," she said to me as she motioned toward the screen door.

How could a person be sweating from the heat and suddenly have a chill surge through their entire body? It was a paralyzing chill causing my knees to lock up on me. Where it came from, I don't know, but I was about to find out why.

My legs obeyed my command to climb the few rickety stairs, and, taking a deep breath, I opened the screen door. Peering inside, I hesitated for a moment. It was dark except for the light being let in by the windows. Shadows crept up and down the walls. Did I see something move? Or someone? Was it just my mind? I took a step inside, turning back to see if Anni was behind me.

She stood back away from the house and shook her head. "This is your journey. You must face it alone. Be strong and courageous. Don't be afraid to face it. I'll be waiting for you," she said, a look of concern on her face.

Stepping inside, I waited for a moment to allow my eyes to adjust to the partial darkness of the house. It smelled musty, not in a bad way like sweaty clothes or rotten food. No, it smelled of dust and wood and soot. The soot had settled here as well, inside the house. My eyes slowly began to focus.

The room that I was standing in was a small room with a dining table to my left and a kitchen to my right. I turned my attention to the dining room. The wooden table had five wooden chairs spaced around it. It was clearly well used. I felt drawn to the table. Something about it was so familiar. Four of the chairs were normal-sized, but the fifth chair was a high chair for a baby or a toddler. Again, it seemed so familiar. I ran my hand across the tabletop. Soot and dust kicked up and caked my hand. There were nicks and dimples strewn across the table, again a sign that it was well used. In the midst of the haphazard marks of the table, someone had clearly etched in a childlike script the letters, "S T E." I traced them with my finger.

Another chill.

Turning away from the dining and kitchen areas, I followed a short hallway toward the back of the house. Two bedrooms faced each other toward the end of the hallway. The bedrooms were equal in size. Nothing out of the ordinary. In one bedroom were two single disheveled beds. Disheveled because of use, not because the room had been ransacked (though sometimes there's no difference between the two). A two-drawer wooden dresser stood against a corner wall, and the window was covered with a makeshift curtain that was really just a blanket hung in the opening. Light oozed from around the edges of the curtain, giving an eerie glow. The wind caught the curtain randomly, causing the light to shift and dance. Shadows joined in the dance too, both playing with my mind.

In the second bedroom, a large bed took up the middle of the room. Again, a dresser stood against a wall, but unlike the first room, there was a crib next to the dresser. On top of the dresser appeared to be toys. Toddler toys. A similar makeshift curtain hung over the window opening, once again, giving an eerie glow to the room.

Weird.

Familiar.

Why had Anni brought me here?

And then I heard her voice again, "Be strong and courageous. Don't be afraid to face it." Ominous.

Another chill.

I retreated back down the short hallway with every intention to walk right through the dining/kitchen room to locate Anni when I was suddenly overcome with thirst. "Don't be afraid to face it!" came the ominous encouragement again. Not even sure if the water in this place worked, I made my way over to the kitchen sink and grabbed a dusty glass cup out of an overhead cabinet. The cup had other plans. Covered in soot, it slipped through my fingers and tumbled as if in slow motion toward the wooden kitchen floor. I batted at it feebly as my hands followed its path all the way to its shattered end. The glass exploded just below my outstretched hands and sent shards of glass plunging deep into my skin. Blood began to flow. Ouch! Again, if this was some sort of dream, it felt all too real. *Is this what I'm supposed to be afraid of?* I thought. *A few shards of glass? A little blood?* I knelt down onto the soot-covered wooden floor to check out the wounds on my hands and pick up the remains of the cup.

Assessing the damage, I concluded I could move my hands even though they hurt. But the blood. It kept flowing. I must've hit an artery. The blood began to pool around my knees. I leaned forward to steady myself with my left hand leaning on the glass and blood/soot-riddled wooden floor. Suddenly, a wave of dizziness came over me, and I felt myself slowly going the rest of the way down to the floor. I stretched out my right hand to catch the weight of my body, but my hand didn't hit solid ground. No, it landed on something. Instinctively, my hand gripped the object, but in the mess of the blood and glass, my arm slid out, causing me to land facedown in my own blood. The light of the screen door was illuminating the spot where I lay as I felt the object still in my right hand create a hazy glow. What? "Don't be afraid to face it," came Anni's ominous voice again. I brought the object in front of my face and began to study it. The object was a knife, and I was holding the blade. I ran my hand down the length of the handle, where I was surprised to discover something etched in it. What was it? A symbol? It was hard to tell because of the blood. I wiped it as best as I could. No, it wasn't a symbol. It was a letter, a single letter. Instantly, I was jolted awake. Blood or no blood, I was fully aware of everything, and I was afraid!

My mind began to race, to flood. The letter "S" was etched into the handle of the knife and looked like the same "S" that was on the dining table. It was my brother's knife. Memories began to flood. I was in my old house. This was my brother's knife. But how? He had left home four years before…

Through the pain, I pushed myself up onto my feet, the bloody knife still in my hand. I stared out the kitchen window, my mind racing, the memories almost overwhelming. It was the kitchen window of my house. My family's house.

Staring out the window, I felt time and memories come back.

The last time I stood here, at this window, was the day that the Chaos came for us. I was in the kitchen doing the dishes from breakfast. Mother was outside at the clothesline, gathering the dried laundry. And Em, my little sister, only three years old, played a few yards away from her mother.

How have I forgotten about my older brother! How have I forgotten about my house? I wondered in despair. This must be what Anni had been referring to, "Don't be afraid to face it," her words in my mind. But this was just the beginning.

The day started off as a typical day. I was doing the chores while mother and I took turns keeping an eye on Em. The day seemed a lot like today. Hot and sunny with a slight breeze. Standing there, looking out the window, I saw what looked like a storm coming. The sky grew darker and darker. Mother hurriedly tried to take down the laundry that she had been hanging before the storm hit.

Still looking out the window, I stopped what I was doing. To my shock, out of the blackness of the encroaching storm, someone or something came running toward mother and Em. My mother, so intent on taking down the laundry, didn't notice. Then I heard Em squeal in delight, "Daddy." Her arms were outstretched as she ran toward him. It had been a little more than a year since he'd left to "find himself," but all I knew was that this person/creature wasn't the dad I knew. Watching through the window, I saw a nightmare unfold right in front of me. A nightmare that you don't wake up from. A real-life nightmare. He approached Em and, with a wave of a powerful hand, flung her aside like a rag doll. She flew through the air and lay limp on the ground near the base of the smiling scarecrow. My dad didn't slow down as he made his way straight for my mom. He was on top of my mother in an instant. His breathing sounded like a high-pitched wheeze, and his body was different. Animallike but not completely. This animal was going to kill my mom!

"No, Jay, no!" she pleaded with him. "This isn't you! I know the real Jay is in there," she continued pleading.

A snarled, wheezing response came from my father, this hideous creature. "You're better off dead!" he roared into her face.

His powerful hands wrapped around her throat. She was fighting, kicking, and then she wasn't.

I just reacted. The knife was in my hand. I bounded down the steps as fast as I could but lost my footing and dropped the knife as I tumbled to the ground. Back on my feet, I sprinted to my mother's rescue, jumping onto my father's back to try to stop him. It wasn't my father's back, though. It was something alien. No amount of force was making a difference. He was too strong. He just held on to my mother's neck. I pleaded with him, but he wasn't responding.

And suddenly, from somewhere in the distance, I heard a noise, a hideous sound like an alarm or a war cry. I felt my father release his grip on my mother, and he sprang to his feet and, with demonlike eyes staring dead into mine, snarled, "You're better off dead! You should run!" He bounded toward the base of the scarecrow, grabbed Em like a rag doll, and fled. That was the last I saw of them.

A storm was coming.

I grabbed my mother, and with all the strength I could muster, I helped her into the house. We couldn't be there long because the approaching storm was closing in fast, and it was no ordinary storm. My father came from the storm. I sat my mother down in a chair at the dining room table and got her some water. In the cabinet was a leftover piece of bread that she told me to grab for her. She put it in her pocket. The sky was almost pitch-black at this point. My mother had regained her strength, but just barely when we made our escape.

I vomited into the kitchen sink as the memories took over. I stared out the window and felt very lonely and dark. And angry. In a rage, to be more specific. I started to shake. I gripped the handle of the knife tighter. I exploded out the screen door, knocking it off its hinges, and ran toward the scarecrow. As I approached it, I raised my knife and began to hack away at the inanimate figure. Over and over, I stabbed the innocent scarecrow, its smile somehow mocking me. Hay and fabric floated through the air as I dismantled it. The anger was still there. The rage still flowed through me, and I would have continued slicing and dicing the scarecrow had my body let me. Physically exhausted, I sat down against its base. Now, I was the one that sounded and looked like an enraged beast. Blood and soot covered my arms and face. My hair was littered with hay. My breathing sounded more like wheezing. Hate enveloped my heart. I hated my father. I hated the evil and the Chaos that ruined my family. Hatred mixed with despair. The hurt was raw and real, and I was afraid…afraid to let it go. Afraid to face it. I began to shake once more. I dropped the knife and just sobbed.

I don't know how long she'd been sitting there, but she was. Not saying anything. Just sitting. I continued sobbing and shaking. Soothing fingers caressed my hair. And then I realized that I was being held. "Mother?" I wondered and hoped. That's exactly what mother would do as I was dozing off to sleep at bedtime.

"No, child," came Anni's soothing voice. "Just be still," she said.

So, we sat on the ground at the base of the scarecrow, and she continued to caress my hair. We were silent for a long time.

Finally, she spoke, "T, what is it that you need to face? The thing that you are afraid to let go?"

It was hard to speak. I knew what it was, but to actually say it…I took a deep breath. Tears formed once again in the corner of my eyes.

Anni coaxed me again, "What did you see here? What do you need to be cleansed of?"

"Cleansed of?" I asked, confused.

"Yes, cleansed of. You see, T, there are some things in your life that are holding you down, holding you back. Things on the inside, dark things. Very dark things. Things that dirty the soul. Things that, if not dealt with properly, will bring you to ruin. Things that Antioch and the evil feast on and delight in. Let me tell you how evil does its work. It doesn't do it by ransacking towns and villages as it did here at your house. This is the fruit of the evil. No, it starts subtly on the inside. A seemingly innocent evil thought. A 'white lie.' A perverse idea. A grudge. Too much pride. Too little humility. Maybe it's anger that starts out as a small flame and grows into hatred, which is manifested in the form of rage. Like your father. He set out to 'find himself.' He abandoned you and your family. It sounded like such a great idea, innocent enough. Leave for a while so he could figure out who he was. But he left you and your mother and sister to fend for yourselves. And what did he find? Himself. He found the selfishness of one who abandons their family to find themselves. He found himself and lost everything that mattered. Ultimately, though, he found darkness, and the darkness welcomed him. He was miserable and saw the same fate for your family. That's why he said, 'You're better off dead!' In his mind, everything is evil. He had given in to it fully and completely." She had stopped caressing my hair at this point, letting what she said sink in.

Finally, I spoke, a million thoughts speeding through my mind. "So, I have to 'deal' with my anger and hatred, or else the evil will consume me?" I asked.

"Yes," was her reply.

"But how?" I wanted to know.

"You have to do the hardest thing you've ever done," she said. She turned my head with her hands to look me directly in the eye. "You have to forgive your father."

"*What?*" I yelled, pushing away from her. I stood to my feet and just glared at her. "*How could you ask me to do that after everything he has done to my family? No, I can't, I won't,*" I yelled at her.

"T," came her soothing voice, "T, I know what I'm telling you seems impossible and even sounds crazy, but it isn't. It has to happen."

"*Why?*" I exploded. "*Why is it so important for me to forgive him? What does it matter?*"

She gave me a faint smile. "Let me ask you a question. When you and Sampson came to Three Sisters, where were you going?" she cocked her head as if to say, "Got him."

"*I'm going to rescue my mother!*" I said tersely.

Grinning again, she said, "Oh really? Are you sure that's who you are rescuing?"

She stood up and walked toward me, her brilliant white hair flowing in the gentle breeze. "You asked, 'What does it matter that you forgive your father?'" she said, grabbing my hands. "You will never be free until you do. You will never know your full potential. You'll be fighting the enemy both outwardly and inwardly at the same time, a battle that's exhausting. Like a civil war inside of your heart. Freedom is found in forgiveness. Cleansing is found in confession."

She looked me straight in the eye and continued, "T, you have no idea of your true potential. You think you do. You've done a few amazing things with the torch, but you have so much to learn, so much to do. You were created with a purpose. You were chosen to do incredible things. Some might even say that you are the game changer between good and evil. *But*—and I emphasize the '*but*'—the only real hope for your mother, for your sister, for yourself, and possibly the world lies in this freedom. The freedom to forgive. And this freedom will allow you to truly soar. To reach the potential you were created for!" She was full-on grinning at this point.

"I, I, don't know…" I said cautiously, hesitantly. "I don't know." My thoughts returned to my mother and sister and even my dad. Out of nowhere, the tears flowed again. My heart hurt.

"Come, child. You've dealt with enough for one day. Let's get out of here," Anni said tenderly.

I blinked back a tear, and we were gone.

TORCH

BACON ME CRAZY

I woke up to the smell of bacon and cinnamon and snoring. Snoring? That's right, snoring. Maybe not so much snoring but a mix of snoring, purring, and growling. And fur. Fur? Something was in my bed! *What?* I jumped out of bed so fast I lost my balance, tripped over my feet, and careened into the wall. There was just the slightest bit of light coming from under the bedroom door, making it nearly impossible to see what was in my bed. It was then I realized I was screaming at the top of my lungs! *What is going on?* I thought, my mind racing with possibilities. I made a break for the bedroom door. As I reached for the handle, I got hit from behind. *This is it,* I thought, *I'm a goner!* I got hit again and again and again! What was hitting me? I turned back, trying to see my assailant when I got hit in the face this time. Next came a chuckle. A familiar chuckle. I opened the bedroom door to flood the room with light. Looking down at the floor around my feet, I saw the objects that were supposed to be my demise: pillows. A pile of pillows. Sitting up in the bed was a laughing lion-boy, Judah.

I was pretty ticked at him when I asked, "What are you doing here?"

"Dude, it's okay!" Judah said. "Anni told me I could crash here since we aren't ready for the big house yet."

"How long have you been here?" I asked.

"Long enough to know that you talk in your sleep, and you have wicked smelling gas. Do you always fart in your sleep?" Judah inquired, quite concerned.

"I...I...I don't know. I'm asleep!" I said, slightly perturbed.

"Dude, I would think about getting that checked out sometime. It can't be good," he said, once again quite concerned.

"The only thing I'm checking out is the bacon," I replied tersely, still a bit miffed at Judah's assessment of my flatulence and his pelting me with pillows.

I wandered out to a familiar scene. The small cabin was just like I remembered it. Anni stood at the kitchen counter, her back to me, plating up bacon, eggs, and pancakes. My mouth began to water, and my stomach began to growl.

Before I could say anything, Anni asked, "How did you sleep?"

"Good, I guess," I said a little guardedly because honestly, I wasn't sure if it was good or not.

"You're wondering if everything you experienced yesterday was a dream or not. Or maybe it was a nightmare."

I hesitated in my answer. Her back was still to me, and I noticed that she was humming a little tune under her breath as she was putting bacon on the final plate. She stopped flatly and turned toward me.

"T, one of my gifts, as a mom, is I can read people. You wear your emotions on your sleeve, which makes it pretty easy for my motherly instincts to tell what you're thinking. And I'm usually spot on."

She resumed her merry humming while washing her hands, but this time, the humming sounded merrier and more enthusiastic. "You know what makes me happy?" Anni asked rhetorically, drying her hands, "Bacon. It's the perfect food. Bacon is savory and salty and crunchy and chewy and even has a hint of sweetness. You can also taste the smokiness in it. And the smell..." with that, she turned to me and shook her head back and forth. She tilted her head back and began to sniff the air. I was mesmerized. I loved bacon too, but I'd never had anyone describe it like this. It was almost poetic. And as if reading my mind, she raised one hand in the air and said somewhat a mix between a poem and a prayer:

"Bacon, no fakin'.

Get in my mouth, no doubt.

Praise."

This very wise woman was very wise indeed.

"Let's eat," she said as the punctuation of her prayer/poem.

Instinctively, I said, "Amen!" with one hand raised in the air as I said it.

Judah seemingly appeared out of thin air when he heard the words, "Let's eat." From what I would learn, this was his all-time favorite phrase.

I grabbed two plates and took them to the table, and Anni followed with two plates as well, and we sat down and began to eat. There was an extra plate on the table that caught my eye. I stared at it briefly, wondering if the extra plate was leftovers or if Anni was expecting someone to join us.

"Yes," she said after noticing me staring at the plate.

"Yes, 'what?'" Judah asked.

"We have a guest joining us. They'll be here in a few minutes once they wrap up a few chores."

We all dove face-first into the plates of food before us. With our munching and savoring the deliciousness of the spread, the silence was praise enough for the chef.

I made it halfway across my plate, mounding up the perfect trifecta of bacon, eggs, and pancakes dripping with syrup when Anni spoke.

"The answer is yes and no," she said. The plate in front of her was completely clean! Now, I'm a fast eater, but this? This was crazytown! Well, she did say that she loved her bacon!

"Yes and no?" questioned Judah, never missing a bite, his mouth bursting with food.

"Were you dreaming last night?" Anni asked rhetorically. "Yes, but you weren't. You needed to go back to a time and place that you had blocked, walled off in your mind. A dark place that you needed to relive as if it really happened last night. You had to confront some locked-up demons so that those locked-up demons don't overtake you." At this point, I dropped my fork onto my plate, and it clanged against the stoneware. She reached over, grabbed my hand, and continued. "You were very brave last night, but that was just the beginning. There are still some demons inside of you that need to be dealt with. You will deal with them when you are ready. Or you won't. Let's hope you do for all of our sake," she said as if saying, "or else."

"Demons?" I said uneasily, realizing that I had unchewed food in my mouth.

"Yes," she said. "Every human has them. Some choose to deal with them. Others try to ignore them. Either way, they're there. That is why the evil is spreading. Antioch's job is made so much easier by those who simply ignore the evil that is inside of them. They go about their daily lives like everything is fine and dandy when, deep down, there are hurts and pains and anger and hatred and frustrations and doubts and insecurities, and, well, all the demons you're dealing with that aren't dealt with," she paused for a moment to let her words sink in. I looked down at my plate of partially eaten breakfast. She released my hand.

"*Oblivions*," Anni continued. "That's what I refer to them as because they're oblivious to the demons, the evil. And yet, sadly, it affects every part of their lives: work, relationships, children, themselves. So, they are easy pickings for Antioch. They're so engrossed in the demons that are harassing them on a daily basis that they can't remember a time when they weren't. And then they look around and see everybody else acting and doing the same things they're doing, so they just accept it as that's just the way it's gonna be. So, their marriages are in shambles, their relationships with their children are strained, and most of all, they're lonely. They do whatever they can do to drown out the darkness…So, they drink too much, they party too much, they fill their spare time with entertainment. They make excuses and blame others for everything. Whatever it takes to drown out the demons. Whatever it takes to avoid the darkness, the loneliness. But the demons are still there, and there is little light left in them at all."

She pushed her chair back from the table and stood up. We were paying full attention. She bent down and began to draw on the table with her finger, and as she did, the scene that she described came to life.

"Imagine if you had a chicken coop and one night, because you were so tired, you forgot to close the coop. Every raccoon, opossum, snake, badger, owl, you name the predator, anywhere near that coop is going to come around for an easy meal. The chickens just climb up on the roost inside the coop just like their little chicken brains tell them to and go to sleep." Again, as she was telling us this illustration, it was coming to life on the table. "They don't say to one another, 'Last one up, please close and lock the coop door.' Nope. They simply go to sleep without a thought for their safety. People today have left the coop door open and are asleep. This makes for easy pickings. The evil is inside the coop and must be driven out, or the whole flock will be devoured." She let the word "devoured" hang in the air. It reminded me of the Offspring and the Arachne. A chill went down my spine. The table turned back into a table, and we were reminded about the purpose of sitting here: breakfast.

Anni, still standing, grabbed her plate to take it to the kitchen sink. As she passed by Judah, she rubbed the top of his mane quite roughly. "Good little kitty," she said with a laugh, "you were brave last night. Thank you for keeping an eye on him!" He purred in delight, and she continued to the kitchen.

"An eye on me?" I said with an air of credulity.

Judah, with a big piece of pancake stuck in his mane and an even bigger toothy grin, chuckled, "Yep, Judah the brave, my lord." He bowed as he said this and, although he was chuckling, there was an underlying hint of seriousness in his voice.

Anni was standing at the kitchen sink, staring out the window, humming when she excitedly exclaimed, "Oh, it looks like our visitor is coming!"

She broke away from her washing and headed to the front door of the cabin. Passing by us, she stopped and said matter-of-factly, "You are on a mission to rescue your mom. Our guest is going to help you."

TORCH

UNLIKELY TEAMMATES

The only reason that Judah's mouth dropped below mine was because he, by far, had a bigger mouth. In fact, his jaw was literally resting on the dining table. Mine was agape further than it had ever been in its existence. Fully open and fully full of food simultaneously. Pancakes, to be exact.

The visitor walked in. No, the visitor floated in as if walking in the air. Each stride was effortless, natural, and…Whoa! Stop everything! Are you kidding me? What? Just what?

Of course, Anni knew exactly what we were thinking.

"Boys, this is my daughter Tre," she said with a smile as she stepped forward to give Tre a hug.

I froze. I wasn't sure what to do other than show her my mouth full of food. I couldn't speak. My heart began to race. "What was in those pancakes?" I whispered to Judah.

Anni looked at me, "It's not the pancakes. It's a girl." And she winked at me.

I was still at a loss for how to react. Do I shake her hand? Too formal. Do I bow? Way too formal. A hug? That would be fantas…Anni caught my eye. *You're right*, I thought, *Too soon and not appropriate.*

Anni took the lead, "Tre, this is Judah" (who was trying to make a smooth recovery) "and T."

I just stared.

"Are you sure?" Tre asked her mother. "You were right; they don't look like much," she said sympathetically.

"Yes, I am sure," Anni replied. "Let me remind you, dear, that those who are chosen aren't chosen because of their physical stature. Strength is important, courage even more so."

Wow, wow, wow! We just got sauced by a girl. A hot girl. Anni shot me a look with a sly grin.

An intelligent girl with a beautiful mind, I corrected my thoughts, knowing that Anni was completely reading my mood.

"Yes, T, she is beautiful," Anni said. I was completely red-faced. Anni continued, "But she is a warrior the likes you've never met."

"Mother, the perimeter of the cave entrance is secure. I drove off a small legion of Offspring—a couple hundred or so—but all is quiet now," Tre said matter-of-factly.

That was the chore she was finishing up. While we were stuffing our faces with pancakes and bacon, she was decimating a legion of Offspring. Her street cred just went through the roof, but how did she do it?

"Are you for real?" Judah mumbled to me with a mouth full of pancakes, in disbelief like me.

"How did you do it?" I asked Tre, a little too incredulously. "You defeated a legion of Offspring by yourself? What I mean is that, well…" already sorry I'd opened my mouth, "you don't look like someone who could defeat a legion of Offspring," I gulped as I said it, realizing that I just made a fool of myself.

Mother and daughter exchanged a look and laughter. The kind that, for a boy, can either be flattering or humiliating. The latter would be the case as Tre spoke up.

She looked directly, unnervingly at me as she spoke.

"T, you think that I couldn't defeat a legion of Offspring because I am a girl? Before you judge me as just a 'girl,' this is how I would describe myself:

"I am *average* in these areas:

"Height: we're about the same height. I may be slightly taller now, but you'll be taller than me in six months.

"Hands: a bit small, but I'm a girl and should have small hands.

"Feet: probably my least favorite feature, good for running but not much else. In fact, never look at my feet!

"Eyes: green. Not much exciting about green eyes.

"Nose: well placed on my face with the ability to smell bacon; what else is it good for?

"Hair: always trying to figure out what to do with it, so it's easier if I just keep it short. As for the color, it's dark brown, not black as most people think.

"I'm *above average* in these categories:

"Strength: don't let my size fool you; I'm very strong.

"Brains: yep, I'm pretty smart; don't underestimate me.

"Courage: I've got lots of it.

"Skin tone: dark tan, almost brown, I have a great complexion that I got from my mother [she glanced at her mom for emphasis] as well as a few freckles around my nose which I used to hate but now find very exotic," she paused. She had my full attention, and she knew it.

"Also, I like control," she began again. "This is a great strength, but it is also one of my greatest weaknesses. That and my temper. In moderation, they are a force to be reckoned with, but in large doses, being in control and having a temper can be my worst enemy."

"Now, my mom calls me beautiful, T, but beauty depends on the person and the object. Take Judah, for instance." Tre walked over and rubbed the top of his head. He blushed. "Judah," she continued rubbing his head, "thinks I'm beautiful too but, I'm just not hairy enough," as she said this, she fluffed his mane with both hands. "Nope. Judah likes hairy ladies." By now, Judah was about to burst with embarrassment! She turned away from Judah's mane and made her way to the seat with the extra plate of food. She dug in.

"But what do your height, size of your hands, and Judah's love life have to do with fighting Offspring?" I asked Tre.

"I guess we'll find out; just don't underestimate me," Tre said with a mouth full of pancakes.

As she devoured her food, Anni addressed Judah and me, "Boys, you need to get ready to go. You have a few-day journey ahead of you, and time is quickly slipping away."

"What about the big house?" I inquired. "We took a bath and got cleaned up so we could go inside."

"Ah, the big house," Anni said, looking at Judah and me, "You came here to rest and recover. And if I can be so honest, you really smelled awful. I mean disgustingly horrendous." She said that plugging her nose, "So, you needed a good bath. One day, you will be ready for the big house, and it will be ready for you. Right now, you have a mother that needs you. So go get ready!" sounding like a pep talk and a scolding rolled into one.

We retreated to the bedroom to gather up a few items: shoes for me and a knapsack for Judah. What Judah had in his sack, I could only imagine.

In the two minutes it took to get our stuff, Tre had finished her plate of food (must run in the family). She was standing near the front door and pacing. A small bag was slung over her shoulder, and the handle of a sleek sword protruded from a sheath that was also slung over her shoulder. She was wearing black trousers that went down just past her knees and a matching sleeveless shirt that was cinched around her waist by a fat black belt that was tied in the back. A red headband held her hair back, and a pair of black boots completed her look. Her outfit was more warriorlike than ladylike, but where we were going, it didn't have to be ladylike. She was anxious to leave. Anxious to fight.

Anni was also at the door waiting for us. She, too, seemed anxious. With concern in her voice, she spoke, "Tre and Judah, I've put provisions in your sacks, so you don't have to worry about stopping for food. This should last you until the town of Helen. When you get to the town, ask for the 'special girl.' Her mother is an Oblivion and will help you. This is a good place to plan your rescue attempt." With that, she opened the door to the cabin and led the way out.

We stood there awkwardly for a moment, no one sure what to say. Anni grabbed her daughter in a long embrace and whispered what sounded like a prayer in her ear. Pulling away from Tre, she walked over and embraced Judah and again whispered what seemed to be a prayer. Finally, she did the same with me. Giving me a hug, she whispered into my ear,

"May the one who is the author and creator of light go before you.
May He help you illuminate the dark places and stamp out evil.
May He protect you, guide you, and strengthen you."

She pulled back, still holding onto my shoulders, looked me in the eye, and said, "Be strong and courageous. Go rescue them all!" The words of Keith came flooding back.

Anni reached in her pocket and pulled out a familiar-looking rag. It had been cleaned as much as it could be, but the name *Sabre* was still clearly visible. Then Tre stepped forward and handed me my torch, saying, "You're going to need this." She wasn't lying.

TORCH

STORYTIME

My family has never been particularly religious. Not in the traditional sense of going to worship somewhere in a building. Religious we weren't, but faithful we were. I got that from my mother. She always had faith in something bigger than herself. Maybe it was this "Creator" that Anni just prayed to. Sometimes at night, I would hear my mom praying, especially when my dad left us. *A lot of good those prayers did us* was a thought that often crossed my mind when I heard her praying. I did believe in something higher, something or someone good, but wasn't sure of the point of it all. In fact, that was the main reason I relied on myself. I didn't need anyone or anything as a crutch. So I thought.

We left Anni standing on the front porch of the small cabin and started following the stream. Everything appeared as it did in the meadow when I first arrived. We were heading in the direction of the big house. I noticed a familiar figure standing at the base of the porch steps. As we approached, I also noticed the little old man, Wallace, standing on the steps. Sampson was so clean; he was radiant. Almost glowing. He was waiting for us.

"Father!" came Judah's happy roar. He came close to Sampson but didn't touch him. They knew something I didn't.

"My *ligo libre!*" came the joyous reply from Sampson. They stood there for a moment, taking it in. "I cannot go on this journey with you.

Wallace and I have a meeting in the big house concerning the approaching evil, and then I must go back and check on our friends."

"The big house?" Judah asked, clearly in awe.

"Yes," came Sampson's reply, "the big house with the big man."

"Whoa!" is all Judah could say in wonder and disbelief.

"You and T will be fine. You are in good hands with Tre. When I make sure that our friends are safe, I will come find you." He gave his son one final look over and started up the steps to the big house. When he got to the top of the steps, he turned and said to Judah, "Be brave, *ligo libre*. I love you," and then he disappeared into the house.

Judah looked away as tears formed in his eyes.

"Let's go!" Tre said firmly. I guess pleasantries were over.

We followed the pathway around the side of the house like before when we jumped off the cliff, but this time, instead of following the stream, we walked into a thick grove of towering pine trees. There was no path. We walked through the pine grove for about an hour when Tre came to a complete stop. *Was she lost?* I wondered. She stood there for a moment, muttering under her breath as if in a conversation with someone.

"This way," was all she said, and we were once again trudging through the thick pine grove. We walked for another hour, maybe two. I don't remember the valley of the Three Sisters mountain being this long. Though it was the middle of the day, if not for my torch, we would have been walking in almost complete darkness—that's how thick the grove was. Walking, walking, walking. No one was talking, which seemed like some unwritten rule. The only sounds were the breaking of an occasional limb, the crunching of leaves under our feet, Judah's breathing, and Tre's mumbling to herself. It was warm, and I paused to wipe my forehead. Ahead of me, I noticed that Tre had abruptly stopped. This time though, she stopped only long enough to yell, "I'll meet you at the bottom!" She disappeared with only a squeal trailing behind her. I sprinted to where Judah was standing.

Judah took a step forward, and then he, too, was gone. A roar of fright trailed him.

What? Where did he go? I stepped forward to see where Judah disappeared too, and the ground gave way beneath my feet. "Ahhhhhhh!" I yelled. I began rushing downward and fast! With my torch the only light now, there was just enough light to illuminate my surroundings—I was sliding down a tunnel. Now, I knew why Tre had squealed! It was amazing! My initial scream of terror was exchanged with the laughter of pure delight! The further I slid, the faster I went. The torch seemed to like it as well because the faster we went, the brighter it shone. Tan-and-brown muddied walls flew by. The tunnel twisted and turned here and there, but other than that, it was smooth. I had no idea how long I was sliding for, but it seemed like ten minutes or more. That may not sound like a long time, but when all you're doing is sliding in the dark, it seems like an eternity. I came to a spot in the tunnel that spiraled down in a corkscrew. Round and round and round I went, still picking up momentum. I was having a great time; my stomach, on the other hand, began to protest. At last, the slide straightened out, and I could see the proverbial "light at the end of the tunnel." I burst out of the tunnel and found myself skidding across a pond, kinda like skipping rocks, except that it was me who was skipping. And except it wasn't wet, it was cold. It was ice! I stopped toward the end of the iced-over pond, my momentum being slowed by a snowbank. I sat there for a moment, trying to collect myself and allow my stomach to catch up to my head or vice versa. Although the snowbank stopped me, I still had to walk a short distance to get off the ice. I'd never seen ice before, let alone walked on it. I tried to stand, my legs and stomach fighting me. I looked completely ridiculous! I gave up and crawled the short distance to the bank. My traveling companions were nowhere in sight.

Standing up, torch in hand, I was still queasy. Before me was a snow-covered path that meandered back toward another grove of tall pines. These pines, though, were winterized, with many bare as a bald-headed man. I started down the path, banks of snow lining each side. Once again, the further into the pine grove I went, the darker it became. Tre and Judah were nowhere in sight.

I heard something. Judah? Tre? A whizzing sound. Kinda like a buzzing insect. Getting closer. And then, *wham!* The insect smashed into the side of my face. It stung. The side of my face was numb. It hurt. And another one hit my stomach, and another one grazed my ear! What in the world? A snowball? And then, out of nowhere, I heard a yell and a roar! *What?* I was being tackled to the ground before I knew what to do. The weight of my assailant pinned me to the ground facedown. *What's going on?* I thought.

Tre plopped down on the ground directly in front of me, looked me in the eye, and said, "Did you miss me?" And then she and Judah began to cackle. Judah got off of me, and I sat up, looking at my companions. They were enjoying this way too much. I vomited. All the pancakes, eggs, and bacon made an appearance on the snowy pathway right at Tre's feet.

"*Gross!*" she yelled. "And don't look at my feet!"

Judah was still laughing. Apparently, he wasn't put off by my vomit. As I sat on the ground, it hit me that although I was sitting on a snow-covered pathway with snowbanks on either side, I wasn't really cold. A well-timed ember landed on my hand. It was the torch's way of saying, "Did you forget about me?" Indeed, I had. Between the sliding and the slipping and the tackling, I forgot I was holding the torch firmly in my right hand, the rag wrapped around its handle. I did feel warm.

Standing to my feet, I gave Judah a sucker punch to the back of his maned head.

"Ouch!" he yelled. Thinking about retaliating, he stopped himself and resolutely said, "I deserved that one," as he rubbed the back of his head.

"If you're done heaving," Tre was saying, "then we need to move on. We can make a camp in an hour or so." She started to walk on, completely in control.

I sat there for a minute. "Who does she think she is? She hits me with a snowball and gets you to tackle me, and now it's my fault we stopped. Well, sorry, not sorry!" I complained to Judah.

"I heard that!" Tre yelled over her shoulder as she continued down the path.

"Heard what?" Judah asked, clearly confused.

"Nothing!" Tre and I said it at the same time.

I helped Judah to his feet, and we both jogged after Tre.

We walked for an hour or more, with tree branches intermingling with glimpses of sunlight. Up ahead, Tre stopped in a spot where the sun was breaking through to the forest floor, making for a dry spot to stop for the night.

"Here," Tre said, "we'll stop here for the night."

Not equipped to camp with tents, sleeping bags, and the like, the only "campy" thing we could do was gather up some tree limbs to make a fire. With a few sticks and the torch's flame, we had a nice fire going in no time. Initially, we sat around and stared at it. That's what you do around a fire: stare at it, watching it jump and dance, listening to it roar when the wind kicks up, seeing embers float high into the air and disappear. It was a pretty scenic scene. A couple of young people out in nature, sitting around a campfire. What campfire would be complete without scary stories? Cue the Spooky Stories by Tre.

Spooky Stories by Tre

I. "The Shape-Shifting Forest"

When the sun finally set, Tre stood in the glow of the fire and, with much drama, began to tell us this story.

"Boys, are you afraid of these woods?" she asked rhetorically. "Well, you should be!" she said, trying to make her voice sound ominous while flailing her arms like she was possessed. I was on my back with my head resting on a log and trying to hold in a chuckle. Judah was laying on his stomach, completely stretched out like a cat. I half expected him to start licking the back of his hands/paws. Tre chuckled. "T, this isn't funny," she scolded me while still laughing.

"What isn't funny?" Judah asked, clearly confused.

"What I'm about to tell you," Tre said to Judah. She then got stone-cold serious. I've never heard a better, more frightening, and realistic storyteller in my life! She began.

"These woods, the ones we're about to spend the night in, are here for a reason. You see, these are on the back side of the Three Sisters mountain and stand as a natural barrier."

"Woo. Sounds scary," I said mockingly.

"Just you wait!" Tre said out loud.

"Wait for what?" Judah asked, clearly confused.

"Some campfire stories are made up simply to scare people. Not this one. As I was saying," Tre began to pace back and forth and use her hands to tell the story, "these woods are known as the Shape-Shifting Woods. At night, the entire forest transforms itself. Nothing is as it seems. I picked this spot because it is an opening with few trees to watch. Stay here, in this clearing, and we have a chance to make it through to first light." She paused so we could think about what she just said.

"So, we sleep here all night and don't move, and we'll be okay?" I asked, thinking she was being overly dramatic.

"If only it were that easy. You see, Antioch has cursed these woods to prey on people's emotions. They play with your mind and your feelings. You start to see things. Good things. Evil things. One minute you think one of us is being hurt, so you come to our rescue only to find it's a trap! The next minute you see a boyhood chum, and you run to greet him, only to discover that it's really a Wolf Terror ready to devour you! No one who enters these woods has ever made it out alive. Except for me."

I was sitting up now. She had my full attention. "How…how…how do you know all this?" I asked hesitantly.

"I know someone who came here and hasn't been seen since. And, when I came looking for them, I had to spend the night here. My mother tried to dissuade me from coming and even tried to warn me of the dangers." Tre looked down at the ground, and for the first time, I noticed she was wearing a necklace with a charm dangling from it. Instinctively, she was rubbing the charm with her thumb and pointer finger. It seemed to give her comfort.

"Did that necklace belong to them?" I inquired.

"*Don't worry about it!*" she snapped. She took a minute to gather herself. "There are more important things to worry about than this stupid necklace."

"Like what?" Judah said almost sleepily. Did he not hear what Tre just told us about the very woods we were spending the night in? How could anyone be sleepy?

"The Wolf Terror. Have you heard of them before?" she asked us both.

"I thought those were myths," I said quickly, hoping it was indeed a myth.

"Let me tell you about them in case you encounter one…or more," Tre said, making her voice ominous once more.

Spooky Stories by Tre

II. "The Wolf Terror"

"A single Wolf Terror has been known to wipe out an entire village in a single night. They are drawn to the smell of human flesh and flames," she stopped and looked back and forth between Judah and me. She got the reaction she was looking for. "Just kidding. About the second part. They love the smell and taste of human flesh but are scared to death of fire. They are themselves shape-shifters that can blend in perfectly with the scenery. You could walk right past one and not even know it. Well, until it is eating you," she stopped again, sensing questions.

"So, what do they look like? How can we tell it's a Wolf Terror?" I asked, fully intrigued and somewhat terrified.

"That's part of the problem; we don't know for sure. All but one person who has encountered a Wolf Terror is dead. They blend in and can take on any form. The one person who saw its true form, though, said it was incredibly strong and that it looked like an oversized dog or a wolf. Some villagers have even been known to take a Wolf Terror, thinking it's a stray dog or an orphaned child, only to end up dead by the morning. The only traces that it was a Wolf Terror were the large bloody paw prints left throughout the home." Storytime was over. She sat down on the ground, gathered her knees in her arms, and started to shake.

"So, these are just harmless campfire stories?" I asked, immediately thinking what a stupid question that was. She didn't have to answer. Her face said it all.

TORCH

A SHORT WINTER'S NAP

The campfire danced before us, oblivious to the danger which Tre just warned us about. It bobbed and weaved and gave a happy little snap, crackle, and pop every so often. Embers floated into the dark night sky, disappearing into the blackness. We stared at it, enraptured by its comforting glow. Instinctively, we huddled closer to it.

Besides the crackling of the fire, there was only the occasional sound of a stick breaking in the woods as if a small nocturnal creature was out foraging. The breeze was barely felt, and what little wind was blowing smelled of smoke and the crispness of a winter night's air.

Nothing seemed off. Still, sleep would be scarce for all three of us. Well, make that two of us. Off to my left, Judah was still sprawled out on the ground, and he was beginning to snore/roar. It wasn't terribly loud, but it was rhythmic. Dare I say it was somewhat comforting? It was like ambient noise that drowns out your racing thoughts. The only thing that would break up his snoring was the occasional snort or delayed snore and the occasional fart. This also happened rhythmically every couple of minutes or so.

All was quiet around the campfire. Tre and I were lost in thought, and Judah was snor…Judah wasn't snoring. I looked over to where he had been sleeping only to see the outline of his body indented into the snow but no lion-boy. Tre and I had been so transfixed on the fire that when Judah stopped snoring, we didn't even notice. Where did he go? Did I doze off and not realize it? Having adjusted my eyes, I saw that he was standing on the edge of the clearing, just feet away from the tree line. His back was to us, and he appeared to be waving at someone.

I got up and started toward him. "*T, sit down!*" came a firmly whispered command from Tre. She meant business. I stopped halfway in between Judah and the campfire.

"Hey, guys, it's my dad!" Judah yelled gleefully over his shoulder. "He said he would join us once he made sure the others made it to safety."

Sure enough, I saw him too. You can't mistake Sampson. I started toward the edge of the clearing, Judah, on the other hand, bolted toward his dad.

"*T, stop!*" Tre commanded. I stopped but just long enough to see Judah getting attacked by his father.

"Dad!" he yelled in disbelief.

I started to run toward him but realized, like an idiot, that the torch was back by the fire. Sprinting back, I grabbed the torch and, to the cries of my friend, dashed to the scene. Tre, meanwhile, sat by the campfire, shaking.

Judah was beginning to lose consciousness in the short time it took me to get there. Judah's feet were dangling in the air as "Sampson" had him by the throat and was trying to strangle him! *What?* My mind was racing. How come Sampson was doing this? Instinctively, I swung the torch and struck "Sampson" in the back. It didn't seem to faze him. He was *so* strong! I took another swing, this time at the back of his head. Nothing! Another swing, this time at one of the arms. This seemed to do the trick! I struck it again and again. One hand released Judah.

Flash!

Instantly we were in some other world. There were still trees everywhere, but it was hot and sticky like a jungle! The snow changed to sand, and the sun was high in the sky, scorching everything with its intensity. Sampson still had one powerful hand wrapped around Judah's throat. Sampson's eyes were glowing red, and he was now trying to bite his son, his mouth snapping at Judah's flesh. Even after I smashed him with the torch, he was oblivious to my presence. It was like he was in a trance. I began smashing his arm with the torch, but this time, a strong paw sent me flying backward!

In desperation, I cried out to Tre, "Help!" She was nowhere in sight. In a last-ditch effort, I charged Sampson, knowing that Judah's life was on the line! The torch roared to life, and we rocketed through the thick jungle air, the torch embedding itself in Sampson's abdomen. He released Judah, and immediately, he turned into his true identity, a Wolf Terror! An oversized werewolf stood before me, bleeding from his side and seething. Raspy, hot breath poured out of his hairy mouth. I grew sad, though, when I looked into his face. Through the fur and the fangs, there was the hint of a man reminiscent of the Offspring or the Chaos. In another life, his name may have been Bob or Stu or Lenny, and he may have had a wife and kids and, ironically, a dog. But this was a man who the evil punished by making him a hideous, terrorizing creature! I would find out later that these Wolf Terrors weren't made this way against their wills. No, they made a deal with the evil, and this was the result. The Wolf Terror in front of me looked as if he might attack me but thought better of it. Holding his side, he snarled at me one last time before limping away into the jungle.

Judah lay there for a minute unmoving, but as I leaned down to check on him, he let out a big sigh. Or was it a snore? I shook him, and he just looked up at me quite strangely.

"What'd you do that for? I was in the middle of this awful dream about my dad trying to kill me, but in the end, Tre saved the day!" Judah said, a bit groggy.

Flash!

We were back by the campfire. He was lying down in the snow in the same place he'd been lying before he went looking for his dad. Before long, he was snoring. Tre, on the other hand, was nowhere to be found. I scanned the perimeter of the clearing, half expecting her to be standing there waving at a Wolf Terror. What to do? Go looking for her or sit down by the campfire and wait? "She's a warrior," her mother said. Plus, she's been out here before, so she can handle herself. So I sat and stared at the fire. Once again, Judah's snoring was comforting. The fire crackled but still no sign of…A scream broke the silence. It was Tre! Or was it?

"T, help me! I'm lost!" Tre yelled.

I was conflicted. She wasn't sitting across from me but after what happened with Judah…

"T, please! I'm so scared!" she pleaded.

I closed my eyes and tried to ignore her.

"They're so close! I'm surrounded!" came Tre's cry.

I couldn't take it. I jumped up and grabbed the torch. I jumped over a still snoring Judah as I ran in the direction of her voice. I made it across the clearing in no time flat and began to weave in and out of the trees. Out of nowhere, something grabbed my hand and pulled me to the ground. It was Tre!

I breathed a sigh of relief. Sitting in the snow at the base of a tree, she put a finger up to her lips, not wanting me to say a word. We sat there for a moment before it dawned on me that she was still holding my hand. With that knowledge, I got nervous and began to sweat. Other than my mom and Em, no girl had *ever* held my hand. Although I was nervous, it seemed so…so natural. *Wait a minute!* I thought to myself, *You are out in the most terrifying woods ever with the most terrifying beasts ever, and you're thinking about a girl, this girl, in those terms! Wake up!* (I would learn later on that what I was thinking at that moment was perfectly normal for boys my age, or any age).

Tre leaned over and whispered in my ear, "We need to get out of here. When I count to three, we'll run. Got it?" her breath was warm and comforting, and it tickled my ear when she whispered and caused me to get goose bumps all over. I couldn't wait to tell Judah!

"Got it?" she whispered again. I wasn't exactly sure what I got or what I was agreeing to…I was still in la-la land. I shook my head none- theless in agreement.

She whispered, "One, two, *three!*" She sprung to her feet, pulling me with her, and we dashed through the woods. All around us, I heard creatures that sounded like they were trailing us. We zigged and zagged, Tre still holding my hand and leading the way.

White flash!

Suddenly, instead of running through the snowy woods, we were running on a tropical beach. The warmth of the sun was welcome, and the smell of the saltwater was refreshing. We ran a considerable way down the beach before coming to a stop. A few people were laying on beach towels, appearing to work on their tans. I realized that Tre still had my hand. My pulse quickened, not that it had slowed down or could get much faster. We stood there for a moment, admiring the scene, a far cry from the snowy woods. I wondered if Judah was still snoring.

"T," Tre said, "you were brave, coming for me." She took her hand and ran her fingers through my bangs. "I don't know if anyone else would have come for me, but you did." She giggled and then turned away as if slightly embarrassed. And then she turned back and gave me a kiss on the cheek. "Thank you," she whispered into my ear. I got goose bumps again.

She was still holding my hand.

"T, get away from her!" a voice came from behind us. As I turned to look, Tre squeezed my hand tighter.

Turning, and quite confused, I saw Tre, or someone who looked like her, coming toward me from up the beach. My mind began to race.

"T, get away from her! That's not me!" came the voice of the identical Tre.

Leaning in and talking through her teeth, the Tre holding my hand said, "Don't listen to her, sweetie! I'm the one holding your hand!" She squeezed extra hard as a reminder.

The other Tre was almost to us when the Tre holding my hand let go and shoved me back. In one continuous motion, she grabbed the sword from the sheath in her back and brought it across my abdomen. I doubled over, and immediately, my blood began to soak the sand. I fell facedown in the sand; this was where I'd watch the ensuing scene.

She looked down at me and said, "It's nothing personal, but then again, it is." She turned her attention back to the approaching Tre and, with quite a bit of delight, said, "Isn't that sweet! She's coming for her boyfriend!" She cackled.

"*He's not my boyfriend!*" screamed the approaching Tre.

"Hey, T," the nearby Tre said, looking down at me, "if you like one Tre, how about six of us!" She laughed a hideous laugh and then yelled in a demonic voice, "*Now!*"

Instantly, the sunbathers on either side of her transformed to look like Tre. The four of them, along with the one that sliced my belly, began to charge the one who just proclaimed that I was "not her boyfriend." They were about twenty feet away from me; the fight was on!

(cue the techno music)

Six swords were out, and they started to move around in a circle, each waiting for the other to make the first move. Tre, the real Tre, was by far outnumbered. One of the adversaries made her move.

She lunged at Tre, real Tre, with her sword. She moved to the side and knocked the sword out of her assailant's hands. Tre, with lightning speed, sliced off one of her hands, which went flying down the beach. The creature howled, now halfway in between looking like Tre and a Wolf Terror. The creature scurried after its sword. Another Tre attacked the real Tre, who this time was going for the assailant's legs. She jumped over the fake Tre, pushing off her back and standing directly behind her. A swift swing of the sword and this Tre was sliced from the top of her back to her butt. The creature fell forward in pain, letting out a hideous demonic scream and flickering between looking like Tre and looking like a Wolf Terror.

The next two Tres attacked together. Now three Tres were fighting it out, swords clanging, the air filled with sweat and death. They fought round and round, moving up and down the beach with ferocity. Tre, my Tre, was holding her own but for how long? She knocked one of her counterparts to the ground with a well-landed kick to the stomach. The other she nailed in the face with the flat side of her sword, which sent the creature tripping over her teammate. She looked poised to take them out when the original two came back into the fray. She raised her sword to finish off the two on the ground when she was tackled. One of the Wolf Terrors (fully a Wolf Terror now) was on top of her with its full weight and fury unleashed on her! She was in trouble!

All the while, the Tre that sliced my stomach stood back and watched in delight.

I lay there watching it all, feeling helpless and sorry for myself. Sure, my stomach was sliced in two, and I was bleeding to death, but this was a bad time for a pity party. I began to blink away a few tears that were left over from the initial stomach pain. Blink, blink, blink. The tears covered my eyes, making everything blurry. I couldn't see what was happening to Tre but what I heard, though, made me cringe. It sounded like a demon-feeding frenzy. Blink, blink, blink. Eyes focusing on... What in the world? Keith? Walking toward me, wearing board shorts. What? With all the blood I've lost, I must definitely be hallucinating! And then, the oversized rodent spread out a towel next to where I lay dying in a pool of blood and began to sun himself.

"Keith..." I called out to him. But he was in his own world, enjoying the sun. I tried again, "*Keith!*" yelling this time. This got his attention as he rolled over on his side and looked at me. He was wearing sunglasses. *Weird*, I thought.

"Oh, hey, Milky White! Whachu doin' here?" Keith asked. He smelled like sunscreen. "I thought I was the only one that knew about this place." Then he noticed the blood. "Looks like you've got a little cut," he said. "Is you in a pickle, Milky White?" he asked.

"*Yes!*" I screamed in pain. "Yes, and I can't do anything about it!" I blurted out.

"Well, it looks like someone's havin' a little pity party. I like parties, can I come?" Keith said mockingly. "Your girlfriend is being attacked by a pack of Wolf Terrors, and you're worried about a little blood and perhaps losing an innard or two! Some boyfriend you are!" And he scowled, looking over the edge of his sunglasses at me.

"She's not my girlfriend!" I protested painfully.

"Well, if you care about her, you'll figure out a way to save her!" Keith said as he pointed at me. "By the way, I found this down by the water. I think it belongs to you." He tossed an object that landed by my face. My torch! A foot stomped down on the handle of the torch. Tre, the one who sliced my stomach, stood on top of the torch, trying to bury it into the sand.

"Oh no, you don't!" she said, looking down at me. "I know all about these things!" But as she bent down to grab it, she violently rocketed over my head, landing headfirst in the sand. Keith stood there smiling, pleased that he was that strong. He put the torch in my right hand, and I squeezed. Warmth, strength, and healing flowed through my body.

Keith lay back down on his towel and folded his hands over his chest as if nothing just happened. And casually, he looked over at me and said over the top of his sunglasses, "Save them all, T! Save them all!" And then he was gone.

Her screams will go with me for the rest of my life. The Wolf Terrors had Tre pinned down and were trying to tear her apart. *Not for long!*

I rose slowly, dramatically from the blood-soaked sand. The torch was roaring in anticipation of the fight that was about to ensue. I charged! The closest Wolf Terror had no idea what hit it. I ran full speed and swung an uppercut at the back of its skull. The skull was crushed instantly, and the hair on its head was singed. This time, it wasn't injured; it was dead.

A second Wolf Terror, holding down one of Tre's arms, leaped to its feet to attack. I spun around and smashed it in the stomach, which was now on fire. It tried to advance on me, but I parlayed its attack and crushed its kneecap as it went by. I jumped on its back and shoved the torch in its ear. The cries of a dying demon filled the air, as did the stench! It toppled to the ground in a heap!

The third Wolf Terror lay on top of Tre still. It was trying to bite her face as she struggled beneath its grip. I ran and jumped off the carcass of the most recently deceased Wolf Terror and drove the torch down and through the Wolf Terror's back. It released its grip on Tre, who wriggled her way out from under it. Surprisingly, it whirled around to confront me, knocking me backward in the process. How it was alive, I had no idea! There was literally a flaming hole in its body. You could see daylight out on the other side. It smiled a hideously awful smile and ran at me. I pushed off to meet it, but my foot gave way slightly in the sand just enough to cause me to be off-balance when we collided. We tumbled backward over and over in the sand. It was on top of me, and the torch, having come out of my hand in the tumbling, was just out of reach. It pinned down my arms and put its hairy knees into my open abdomen. Without the torch, the wound opened back up, and the pain overtook me. The Wolf Terror was snapping at my face over and over again, trying to rip my face off. The pain was so fierce that I knew that I could only hold it off for so long. Closer and closer, it got to my face; its hideous breath was stinging my eyes and my nose! I felt a canine graze my cheek and felt the coolness of blood run down my face. I was losing. I couldn't take it any longer. The pain, the fatigue, the…what? It took me a second to realize that the creature had tumbled off me. Unbeknownst to me, Tre had sliced the creature across its back.

"*T, grab the torch!*" Tre yelled. I crawled over to where it laid in the sand, just a few steps away. Grabbing its handle, I sensed strength, warmth, and healing flow through my body again. I lay there, allowing the sensation to envelop me for a moment. A very brief moment.

"*Watch out, T!*" came the cry from Tre.

Out of the corner of my eye, I saw the Wolf Terror crawling toward me. It was coming to finish me off. I had other plans. I rolled over with the torch firmly in my hand and lunged at the beast. As I did this, I made sure to strategically shove the torch into the hole in its body and embedded it in its abdomen. The creature landed on its back, and I landed on top of it. The smell of a burning demon is noxious. I wanted to vomit, but I wasn't pulling the torch out until I was sure this one was dead. It continued to struggle and tried to bite me until it finally breathed its last, and I finally breathed my first in quite a few minutes, something I hadn't done due to the vile odor. I extracted my torch from the creature's abdomen and just stayed there for a minute, kneeling in the sand. Looking at this Wolf Terror, I realized that this one used to be a woman. A young woman. For some reason, in my mind, I thought that the Wolf Terrors were only men who'd lost their lives to the evil. I guess both sexes made deals with Antioch. Studying her face, I tried to imagine what she looked like prior to her hideous transformation. She may have been somewhat beautiful. Those days, though, were well past her. All her days were well past her. I took solace in possibly putting her out of some tormented misery.

"You can thank me later," Tre said as she walked toward me. I stood up and made my way past her, ignoring her snide comment, and down to the water's edge. I sat down in the sand just enough so that the ebbing water could lap against my feet. My shirt was a bloody mess, and my stomach was still tender but was healing. The scene was so picturesque. My mom told me about the beach, about a beach like this. It was more beautiful than I imagined. Weird are the things you think about at times like these.

To my right, Tre came and sat down. She began to bury her toes in the sand, mostly so I wouldn't stare at her feet. We sat there for a few minutes, just taking it all in: the scenery, the battle with the Wolf Terrors.

Tre broke the silence. "I'm not your girlfriend," she stated matter-of-factly. "And I'm not here to bail you out every time you get yourself in trouble." She punctuated this statement with a "humph" and a stern stare.

"Every time I get in trouble?" I asked, a little perturbed. "You were the one who called out to me because you were scared and lost in the woods!" I shot back.

"I wasn't lost in the woods! I told you to stay put by the fire! You went running after a Wolf Terror disguised as me, and we both almost died because of it!" She was shaking but looking me straight in the eye. "Your feelings for me almost cost us everything!" She let that sink in.

She was right: I acted foolishly. I was embarrassed, and my pride had been hurt. I couldn't deny the fact that I was extremely attracted to her and even more so now that I saw her in action. She was a mighty warrior, and I, well, I just had a silly torch. I had to act more rationally.

Her hand was on my arm before I knew it. Once again, the goose bumps returned. She knew I was angry with myself, but she also knew that she needed me.

As if taking a cue from her mom and reading my body language, Tre said, "That torch in your hand, it's not so silly. It saved my life today while I was trying to save yours." She let go of my arm. "We have more battles to fight. Many more."

TORCH

FAMILY REUNION

"We need to get back," Tre said, still wiggling her toes in the cool sand. She stood up. I watched her out of the corner of my eye, trying not to seem like a creeper. Instead of walking away, though, she just stood there. I thought she was waiting for me, but when I turned to get up, I realized she wasn't waiting for me, she was staring down the beach at someone. Clearly, she knew who this person was.

"Tre! Tre!" came the excited greeting of a familiar voice. Walking down the beach and waving enthusiastically was Anni.

"Come on, T, we need to go...*now!*" Tre said and started to tromp off in the opposite direction of her mother. I thought she'd be excited to see her, but apparently not.

Anni was jogging toward us now. Tre was walking more briskly now, and I had to jog to catch up with her.

"Tre, sweetie! I need to talk to you!" Anni yelled at our backs.

And suddenly...

Flash!

She was in front of us, and we were in the meadow of Three Sisters right outside of the little cabin.

Anni and Tre just stared at each other, Tre seething now.

"Of course, you'd bring us here!" yelled Tre.

"Why, this is where we live, honey," Anni said with kindness in her voice.

Tre was still seething. "And of all people to impersonate?" she roared.

"Sweetie, I don't know what you're talking about," Anni said with a note of concern.

"I'm not your sweetie, and you're not my mother!" Tre yelled and grabbed her sword.

Turning to me, Anni said so sweetly, "T, can you believe how ungrateful children can be? Can you imagine saying such cruel things to your own mother? And a sword? That's a bit dramatic, don't you think?" she asked me.

My mind was in a fog, trying to process what was happening.

"The sword is exactly what you need!" Tre roared as she charged her mother.

Anni wasn't looking at Tre. No, she was looking at me, her eyes pleading with me to see things her way. It was starting to work.

At first, Anni was merely blocking the blows from her daughter. It seemed relatively easy for her. She was very agile for being middle-aged! My mom would never have been that spry!

"You are an imposter!" Tre said through gritted teeth as she continued her assault.

"No, dear, you are confused. The forest does that to people. I would never harm you," Anni answered.

"Maybe she's right, Tre?" I spoke up. "Maybe this is your mom, and that's why she's not fighting back? Maybe the forest has completely twisted your mind?"

"Shut up, T! I know my own mother!" Tre yelled as she continued her assault. She landed a blow to Anni's skull, causing her to tumble back onto the grass near the stream. "And this is not my mother!" she growled.

Anni pleaded with me, "T, help me. Please!"

Tre was going in for the kill! In three quick steps, I was in between them, torch in my hand. Tre stood in front of me, sword drawn. Anni was behind me on the ground, cowering.

"*Get out of my way, T, or I will kill you too!*" Tre growled.

"No, T! Don't let her kill me!" Anni pleaded.

"Tre, put the sword down!" I yelled, anger building.

"*No!*" yelled Tre as she swung her sword toward my stomach.

Instinctively I sidestepped her sword, but, midswing, her sword ran into something...her mother. I felt the blood before I saw it. It was pooling at my feet. Not just Anni's blood but mine, too. I looked down to see the tip of Tre's sword sticking out of my abdomen not too far from my previous puncture wound. My knees began to buckle. Tre had stabbed us both in one blow!

"Hold on to the torch!" Tre demanded.

My world was spinning, and if not for the torch, I would have been dead before my knees hit the ground.

A ghastly cackle echoed off the valley floor and seemed to go on for hours. It was not Anni's laugh; it was the laugh of a demon, a Wolf Terror!

Tre walked past me and straight to the monster, speaking with authority, "I will not kill you today, sister. I will let you live so that you can go back to your demon pack leader and tell him that the One is coming!"

She took the flat of her sword and crushed the creature with it, sending the demon fleeing in the wake of stench and bloodcurdling shrieks.

I was kneeling on the ground still, the pooled blood soaking into the ground.

An odd sensation: having a sword pulled out of your body. An odder sensation: feeling your body heal from the said sword. My body was working overtime, in conjunction with the torch, to repair itself. I was tired. I just needed a nap. I closed my eyes.

When I finally opened my eyes, it was dark. The fire crackled. The lion-boy snored. The scene was almost the way I left it, except Tre was now sitting next to me on the log, still holding her legs in her arms and still shaking. I wanted to put my arm around her and comfort her, but the last thing I remembered was her saying she would kill me if I didn't get out of her way. Oh, and her swinging her sword at my head.

Thinking she was awake, I ventured a conversation about what just happened, "Tre, what happened? What was that all about?" She just stared at the fire, continuing to rock. I decided to let it go. Maybe she'd want to talk another time.

Daybreak came and was a welcome sight. Somehow, I managed to get some rest, but not much. You know the stinging sensation in your eyes when you are overly tired? That was me. Judah, on the other hand, was wide awake and full of energy.

"I love sleeping in the great outdoors!" he said cheerfully. "The fresh air, the smells, the trees…"

It was my turn to throw a snowball. It hit him smack in the side of his head.

He looked at me as if to say, "What was that for?"

"Anything but the trees. You can talk about anything but them," I said to him.

"T's right," Tre said, stretching. "I've had enough of this place. Let's get out of here." She reached in her bag, grabbed a roll, and tossed it to me. "This is a to-go meal." She stood up and headed toward the path to continue our trek toward Helen.

Thankfully, after an hour of walking, we cleared the forest. The pathway turned into a narrow road, and the terrain was hilly but with few trees. The air was foggy, waiting for the sun to burn it off. The snow was gone, and though cool, it was more like a fall day. After a few minutes' walk away from the forest, we trudged up a hill, and from the top of the hill, we could see a little hamlet with about a dozen or so small wooden homes lining the road. Each house had a chimney, but not a wisp of smoke was evident. As we headed down into town, we passed a sign that read, "Forest Glen." An ominous red "A" with a slash across it was painted on the sign.

Tre spoke up, "This is strange. I wonder who did this?"

"Ominous is more like it," I said.

We continued into town. It was empty. The tiny pub, the cobbler's shop, the blacksmith's shed, all devoid of life. Not a person or animal in sight. Red As with slashes were painted on all the doors. Footprints in the mud looked much like the paw prints that the Wolf Terrors were known for. "Was this their doing?" we all wondered. This was the closest village to the forest.

Our senses were heightened. Every sound, every smell was cause for alarm. The hair on the back of my neck stood up. The fog was even thicker in the little town than on the hilltop. It was like a damp blanket covering the village and making it difficult to see. It actually looked more like dusk than midmorning.

We made our way through to the opposite side of the village where, just off the road, was a quaint white church. On another day or in a different setting, this would be an inviting place to stop. A few wooden steps led to a set of double doors. These doors, unlike every other door in town, did not have a red slash across them. In fact, the word "Welcome!" was written on a sign in a cheery font just above the doors. There were four tall stained-glass windows on the side of the church nearest us. We hadn't stopped walking, nor had we stopped staring at the church.

So enraptured were Tre and I in staring at the church that we didn't even notice that Judah had disappeared. We were almost completely past the church when we discovered his absence. I got ready to call out for him when Tre held her finger to my lips. A buzzing sound, slight, but buzzing was coming from the vicinity of the church. We headed quietly, stealthily in the direction of the sound. While we were flanking back around to the front of the church, the buzzing sound got louder. As we approached the front of the church, we noticed the grass directly in front of the steps was red and marked with paw prints. The buzzing was louder at this point and was coming from just beyond the porch railing. A few dozen flies hovered above the porch but high enough that we could see them. Each step had a large bloodstain on it with the form of an oversized paw clearly outlined. The smell made its way down the steps and into our mouths and noses. I had to resist the urge to both vomit and run.

Tre led the way slowly up the stairs, one step at a time. The third step creaked loudly. We both froze. After waiting a minute to see if we alerted anything or anyone, we finished our ascent and were horrified by the scene on the porch.

Just to the right of the double doors with the cheery "Welcome" sign lay the corpse of a Wolf Terror. From its look and smell, it had been dead for several hours. The blood that it laid in was still glossy, and the flies, numbering in the thousands, almost completely covered its face. It smelled worse than it looked! My stomach couldn't take it! I leaned over the porch railing and let loose. Still queasy, I turned back to the gory scene. Tre was squatting down near the Wolf Terror's face, swatting engorged flies out of the way.

"I remember this one," Tre whispered.

With a lump in my throat, I squatted down too to get a better look. I didn't remember that one. Staring intently at the hideous face, sadness overcame me. I don't know where it came from, but it manifested itself in the pit of my stomach. It was emptiness, a dark void. I shook my head, trying to escape the feeling. Tre, too, seemed to be wrestling with this feeling. We stared down at the creature and then looked up at each other. Our only indication that we weren't alone was the ever so slight creak just inside the double doors before they burst open!

The doors exploded as something came flying out, knocking me back and causing me to tumble down to the base of the steps. It took Tre a second to respond. She dismounted the porch over its railing to give chase. The black creature was running full speed around the side of the church with Tre in hot pursuit. I gathered my wits and joined in the chase. Well, it wasn't much of a chase. Turning the corner of the church, I saw Judah sitting on the ground, a sandwich in one hand, the runner in the other. Judah was grinning when he saw me.

His mouth full of sandwich, he said, "Tre's mom makes the best sandwiches!" as if the creature struggling to flee in his other hand didn't exist.

The creature in Judah's hand wasn't a creature at all, just a frightened man. Tre went over and spoke to him in soft, hushed tones. His struggling slowly abated.

"Judah, you can release our friend," Tre commanded Judah, to which Judah dropped him on the ground.

"This is Simon," Tre told us, "He's going to tell us what happened here."

TORCH

SIMON SAYS

Simon sat still for a few minutes before talking. Like Tre last night at the campfire, he held his knees in his arms and rocked ever so slightly. It was very odd to see a grown man do this. He was wearing some sort of religious robe that was black with a white collar. I assumed it was a religious robe since he came out of the church, but since I'd never been to church, this was just an assumption. He wasn't too old, maybe in his early thirties, but his face was hidden by an impressive beard. His hair was unkempt, and he smelled of cigars or a pipe. Centuries later, they would call Simon a "hipster." Now, though, it was just a practical look. He had blue eyes that darted to and fro and sat squarely atop a slightly crooked nose (not like a witch's nose at all but like somewhere along the way he'd broken it). When he finally spoke, it was in a surprisingly rhythmic fashion, although he was still terrified.

Simon began:

"Little town,
It's a quiet village.
Every day
Like the one before.
Little town,
Full of little people
Waking up to say—"
(dramatic pause)

Simon paused for a moment and looked over at Judah. He continued his story, and Judah began to make a beat with his mouth.

Judah continued his beat; Simon continued his story:

"Now, this is a story all about how
My life got flipped, turned upside down,
And I'd like to take a minute,
Just sit right there,
And I'll tell you how I became the Prince of Despair.

In West Mountain Glenn, I was born and raised,
In the village where I spent most of my days,
Chillin' outside cause the weather was cool,
Tippin' some cows outside of school
When a couple of dudes who were up to no good
Started makin' trouble in the villagehood.
They promised wealth, fortune, and fame;
The town folks ate it up, what a shame.
Sign on the dotted line, the people agreed
They gave up their rights for an ounce of greed.
Rounded up, chained up, and taken away
To the evil creatures, mines to become his slaves.
Those that straight up refused to sign
Were captured, eaten, or resigned to hide.
Now, I'm the only survivor, the only one spared,
So this is how I became the Prince of Despair."

Simon glanced over at Judah, who stopped his beat by saying, "*Yo!*" and holding out his arms and laying on his side.

Peculiar, I thought.

"Peculiar indeed," said Tre. "It will never catch on."

If the story wasn't so horrific, I would've applauded.

"Simon," Tre started to ask, "were you the town truth minder?"

Simon shook his head. "No, I was just the assistant truth minder. Along with the head truth minder, Glenn, we tried for days to stop people from signing the contract. 'It's evil!' Glenn told the people.

'You don't need money to be happy,' he would plead. At least, I tried for days. When the wagons pulled up to whisk the villagers off to their 'fame and fortune,' Glenn was in one of the wagons. He met the men in the middle of the night and signed the contract. Within a week, the whole town had either signed or were being rounded up against their wills. I escaped to the edge of the forest and waited. When it all died down and the men moved on, I snuck back here to hide in the sanctuary. When you came up, I thought you were here to take me to the mines," he paused for a moment.

"I don't know how it happened, but Glenn was changed into a Wolf Terror. As he was wheeled out of town with the others, I heard him screaming, 'I take it back! I take it back!' Perhaps that's why he was transformed," Simon said distantly.

"How do you know that Glenn was turned into a Wolf Terror?" I asked inquisitively.

"That Wolf Terror on the porch of the church? That Wolf Terror is or rather was Glenn," Simon said. This is why he dubbed himself the "Prince of Despair."

"He either wanted to die in a place that brought him comfort, or more than likely, was seeking forgiveness," Simon said, forlornly.

The only one who didn't seem phased by Simon's story or by the condition of the village was Judah, who was now lounging on a tree limb above our heads, eating another sandwich. Who could eat at a time like this?

Simon turned and asked, "Where are you heading?"

Tre looked at me as if not to reveal too much to Simon. His story sounded credible enough, but he was a stranger, and at times like these, it's best to be on guard.

Tre spoke up. "We are looking for someone," she said, true enough but not nearly the whole story. "And we are on our way to Helen to see if they are there."

"Hmmm…" Simon said. "This is the furthest village to the east of Helen, and past this village are the Shape-Shifting Woods," he paused, thinking. "So you came here through the woods?" Simon asked.

It was my turn to speak up. "We got a little lost, off track, and ended up there. Look at us; we're just kids," I was playing dumb.

"But you survived the woods?" Simon said incredulously. "No one has ever survived those woods," he said with skepticism.

"Are you for real?" I said, still acting. "We heard the myths about those woods but thought that it was made up just to scare people. You know, 'small-town folklore'?"

"You didn't notice anything weird or evil?" Simon asked in disbelief.

Judah, mouth full of sandwich, spoke up. "Sir, have you ever been camping?" Judah asked rhetorically. "Well, that's what it was like because that's what it was! Loads of fun! We even had a snowball fight!" he finished with a chuckle.

Tre and I exchanged a look. It was anything but a fun camping trip.

Simon didn't know what to say.

"Anyway, we must be going now. Boys!" Tre summoned us. Judah jumped down from the tree, and the three of us turned to leave. We couldn't get out of this creepy town fast enough.

"Wait!" Simon yelled. He ran in front of us and stood facing us, his arms out in front of him to stop us. "Wait!" he said again for good measure. "Let me go with you. Don't leave me in this cursed town!" the Prince of Despair cried.

"No!" Tre said without even thinking about it.

But Simon wouldn't take "no" for an answer. He got down on his knees like he was about to pray and said over and over again, "Please, please, please!"

"No!" Tre said again, more firmly this time.

Simon groveled some more, but we had no time for the likes of Simon. We needed to leave. We walked right past Simon, leaving him on his knees on the side of the church. As we got back to the main road, we heard his footsteps behind us.

"But I know Helen: the streets, the people, the places. I used to live there, and it's not a place to get lost in!" Simon pleaded to our backs as we kept walking.

"What if he's right? What if he does know Helen as he says. He could be valuable," Judah whispered.

"No!" Tre whispered back as we kept walking.

"I agree with Tre. How can we trust him? He's the only witness to what actually happened here," I whispered.

Judah gritted his teeth and, hardly whispering at this point, pleaded Simon's case, "I don't want to live with having this on my mind, thinking that I left someone out here to fend for themselves."

Without giving us the opportunity to say anything, Judah whirled around and said to Simon, "C'mon, let's go! Catch up!"

Tre and I were thinking the same thing…

TORCH

DIDN'T SEE THAT COMING

The thought was simple. The thought was disturbing. The thought hung in the air between Tre and me for about an hour. The thought will come to fruition in the next few paragraphs.

The road undulated up and down as the terrain still rose and fell over hills of varying heights. It might be picturesque save for the fog that continued to follow us. Like a veil or a fabric scrim, it gave us just vague glimpses of the landscape around us, which appeared mostly like groves of trees and fields. I thought I saw a scarecrow similar to the one from my family's field. When I looked more intently, though, it appeared to be grimacing in pain with drops of blood trickling down its face. I got a chill.

I'd never been to Helen, but I thought by now we should be nearing the outskirts of the city. At the very least, I expected a directional sign. Something like "Helen: 21 Miles." Nothing. We just kept walking.

It was about midafternoon, as far as any of us could tell. Judah was quite cheerful. Every once in a while, he would scan the sky. Not sure what he was looking at or for, I just kept plodding along with the rest of my party.

The road flattened out at the top of a hill, and we found ourselves surrounded by trees. We were in a forest. The tall pines rose to the sky and blocked what little sun was trying to break through the dense fog. The road narrowed to just a small path. On either side of us, snow was mounded up, and there was a light covering of snow on our pathway. Weird. This looked so familiar. As we plodded along the path, the trees up ahead gave way to a clearing, and the closer we got to the clearing, the less snow was evident. The pathway got wider as we approached a road. Up and down a few hills until we stood atop a hill and overlooked a familiar scene.

Walking down the hill, we passed a familiar sign saying, "Forest Glen" with a red "A" and a slash across it. We hadn't walked in a circle, had we? No, we were supposed to be here. We continued into town, passing familiar homes—doors with red slashes across them. The fog still clung to the ground. This time, though, there were whispers coming from all around us. Something in between human and animal whispers. As we neared the simple town square, Judah stopped to get a drink from the town's well. He took his time drinking and stopped to look up into the sky.

We heard the flapping of powerful wings and, to our relief, saw Sampson. Judah waived at his dad like he hadn't seen him in forever. The chattering around us got louder, though there was no one there. It was unnerving, but with Sampson there, I didn't feel anxious. He would be able to tell us what was going on.

Sampson alighted on top of the town well and sat there like a gargoyle. He was immensely immense! We gathered around him, Tre to his left, me and Simon to his right, and Judah standing directly in front of his dad, a grin of expectation on his face.

Tre spoke first, "So, this is where you want it to go down? Right here?"

"Why not?" said Sampson, a sinister toothy grin plastering his face. "This looks like a great place to die." He was chuckling as he said it.

What's going down, and who is about to die? I wondered, grabbing the torch a little tighter. The torch was much quicker than me and had already started to burn hotter, making a low rumbling sound. It was ready for what was next. Me, on the other hand…

Tre spoke, "Sampson and Judah plan on dying here, in this place. This is their choice. Get on with it!" Tre demanded as she pulled out her sword and smashed Judah on the back of the head. He tried to return the blow, but she was too quick. Sampson jumped down from the well and headed straight toward Simon and me. His strong arms came swinging at us. I somersaulted backward in the air doing a backflip, narrowly avoiding getting smashed in the head. Simon wasn't so lucky. He was sent flying through the air and landed on the thatched roof of a barn. Sampson turned his attention toward me, chasing me at full speed. I ran toward the nearest house, and he exploded through the wall of that house. The whole house came down just as I made it out the back. He was still pursuing me. I ran toward the next house, jumped on top of some crates, and flipped up onto the thatched roof. I waited for a minute, listening. I must have lost him…The thatched roof beneath my feet exploded as Sampson rocketed through the roof, blasting me upward into the sky. We were in midair, and he was swatting at me, trying valiantly to kill me as we tumbled toward the ground. From this height, I would surely die if I hit the ground. I willed myself to stop by pointing the torch at the dirt road beneath me. It worked as I stopped mere inches from the ground! Landing softly on my feet, I struck a defensive pose. Sampson was coming straight down at me. Make that an offensive pose. I had no choice…Believe me: I was just protecting myself. Sampson neared like a speeding bullet, and I swung! Wham! I caught him square in the skull. An explosion of fire and fur. He went flying backward into the nearest house, taking down the entire structure. He wasn't through, though. Neither was Judah. He was going after Tre. She was faster, but he was stronger. Around the town square, he chased her. Every few steps, she'd turn around just long enough to turn and cut him. At one point, she whirled around and ran straight at him; the flat end of her sword sent him careening into the well, completely destroying it. He charged her again, and they began to spar: Judah with his strong arms and hands, Tre with her sword and speed. Tre nicked Judah's arm, and he started to spurt out blood. She didn't see his other arm; however, that drove straight into her stomach, sending her flying backward into a wall. She doubled over and was slow to get up. I could barely see her head above the fog. The chattering of creatures grew louder, kinda like cicadas on a quiet summer night. The noise was growing, becoming almost deafening. Simon was nowhere to be seen.

"*Get up!*" I yelled to Tre as Judah bolted toward her. "*Get up!*" I pleaded as I took off toward her.

"*I can't,*" she yelled, clearly in pain. "*I can't move!*"

Judah was a few steps ahead of me as we both were trying to get to Tre. I willed my legs to go faster, and they responded. Judah was directly in front of me, and Tre was directly in front of him. I raised the torch to take him out; however, I tripped over something in the dense fog. Fortunately, I careened into his back with the torch plunging all the way through his body. Screaming, Judah stumbled, losing his footing. His momentum was propelling him right at Tre. I, too, was still rocketing forward right behind Judah. Judah came to a stop right on top of Tre. She let out a fierce yell! Judah's backstopped my momentum, but now I was staring at the tip of a sword, a sword that nearly took my eye out. Tre! She had plunged her sword through Judah when he landed on her. Judah was Judah no more. He transformed into a Wolf Terror. A dead Wolf Terror but a Wolf Terror, nonetheless.

"Don't touch the ground!" Tre commanded. I was still on the Wolf Terror's back.

Looking into the dense fog, the sound of the creatures almost overwhelming my eardrums, I noticed hands reaching up, grabbing at whatever they could. Tre was trapped not just by Judah; these creatures were holding her down. A gnarly leathery green hand with mutilated fingernails grabbed my leg and started to pull me down. It was strong! I thrust the torch into this corpse's hand just before getting pulled down. I scrambled up onto Judah's back and got a better perspective. The entire town square was crawling with these creatures, which were moving with the fog. Random shrieks and hideous groaning flowed from the fog. These zombielike creatures were crawling around on all fours like animals, but they were clearly human at some point. Tre was being held down by them, but Judah's body prevented them from completely taking her under.

What to do? I thought, *If I move Judah, then they'll take Tre down. If I don't, she'll have to stay here forever. And then, where do we go? How do we get out of here? Are these zombielike creatures everywhere? Think, think, think!*

No time for that. Coming back like a comet, Sampson was heading right at me. My mistake was forgetting about him. His mistake was remembering me. As he closed in on me, I gripped the torch tighter. I bent my knees, almost crouching. *Wait for it*, I told myself and the torch. Wait for it…He was close enough. *Now!* I jumped just as he got ready to crush me. I flipped over the top of him, running the torch down the length of his back, all but splitting him in two. He destroyed the house that Tre was leaning against as his true Wolf Terror self was revealed. I came down on a section of the well wall that was still standing (barely). The only problem was that there was only enough wall left for one foot to stand on. I stood there precariously perched on one foot, assessing the situation. Sampson and Judah, the Wolf Terrors, were both dead. Tre was still trapped by both Judah on top and the zombielike creatures below. I was trapped, standing on one foot, on top of a crumbling wall. I had completely forgotten about Simon.

My foot was beginning to slip; the wall was falling to pieces. I was falling backward in slow motion right into the fog of zombielike creatures. Partway to the ground, zombie hands grabbed me and yanked me hard into the cobblestone ground. They were on top of me in an instant! They weren't big; in fact, they looked like little kids, but they were strong, and there were so many of them! The sound was even more deafening below the fog, like a schoolhouse cafeteria gone mad! My head hit the cobblestone hard, which didn't help me think. The zombie children were biting my arms and legs. Two were trying to wrestle the torch from my hand. The torch melded itself in the palm of my hand. But they kept coming and coming. One sat down on top of my chest and bared its grotesque teeth, shrieked, and made a pass at my face with those same teeth. I moved my head just in time, and instead of biting my face, it got a mouthful of cobblestone. It reared back again for a second go at my face. I dodged it again, but this time, it nicked my ear. They were winning. I was dying.

I saw movement out of the corner of my eye and assumed it was another zombie child. The creature moved smoothly, though, not like these zombie creatures. The creature laid down on its stomach and just stared at my face. I turned to look, and to my shock, it was Simon lying down in the fog, zombie children oblivious to him. He was grinning at me like he knew something I didn't.

He spoke through the noise. "What on earth are you doing down here?" he asked. "This is quite a silly place to quit. It seems like, once again, you're stuck, this time allowing some little zombie children to get you down. When are you going to learn? When are you going to stop reacting and start acting? Stop looking with your eyes? Stop fighting with your fists? You lie here, on the ground, because you choose to. You look around and blame this situation on Sampson or Judah or these zombie children or even me. But you make your choices, and your choices make you. You are a scared little chicken. You will always be a scared little chicken. Although you weren't created to be a scared little chicken, a scared little chicken you will be because that's how you see yourself and how you see yourself determines what you will be—nothing else. So keep pecking along the ground; believe the chicken spit that you've believed your whole life. Go ahead and just stay here on the ground to die!" He lifted his head up toward the sky and pointed up. "'Up.' Chickens don't know about 'up.' Eagles, on the other hand…" He smiled, got up, and walked away through the fog.

I didn't get all that Simon was saying in the moment, but I did get the fact that I was about to die at the hands of zombie children, and no way was I going to allow the likes of former Coopers, Peytons, and Baileys be my undoing! I gripped the torch tighter, and the warmth flowed through my veins. My body temperature soared! It didn't affect me at all. The zombie kiddos, on the other hand, started to melt away with the intense heat. I shook the last couple of hangers-on off (bye-bye Chase and Riley!) and sprung to my feet. I dashed through the fog, knocking zombie kids out of my way. Judah's dead Wolf Terror body was still on top of Tre when I got to her. With one hand swatting away zombie kids, with the other hand, I lifted Judah enough for Tre to roll out from underneath him. She was in bad shape. Bite marks up and down her arms and legs; she was still bent over at the waist, holding her stomach where Judah had punched her. Still batting away zombie kids,

I reached down with my free hand, grabbed Tre's arm, and swung her up and onto my back (I didn't know that I was *that* strong). We bolted toward the edge of town, Tre on my back, swatting occasional zombie kids until it was just Tre and me. I only slowed down to a walk when we passed the white church.

Flash!

TORCH

HELEN OR BUST (FOR REAL)

The fire crackled in front of me. Sprawled out to my left on the snowy ground was Judah, still snoring. Much to my delight and my nerves, to my right, Tre was leaning against me, dead asleep with a hint of drool in the corner of her mouth. Or was that blood? I was curious but didn't want to know the consequences if she woke up to find me staring at her mouth (creeper!). Besides Tre leaning against my shoulder, the scene was exactly the same as before. The three of us were on one side of the fire. I was the only one awake to notice a man dressed in black, priestly robes sitting on the other side of the fire. It was Simon. He sat there for the longest time, staring at me and the fire.

Finally, as the sun began to make an appearance, Simon walked slowly toward the fire. He was staring at the fire when he simply said, "Now that you're back in reality, T, it's time to choose. You have been created for greatness. Are you going to embrace it or keep pecking along at the ground? There are too many chickens in this world and not enough eagles. The world is waiting. The world is desperate. The world is longing. The darkness is growing." Suddenly he was standing directly in front of me. Simon snatched my left arm, and before I knew it, he was searing something into my forearm.

I let out a scream of pain as I felt and smelled my flesh burning. My scream woke Judah and Tre up.

"What? What happened?" a groggy Judah asked.

Tre had sprung to her feet, embarrassed that she was leaning against my arm. Simon had vanished.

I sat there rubbing my burned forearm. Tre came closer to inspect the wound and, realizing it was a burn, bent down and picked up a small pile of snow and covered the wound. The throbbing began to ease. The redness was still there, and now you could make out a distinct shape. Tre was looking intently at the wound.

"A tree. It looks like a tree," she said confidently but still staring.

"It's a feather. An eagle feather," I told her.

"Really? You really think it's an eagle feather? It's definitely a tree," she responded and rolled her eyes.

"It's an eagle feather, and it's a long story that I'll tell you later," I responded.

"Whatever!" she said, miffed that I thought it was a feather. She didn't like to be wrong or at least told she's wrong.

I took a quick glance at the corner of her mouth. It was blood, indeed.

"We need to get moving as soon as we can if we want to make it to Helen before nightfall," Tre said.

Standing to my feet, I noticed that my abs were sore like I'd been in a fight. I hobbled around the fire, trying to wake up. I ached all over. Not just my abs but my head, my back, my legs. I wasn't the only one in this boat. Watching Tre, I could tell that she was moving gingerly as well. It looked like she was favoring her stomach, too. She grabbed her bag off the ground, reached in, and tossed me a sandwich.

"Maybe this will help with your aches and pains," she said with a wry smile.

Judah had his own sandwich stash and had a sandwich in both hands.

"T, you feeling okay?" Judah asked as I hobbled around, clearly in pain.

"Ya, I'm okay. Just had a rough night of sleep," I responded. Tre chuckled at my response.

That's it! She was really there the whole time! On the beach, in the meadow, and in the creepy town. She was there for it all!

"You were there last night, weren't you?" I asked.

"Yes, I was," she responded out loud.

"Yes, you was what?" Judah asked, clearly confused.

"Yes, I am ready to leave," Tre said with a chuckle, patting Judah on the head as she passed by him. We left the clearing and headed to the pathway that led out of the forest.

Before long, we cleared the forest, and, once again, the snow gave way, and the pathway meandered up and down rolling hills. An hour or so beyond the forest, we crested a hill that overlooked a tiny hamlet. Just down the hill was the town sign, "Forest Glen." No red slash across it. I noticed the scarecrow in the field protecting the farmer's crop. It just looked like a happy scarecrow, no blood trickling down from its eyes. As we neared the town, Forest Glen looked just as I had imagined it, but this time, it seemed to be alive. People were up and about doing their daily chores. It seemed quite quaint. People exchanging pleasantries. The clanging of the metal in the blacksmith's shop. The delightful smell of freshly baked goods and the comforting smell of freshly cleaned laundry hung in the air. No fog. No creepy zombie children. As we strode into town, no one paid attention to us. In fact, that was the creepiest part. It was like we were nonexistent, not that we minded. We stopped at the well in the town center to refill our water.

"Keep your eyes open for anything suspicious," I said to Tre and Judah.

"I agree," Tre said, "my nerves are on edge too."

Judah filled his water bottle up first. Then it was my turn. I cranked the bucket all the way down to the water. It was really deep.

The squeaking of the well handle.

A gentle breeze on a warm day.

The smell of pies and laundry and livestock.

The sound of the bucket splashing into the water.

Weighted down with water, cranking harder.

The bucket rising out of the water, cranking harder, still.

Higher and higher, the bucket rose. The heavier.

The bucket passed in and out of the shadows as it made its ascent.

I was staring intently at the bucket. Never had a bucket of water been this heavy!

Judah got his water so easily.

Staring down at the bucket filled with water, I hardly noticed Tre standing beside me.

She noticed my struggle with the bucket and was checking to see what the issue was. We were both staring at it. The cranking was becoming all but impossible now. The rope was taut and began to burn against the weight of the bucket. Tre's hand was on my back now as we both stared at the bucket. A face emerged in the water. A head at first, then the teeth, and then the shriek as it leaped up at us, trying to cut us with one of its gnarly fingers. It missed and went tumbling back into the bucket, but its weight slammed against the bucket, and the rope split in two. It tumbled backward into the blackness of the well, chasing the now broken bucket. On its descent, we heard it laughing, cackling in a childlike voice. The zombie child was now at the bottom of the well. When it splashed down, we heard echoes of a sea of zombie children. Tre and I stumbled backward into Judah, who was just getting ready to take his first sip of the well water. All but a few sips spilled all over him.

"Hey, watch what you're doing!" Judah yelled as he got ready to drink the remaining drops of water. Lifting his water bottle back, he had a few drops tumble through the air toward his long, outstretched tongue.

Instinctively, Tre and I dove at him, tackling him to the ground.

Judah was furious! He shoved us off and jumped to his feet. He was ready for a fight.

"Come on and get up, you two! You don't think I haven't noticed what's going on between you two? Trying to push me out of the band? I guess I make a bad third wheel! Let's settle this once and for all, kissy-faces!"

"Kissy-faces?" I said with a laugh.

"Yes, he just said 'kissy faces'!" Tre responded.

We couldn't contain ourselves. We laid on the ground laughing and laughing and laughing while Judah stood there perplexed, his hands still out in front of him in a boxing stance. He was both confused and hurt that we were laughing at him.

Finally, I spoke up, "Judah, she is not my girlfriend." (Even though I would love it.) I started to stand up, and Judah took a slight jab at my head.

"No, Judah, he is *definitely* not my boyfriend," Tre responded as she jumped to her feet.

(Why did she have to use the word "definitely"? Wouldn't just the phrase, "not my boyfriend," suffice?)

"Then why did you tackle me?" Judah asked, still ticked off.

"The water, the well. It's tainted. It's bad," I said as I jumped to my feet.

We all seemed to notice it at the same time. Although the townsfolk looked normal, going through their daily routines, they were all in some sort of trance. That's why they hadn't noticed us. When the quaint becomes creepy, you leave!

"Let's get moving," I said, for the first time taking the lead. Judah and Tre complied.

On the opposite side of town near its outskirts, we passed by the white church. On the porch was a person dressed in a black priest robe, sweeping. He stopped long enough to wave at us. We waved back.

"This is how it all began," he said as he returned to his sweeping.

Simon, thought Tre and I at the same time. We weren't here for a social visit, though. So many people get caught up (distracted) with social calls on their journey and lose sight of their mission. Then they complain about not getting where they want to go. Our mission was too critical for this. We kept walking.

"Godspeed and go save them all! And hurry!" we heard Simon shout to our backs as we made our way out of town.

We walked until around midday, up and down more meandering hills, passing by the occasional farm and the occasional patch of woods.

"Let's stop for lunch," Tre said. Just off the road was a nice shade tree, which would be our lunch destination.

"Good," said Judah. "I gotta go pee!" He trumped off into a nearby grove of trees.

Tre and I sat down and began to munch on a sandwich, both lost in our own thoughts. I was studying the brand that Simon gave me on my arm. It had slightly changed since I last noticed it. It still ached, and even now, it seemed to be changing as it healed. There's not a big difference between a feather and a flame. It could be either. It could be both. Tre saw me staring at it.

"Does it still hurt?" she asked, even though she knew the answer. It was her way of small talk.

"Ya, it still hurts," I said. "How about you? How are your wounds healing?" It was out of my mouth before I knew it.

"My body will heal soon enough," came Tre's response. She looked at me and then off into the distance.

"That's not what I'm talking about, Tre, and you know it," I replied, trying my best to sound gentle and firm.

"You're right. I can't shake that scene. I can't shake any of them but especially that one," Tre said, staring off in the distance. My sandwich was forgotten.

A look came across Tre's face that I hadn't seen before. A sadness. A darkness. She sat there looking out across the horizon. Her sandwich was also forgotten. "The Wolf Terror. I knew her. She was my best friend. She was my sister." Tre continued after a long pause, "Priscilla. Her name was Priscilla."

The next part seemed very difficult for her to say. "T, I've never talked about it. About her. About what happened." She was now staring at the ground and absently playing with the grass with her hands. "We were sent by my mother, Anni, to investigate a disturbance coming from the woods. She had heard reports that the Wolf Terrors were building a camp and using the Shape-Shifting Forest as cover. We weren't too concerned as we were supposed to just go down and scout the forest and report back. The three of us set out, much like the three of us did. It was me, Priscilla, and my younger sister Naomi, whom we affectionately called 'Little Princess' because she was always so…so…pure. Above everyone else. Not in a haughty way. She just didn't get involved in the trivialities of life. They didn't faze her." She continued playing with the grass. "Priscilla and I were shocked when mother sent her with us. She had only been out of the meadow once, and that was to overlook the valley below, on the side you entered. When we got to the forest, we realized that something was indeed off. Not that we'd ever been there, but the fact that it was snowing in the middle of the summer was very strange. In fact, none of us had anticipated snow. Mother told us to be careful at night with the way the forest plays with your mind, but she was shocked when I told her about the snow. She was even more shocked to see that I was the only one to come back from the forest. When we reached the forest, the snow was falling at a pretty good clip. By the time we decided to make a camp for the night, we were in the heart of a blizzard."

I could tell how raw this was for Tre. The depth of her pain resonated in her voice. She kept picking at the grass with her hands to hide the fact that her hands were shaking. She looked up at me as if to say, "You're right," and then continued.

"Again, we weren't prepared. Physically or mentally. That night, with the wind howling and the snow building, Priscilla gave into the darkness. She actually welcomed it. I witnessed the whole thing, and I couldn't stop her! We were sitting around the campfire when the evil visited her. They talked in hushed tones, and a pact was made. What no one knew was that Priscilla was deeply jealous of Naomi. She hid it well, but looking back, I know there were signs. Little signs, but signs, nonetheless. Naomi was naive, and Priscilla played on that. She always looked for ways to make Naomi look like a fool but then would turn around and pretend that she would help her make everything okay. That night in front of the fire, while Naomi slept, the evil sent two Wolf Terrors into our camp and dragged both of my sisters away into the darkness. I tried to stop them, but they were too powerful, and I was inexperienced with fighting such beasts. A powerful paw smashed my head, leaving me unconscious in the snow. When I awoke in the morning, the fresh snow covered their tracks. I spent a week tromping around the woods by myself, looking for them. It was in vain. Part of the reason mother wanted me to assist you is, first of all, you need my help [I couldn't argue that] and to see if I could locate either sister. I located Priscilla. That's why I let her go. That and the fact that I knew that she would deliver a message to Antioch that you were coming." She looked exhausted, as if she'd just relived the entire story.

"Priscilla may be a lost cause, but Naomi..." Tre's voice trailed for a moment, "I'm still holding out hope for Naomi. And you, T. My mother took you to that dark place so that you can begin to deal with the darkness. If not, the darkness will consume you. Look at Priscilla, something as seemingly mundane as jealousy, and she's made a pact with Antioch!"

The grass on the other side of the tree rustled with the somewhat clumsy footsteps of a lion-boy. Judah rounded the corner and had an expression of accomplishment on his face.

"You don't want to go over there for a while," he said with a chuckle while pointing off in the distance with pride plastered on his face.

"That's disgusting, Judah!" Tre said as she wrinkled her nose at him. I was amazed at how quickly her mood could change. Of course, it was easy when Judah was around.

That's when the lion-boy noticed our half-eaten sandwiches. He swiped both of our sandwiches right out of our hands and said, "You don't mind, do you?" as he shoved them both in his mouth at the same time. Mouth full, he continued, "You guys don't know what you're missing!" with a big toothy grin and a burp.

"C'mon, boys, let's get moving," Tre prompted. "Helen isn't too far away now, but I want to get there in the daylight so we can look for the *special girl.*"

TORCH

WHAT IS WRONG WITH THESE PEOPLE?

On we walked, with not much change in the terrain until we approached Helen. As we did, the road widened and went from dirt to paved, and it flattened out considerably. We began to pass a farm or two leading into town with the occasional farmer working the field. The fields, of course, had the customary scarecrow keeping watch (not a fan of scarecrows anymore). A few of the farms had horses while others had cows and goats, and some even had a few woolly sheep. Some chickens also hung out on the sides of the road in front of the farmhouses. This scene reminded me so much of home. But fond memories quickly gave way to darkness as white transitioned into gray, which transitioned into black. So much pain. So much buried anger and rage. Tre looked at me, knowing what was going through my mind, but only said to my mind, "Deal with it." Later she would reveal how, in that moment, it took all her strength to not reach out and grab my arm to stop the pain. We walked on in silence as I was still grappling with my internal demons.

The closer we got to Helen, the more frequent the houses became. The bigger they became as well! Houses two, three, and even four stories tall lined the street. Also lining the streets, besides the occasional wagon or buggy, was a contraption that I had heard about but had never seen before. It was like a metal wagon but with some sort of magical power to make it move. Some people call it a horseless carriage. I call it a miracle!

I had never seen a town like Helen. It was so modern. So relevant. So fast-paced. People scurried from place to place like they were wound up like toy mice.

The women smelled of flowery perfume and wore a tasteful amount of makeup. They dressed in beautiful colored dresses, some adorned with matching hats. The men smelled of, well, men. They wore nicely pressed trousers, button-down shirts, and either ties or bolos. Most wore hats; all wore beards. Boots were the preferred shoe for both sexes. The smell of livestock and gasoline mixed with the smell of fresh-baked goods. The sights, sounds, and smells…It was almost intoxicating. Helen was the place to be! Helen was happenin'!

The men, women all had pleasant looks on their faces. They greeted each other with a grin, a nod, and the tip of a cap exchanging pleasantries like, "Mornin'!" and "Ma'am!" and "Good day!"

Not a piece of litter graced the streets. Not a pothole or a crack in the sidewalk. Kids played chase in the town square but never in the road and never loudly. In fact, they were polite to one another…Too polite. That was my first clue. Either Helen was the essence of perfection, or it was hiding some deep sinister secret, and these people, this town, was being manipulated by something even more dark and more sinister. The evil. Maybe this was a town of Oblivions.

But we weren't here to evaluate the realness or the fakeness of this town. No, we had to find the "special girl." But where? In this crazy chaotic town filled with plenty of girls, how do you find *the* "special girl"? What happened next did not help…At all!

We heard a whistle blow behind us, and a man with a funny high-pitched voice yelled, "Hey! Hey you kids! Stop! What are you doing in this town?" He sounded like he'd just swallowed some helium. How do you take that person seriously? For real?

(Think about it: imagine a teacher or a parent talking seriously about whatever—math, dishes, money—and talking like they just had a hit of helium and taking them seriously.)

We turned around to see a man walking quickly toward us. He looked like the others in town, but he had a gold star button on the left chest of his coat. His hat was tan in color and was peculiar-looking: extra tall and skinny with a wide brim. His body was round except for his long skinny arms and twig legs, which were slightly bowlegged. On his face sat a furrowed expression like he meant business. He was the law! In my mind, I said it like I'd just sucked on some helium, "He meant business!"

Tre burst out laughing because she was thinking the same thing. In fact, she had tears in her eyes. That did it! I started to laugh, and then Judah, who had no idea why we were laughing but caught the contagious fever of laughter from us.

"Stop it! Stop that laughing now!" the man yelled in the high-pitched helium voice. This didn't help the situation, and we all doubled over laughing, Judah leaning against me so he wouldn't topple over. Before we knew it, we were surrounded by a group of high-pitched rotund marshals with overly tall hats and twig legs. They were the law.

"Get 'em, boys," came the command from the original high-pitched Homo sapiens.

Our weapons were confiscated, and we were loaded into the back of a horseless carriage. Wooden panels surrounded the area where we sat, and though a bit anxious, we were still laughing. We had no idea where they were taking us or why. All we could see from the cracks in the slats of the wooden boards were fuzzy glimpses of the town. The miracle wagon seemed to be taking us down some windy side streets. Suddenly, the smells changed. The air changed. I had a feeling that we weren't in Helen anymore.

"Where are they taking us?" asked Judah. It was a question we all asked, and soon enough, we would have our answer.

We pulled up in front of a gray brick building. It was tall and ominous. There were no windows, and green moss flaked the building's facade. The smell was putrid, like a sewer, and the air was thick with the smell of rotting food. The high-pitched police grabbed us out of the back of the wonder wagon, thrusting us into a dank, dirty alleyway. One of the silly-hatted humans fumbled for the right key to unlock the door to the tall tower. The door itself was wooden with a tiny peep window about three-fourths the way up the door. It also had a familiar red slash across it, which seemed newly painted but which no one seemed to notice or care about. I shivered, remembering the last time I saw a red slash on a door. With the door finally unlocked, we were strong-armed inside the building. The door closed behind us, and that was when the screaming began. A high-pitched scream followed by a low moan. Save for the light from the peep window, it was almost completely dark inside, and we had no idea where the awful screams were coming from. They seem to be moving quickly. Footsteps scampering. Moans. Screams. From where?

"Let's take care of them and get out of here!" said a high-pitched patroller. They shoved us further back into the darkness. It was wet and smelled even worse than before, if that was possible. We walked down a long hallway before being shoved into a small cell, tripping over each other before landing in a heap. A thick wrought-iron door slammed closed, sending a grating, clanging sound echoing through the cavernous building. We jumped when it clanged; we jumped more when we heard the screams getting louder as if whatever was coming was getting more and more excited.

The high-pitched patrolman's voice rose above the oncoming noise, "You are hereby charged with: first, laughing at an adult, second, being filthy, and third, not being entirely human, a mongrel!" He paused in disgust, pointing a boney finger at Judah. "All three are forbidden according to the Perfection Penal Code, or PPC: first, there is only one PPC, and you have violated it. Tomorrow morning you will face the judge," he paused again, this time for a dramatic flair, "if you make it till then…"

The group of helium-inhaling haters, in unison, stuck out their tongues and blew raspberries at us. They turned and left, yelling in their high-pitched voices, "Dirty shame! Dirty shame! Dirty shame!" It was both funny and ominous.

"What did he mean by, 'facing the judge' and 'if you make it till then'?" I whispered.

"We're about to find out!" Tre said, staring at the cell door.

"Find out what?" Judah asked, confused.

"You'll see. We'll all see," I responded, suddenly realizing how much I missed the comforting and empowering glow of the torch.

The sounds grew and were now accompanied by footsteps. Some seemed human, others…it was hard to tell. I felt a combination of nerves and adrenaline taking over…The nerves were winning.

We just stood there, back as far as the tiny cell would allow, and stared at the cell door. Judah was breathing loudly. I wasn't breathing at all. Tre stood there cool, calm, and collected, except I noticed her hand just barely grazing mine as if to either reassure her or me. I was reassured, sorta.

The noise arrived in an instant! What sounded so distant a second ago was now standing in front of us, staring at us. Tre grabbed my hand. I exhaled.

TORCH

WEEKDAY SPECIAL

Judah's heavy breathing was drowned out by the creatures' breathing. Heavy, wheezing, pungent, and hot, they pressed against the cell bars. Arms with claws reached through the bars, trying to swipe at us. Arms with hands trying to grab us. In the darkness, we had no idea what "they" were. Their excitement was feverish as they tried getting at us through the thick bars. "This may be the one time anyone has ever been glad to be in jail," I whispered to Tre. Tre squeezed my hand as if telling me to be quiet.

The iron bars were shaking from the weight of these creatures. Clanging and creaking mixed with the squeaking of metal being stressed mixed with crazed creatures and rancid smells and heat and darkness. The three of us just stood there huddled together and waited, thankful for the iron bars of the...

It happened so fast. The jail cell burst open, and they ascended on us! We thought about struggling but thought better of it.

What do you do when being attacked by creatures in a pitch-black jail cell?

1) *Run!* (not an option);
2) play dead (not an option because we were clearly alive);
3) wet yourself and cry out for your mommy.

Option three is what we all chose. At least Judah and me (except I didn't wet myself though I could've). In an instant, we each had two creatures on top of each of us, not necessarily hurting us but using their strength to hold us down.

"Easy, boys!" I heard one of them snarl.

"We can't eat them?" one of the creatures on top of Judah snapped.

"Not yet!" hissed the first voice. "At least not here!" he finished. "Let's get them out of here before the 'perfect' high-pitched po-pos come back and ruin a perfectly piquant picnic!"

They strong-armed us to our feet and led us down the hallway from whence they came.

We stumbled trying to walk, locked arm in arm with our captors. The flooring was made of smooth cobblestone. And it was slick, which made foot traction nearly impossible. Imagine two creatures on either side, locked arm in arm with you, dragging/pulling you along as you try to keep up with them on a slippery floor. Kinda like a three-legged race on ice! The hallway wound this way and that way and seemed to go on forever. We stopped twice so the creatures could loudly whisper to one another.

"What is she going to say about them?" one "whispered" to the group.

"I think she'll like this lot," came a "whispered" reply.

"I hope so," came another, almost giddy reply.

"And if she doesn't?" came another "whispered" question of concern.

"I don't know! She always seems to like them, but there's always a first time for everything!" came a not whispered answer.

"I'm hungry," came another voice. "Let's keep moving."

The three of us gulped at the same time.

On we walked, weaving and winding down the dark walkway. We must be somewhere underneath the town of Helen I surmised, not realizing that our surroundings were changing.

It happened subtly. Very subtly. Kinda like watching the sun rise from pitch-black to full light. I don't know how long it took for me/us to realize it, but we started to see the hallway more clearly. And our captors too. They came more clearly into focus, with some looking relatively human while others looking like hybrids similar to Judah but with different animal/human blends. In our current state, though, it was hard to fully see what our captors looked like.

Up ahead, the hallway appeared to be getting lighter and lighter. The light was coming from the frame of a door, a small wooden door, that was now being backlit by a light source. The smell had changed as well from stinky and smelly and downright noxious to something like sweet yeast and cinnamon.

Is this it? Is this the end? Do I meet my Maker in this room? I thought to myself. I could feel Tre thinking the same thing.

"Slowly now," one of the voices said as a captor reached to open the door.

"Eyes, boys. Watch your eyes," another voice said.

The door slowly creaked open, and light came flooding out, instantly stinging our eyes. We tried to squint the pain away as our captors pushed us into the room. We tumbled in a heap into the middle of the room. Our eyes slowly came back to us.

Sitting in the middle of the room, our captors made a semicircle around us. Directly in front of us was a long table, the kind used in kitchens for prepping meals. Light flooded the room, but it only came from a single torch that was dangling from the ceiling. It was enough light. Behind the table stood a girl about my age. She had her head down and was busying herself with something, seeming totally oblivious to our presence. This must be the "she" the "boys" were referring to.

One of the "boys," who seemed to be higher ranking than the others, cleared his throat, "Huh, hum." The girl continued to work, her tongue hanging out now in a sign of concentration. A puff of white smoke floated from the table. *Magic?* I wondered, *Potions of death?*

A little louder now, the same "boy" cleared his throat, "Huh, hum!" He was clearly human, just a bit disfigured. He had one arm that was strong and muscular-looking and another that was small and shriveled.

The tongue continued to stick out. The girl continued her task, still oblivious to our presence.

"*Hope!*" yelled the "boy." When he said her name, the smaller arm just hung limply from his shoulder while the stronger arm was quite animated.

She finally looked up and grinned at us with a crooked smile, tongue sticking out even more now. She was wearing an apron that appeared to be caked in the white substance.

She squealed in delight, catching us off guard. "Friends! When did you get here?" she said mumbly and a bit hard to understand.

And before we knew it, she was around the table giving us hugs—bear hugs—transferring the white magic powder onto our clothing. As she hugged each of us, she gleefully said, "Hello, friend!" She then proceeded to go around the semicircle and give each of the "boys" bear hugs, caking them in white powder as well and saying, "Hello, friend!"

The three of us were mildly…no, scratch that. We were very, extremely confused.

TORCH

FAITH, HOPE, AND BUNS

With hugs out of the way, the leader of the "boys" asked, "Hope, can we eat 'em now?"

Hope walked around to the other side of the table to resume her task. "Almost time, friends," she said with her tongue hanging out of her mouth in concentration on the task in front of her.

This is it: we're goners for sure! I panicked.

"They're going to eat us, and if they don't," I whispered to Tre, "the special girl behind the table is whipping up some poisonous potion. She set us up with hugs, but you know you can't trust people who hug you the first time you meet them!"

Hope stopped what she was doing and looked straight at me.

"What did you say?" she said a little mumbly.

She wasn't very tall. In fact, she wouldn't be able to work at the table if she wasn't standing on what appeared to be a large silver metallic box, which seemed to be smoking as if on fire. She had red (which is really orange; I never understood why they call orangeheads redheads) hair that was flaked with the white powder. She had a button nose and big eyes that appeared more oval-shaped than round. Her fingers were somewhat stubby but quite agile, from what I could tell. Besides the apron, which was white, she wore a yellow flowery blouse and a matching skirt, similar to an outfit that one of the townswomen would wear, but it was different, more colorful.

"I haven't had anyone call me special in a long time. A very long time," Hope said aloud as she continued working.

The "boys" were licking their lips, if they had them, and they were getting more excited. Then, in unison, they started to clap. *Clap, clap, clap, clap, clap, clap.* The clapping got faster and faster and was now accompanied by a few squeals of delight.

And then a ding! A shout arose from the "boys," and the clapping stopped immediately. Hope hopped hurriedly off the hotbox and hefted up the lid. She reached in and started grabbing brown and white somethings and, to our surprise, started slinging them at the "boys." The "boys" waved their hands and made all sorts of noises, vying for her attention. They wanted what she was dispersing. I think a few of them were actually frothing at the mouth! She was a pro at hurling the brown objects! She didn't necessarily throw them directly at the "boys." No, she made them work for it. She called them out as she threw to them.

"*Thomas!*" she yelled as a brown object whizzed by my ear. I turned to see the ringleader of the "boys" with one muscular arm, somersaulting backward on his muscular arm, flipping over and over before reaching, snatching the brown object out of midair with his mouth. He landed right next to the door that we'd just entered. It was impressive! He had blonde hair, a full beard, and other than his shriveled-up arm, he looked perfectly normal.

"*Edison!*" she yelled as a brown object whizzed by my other ear. I turned to see the (ringleader?) with one muscular arm, somersaulting backward on his muscular arm, flipping over and over before reaching, snatching the brown object out of midair with his mouth. He landed right next to the door that we'd just entered, right next to Thomas. Again, it was impressive! He had blonde hair, and other than his shriveled-up arm, he looked identical to Thomas, except it was his left arm that was fine and his right arm that was shriveled. Again, besides the arm issue, he looked perfectly normal.

"Must be twins," I whispered to Tre.

"Correct!" mumbled Hope cheerfully. Her hearing was incredible and sketchy. When we entered the room, it took one of the "boys" yelling her name to get her attention, but every time I whispered to Tre, she heard it clear as a day.

And then it got good. Hope reached down to grab a few more brown objects, her tongue sticking out still. Pushing her redheaded bangs off her forehead, she hollered, "*Franklin! Teddy! Roosevelt!*" with that, she sent a barrage of brown objects straight into the air over my head. It must've been twelve or so: I couldn't count that fast! I looked up to see three-winged hybrid creatures flipping and turning above me, each trying desperately to get their share of what she was dispensing.

One looked like half ox, half eagle. His upper body was the ox. He was strong and graceful with long wings, but he looked fierce as snot exploded out of his oxen nose. And he had a nose ring. He got his fill and landed surprisingly lightly directly next to me. I could smell, scratch that, I could feel his snot breath on my face.

"*Good job, Teddy!*" a mumbled squeal rang from Hope's throat. She was clapping, tongue still slightly sticking out.

Two of the "boys" were still tumbling in the air above me. One was a brown Pegasus, a horse with wings (I thought they were supposed to be white). If he were white, he'd be regal-looking; I would learn later that this was Roosevelt.

The other winged creature was a mix between a black bear and a man with his upper body—head, face, arms, and chest—resembling a black bear and his lower body—everything else—resembling a man. He had oversized bat wings protruding from his back; this was Franklin. Both, like Teddy, were very agile. They scarfed up the remaining brown objects in midair and made their way down to the ground.

Judah was right there with them! He didn't even know what it was she was throwing, but he didn't care. He was jumping up and down, vying for Hope's attention.

"*Lion-Boy!*" Hope shouted to Judah. She tossed the brown object just over his head. He backflipped in the air, catching the first brown object in his paw and shoving it into his mouth. He was hovering above the floor now, his young wings responding to his direction. This was the first time I'd seen him fly. This may have been the first time he'd seen himself fly. The second brown object was a direct hit, straight into his mouth. And then another and another. Judah was in lion-boy heaven.

"*Torch Boy* and *Girlfriend!*" Hope yelled now, winging brown objects in our direction. We grabbed them out of the air and then studied them.

"You can eat now," Hope said, even though she didn't need to. Each of the "boys" had a hand or paw full of brown and white objects fully disposed of in their bellies.

Tre and I continued to study the objects. We were perplexed. They appeared to be…cinnamon rolls? I had heard of the world-famous Helen cinnamon rolls but never thought I might actually be holding one in my hand. Tre, too, stared in disbelief at her cinnamon roll.

"It's a cinnamon roll," Hope explained, seeing the look on our faces. "Some people call them sticky buns, but here we call them cinnamon rolls. You eat them. You should tell me what you think."

Tre and I gave each other a sideways glance and dove in. As we finished our firsts, a second pair was zinging through the air toward us. We devoured them along with three more rounds. We were stuffed.

Hope made her way around the table as we were finishing up and was now standing directly in front of us. Almost too close. I guessed she didn't understand personal space.

"So, what do you think?" she mumbled expectantly, smile and tongue working in unison once again.

Tre chimed in immediately, "They are amazing! Better than my mo—"

Interrupting Tre, Hope said, "I meant Torch Boy. What did you think?" she mumbled expectantly again.

"They…they…They were delicious," I stammered for no apparent reason but grinning nonetheless.

"Delicious?" Hope asked, sounding a bit disappointed. "I was hoping for more than just 'delicious.'" She looked down as if she were about to cry but then continued, "And I thought you were the One." She let out a sigh of despair, blowing her orange bangs and subsequent flour into the air.

"Well…no…umm…" I stammered again for no apparent reason.

"No! They're not delicious?" she mumbled, now miffed. The redhead was beginning to get red-faced. "Definitely not the One!" she huffed.

"No…I mean, yes," I tripped over my words once again. Hope had her head down now, and her shoulders were shrugging as if she was sobbing. "Hope, I think your cinnamon rolls are incredible! I've never had anything like it, ever," I said quickly. I don't think I'd ever made a girl cry before, and I felt terrible. That feeling was fleeting because, before I knew it, Hope's arms were around me, giving me a hug, squeezing out my innards.

"*Friends!*" she giggled, looking at me. She then looked at Tre and said with a crooked smile, "Your boyfriend might be the One."

"He's not my boyfriend!" exclaimed Tre, a little too forcefully for the occasion.

"It's okay, friend," Hope said as she patted Tre on the shoulder and winked at me.

The two girls stood there facing each other for a moment until they were finally interrupted by a loud bell, like an alarm.

"*Ahh!*" Hope mumbly yelled as she grabbed her head. "*I gotta go!*" She turned and scurried around the table. Lifting up the lid to the steel firebox, she grabbed a couple of trays piled high with cinnamon rolls. She whirled around and quickly made her way to a steep, rickety, circular staircase, which I had not previously seen. Reaching the staircase, she loudly mumbled over her shoulder, "We'll talk when I get back!" She skillfully made her way to the top of the stairwell and opened a door. Light and noise momentarily filled the room where we stood. And we waited.

TORCH

HOPE AT JUST THE RIGHT TIME

Thomas spoke up first, "I know you must have questions, so let's sit and talk." He gestured with his good arm for us to sit. The "boys" sat in front of us in a semicircle.

"As you heard Hope say, my name is Thomas. This is my twin brother, Edison." Edison nodded his head and smiled but did not say anything. "These are our brothers," Thomas said, motioning to the other "boys." "They didn't use to be, though. Like you, we were destined for a meeting with the judge, but Hope came out of nowhere and rescued us. Hope is like that, though. There just when you need her," he paused for a minute as if remembering his rescue, continuing, "We all came upon Helen for one reason or another, but we were all arrested on the same charge, 'being different.' In other words, we weren't perfect. We're strange to look at, and what people don't understand scares them! This town is full of those kinds of people, Oblivions. I guess every town has a few Oblivions, but in the town of Helen, Oblivions have taken over. They live in their own fantasy world where everyone looks perfect and acts perfectly. Perfect kids, perfect women, perfect men. Perfect jobs, perfect homes, perfect marriages. What they are blind to is that it's a facade. Fake. The smiles. The clothes. They've been lulled into thinking their lives are so deep and meaningful, but they are shallow, self-absorbed, and miserable. They just don't see it. It's like they are in a trance. Antioch has them right where he wants them!"

"So," I started, "you were arrested, like us, and Hope rescued you?" I was a little perplexed. "How did she know you were arrested? How did she break you out? Why are you still here?" I tried not to sound too confused, but I was still trying to figure a way out of this place.

"Yes. Hope rescued us...in more ways than you know," his voice trailed off slightly. "I'll let Hope tell you her story when she gets back." Almost as soon as he said this, light broke through behind us, followed by the soft hint of conversation and the faint sound of music. Hope was back.

She made her way down the staircase with empty sheet pans in her hand. When she stepped off the last step, I breathed a sigh of relief. Walking seemed to be difficult for her, and with each step, it seemed as if she would topple over. Maybe it wasn't the walking part as much as the balancing part of walking. How she made it up and down the stairs holding sheet pans was a miracle. After depositing the pans on the table, Hope came over to sit with us. She plopped down right next to me.

"How is she today, Hope?" Teddy asked. He was articulate and sounded very proper. It might have been the slight accent in his voice that made him sound that way.

Hope looked away for a moment before addressing Teddy. It was hard to tell, but it looked like a tear might be stuck in the corners of her eyes.

"She's...she's beautiful as usual," Hope said a bit mumbly with a mix of pride and longing.

"Did she say anything?" Franklin asked expectantly.

Again, Hope looked away, this time for a longer period. It was awkward since we had no idea what was happening.

Finally, Hope spoke, "She glanced at me. I think I even saw her raise her eyebrows," she paused to collect herself, "but she didn't speak." She clearly had tears rolling down her cheeks now. A sniffle came. And then a hug. Unexpectedly, she wrapped her arms around me and was now crying. All out crying. I didn't know what to do. I just sat there stiff as a board but trying, impossibly, not to look awkward.

Tre came to the rescue. "Who is she?" Tre interjected in between the sniffles and snorts of ugly crying. Like a summer rain, Hope went from a full-on downpour to a steady sprinkling of tears to a sporadic trickle of tears before coming in for a not so graceful snot and tear-filled stop.

With a final sniffle for effect, Hope said, "My mom."

"Wait. What?" Tre said in disbelief. "You saw your mom, and she didn't say anything to you? No 'hello' or 'good morning'? Just a glance?" She was miffed.

Hope let go of me and stood up in front of us. The torch hanging from the ceiling was directly above her, and the boys sat in a semicircle behind her. She paced back and forth as she began to speak.

"If...if you couldn't tell..." she was stammering to speak.

Whatever she was going to tell us was clearly hard for her to share.

"If you couldn't tell, I'm not exactly normal. I'm different," she mumbled, finishing her sentence, and paused so that we could get a good look at her. "When I was born, I looked like a normal kid. I smiled a lot and had trouble keeping my tongue in my mouth." (She demonstrated for us.) "But, other than the tongue, I looked normal. However, it took me longer to do things than other babies my age, like crawling and walking and talking. My mother kept holding out hope, no pun intended, that I would catch up one day, but that day never came," Hope said in her mumbly talk. "She tried to pretend everything was fine, but eventually, our neighbors began to notice. People in town began to talk. It wasn't nice. My mom was able to keep me and my secret hidden until I was seven years old. One day, my mother had gone to the market and my father was at work. I was home by myself when a nosey neighbor, Mrs. Elmstreet, came to the door. She said she needed me to give something to my mother. I wasn't even allowed to talk to anyone except for my father or mother, so my first inclination was to hide in my room, but I never got to talk to anybody except for my mother and father. So, I opened the door and did the one thing I do best. I gave her a hug and a smile with my tongue hanging out," she paused for a second to make sure we were paying attention. "Mrs. Elmstreet pushed me away and asked me what my name was. I told her it was Hope but that my mother called me her 'special girl.' Mrs. Elmstreet was tall, boney, and old. Very old. Her hair was dyed black, and she wore makeup and clothes to try to make her look younger. It didn't work. She bent down and put a gnarly finger in my face and said, 'You're not special. You're a freak!' She laughed an ominous laugh and, as she walked away, yelled, 'Wait until the judge hears about this!' I stood there for a moment in disbelief. Before I could close the door, a group of neighborhood kids filled the doorway and started to taunt me, shoving me and shouting cruel things to my face. My mother came upon the scene and shooed the kids away." The look on Hope's face showed that the pain was still evident all these years later.

"Yes, T, that was seven years ago, and it is still painful," she said, completely reading the expression on my face. "But not as painful as what happened next." She looked at me as she said this and then came and sat on the ground directly in front of us. "My mother locked me in my room and ran down to the bakery to fetch my father, who was the town baker. They returned together and, no sooner did they enter the house than the arguing started. They were trying to keep their voices low so that I wouldn't be able to hear them but, more importantly, so that our nosey neighbors wouldn't be able to eavesdrop. I could hear most of what they were saying.

"My dad started, 'I told you this day would come! You didn't want to listen to me!'

"Mother blurted out, 'But she is my baby! My special girl! What was I, what were we supposed to do?' I could hear my mother sniffling.

"'We talked about sending her to live with your cousin out in the country where she'd be safe,' my father responded. 'That was before. Things are different now. We're all in danger,' he said as if my mother did not know that.

"'So, what do we do?' my mother asked. But she already knew the plan. They had discussed it repeatedly for years.

"'We have to stick to the plan,' he said matter-of-factly.

"I don't know all the details of 'the plan' other than my father ran off in the middle of the night, and I moved in down here under the bakery. As far as the townspeople are concerned, my father took off with me in the middle of the night and never looked back." Once again, Hope paused to help our minds catch up. "My mother has said very little to me ever since that day. But she needs my help. You see, she can't bake to save her life. Baking is one of my gifts," she said with pride.

"From what I can gather, my father built this room for me and even connected it to the city's underground sewage system so that I would have an escape route if I were ever discovered. About a year ago, I came across the cell while I was exploring the tunnels and vowed to check the cell every day to see who was locked up. That's how I discovered my 'boys.'"

"So, why don't you escape?" Tre asked a little indignantly.

"Two reasons," Hope said, "one, it's not easy. Not easy at all. In fact, it might be suicide. Everyone, all the Oblivions, have been trained to snitch on any and everyone. You can't trust a soul. They engrain this in children as young as preschool. I don't even know if I could trust my mother anymore. So, it's extremely dangerous," she paused for a moment.

"And the second reason?" I asked.

Standing to her feet, Hope turned to look at the boys. They stood up in unison and gathered around her. She turned back to us and spoke clearly, firmly, no mumbling, "We were waiting for the One."

TORCH

FAMILY SECRETS

The One? I thought, still as perplexed as the first time I heard the phrase referring to me. *What does that even mean? And why me?* Where I came from, kids would talk about different myths and legends, but I mostly chalked it up to schoolyard fantasy. Some were meant to scare you like the Wolf Terrors, and others were meant to give you hope like "the One." Even Helen's cinnamon rolls held legendary schoolyard status. *But can something be real and legendary? Fully true and fully mythical?* These thoughts raced through my mind with the lingering taste of a legendary cinnamon roll from Helen in my mouth.

"Thomas, why don't you explain to T what the One is? Or rather, who the One is?" Hope mumbly directed.

Thomas stepped forward, and the other boys stepped back and had a seat on the ground behind him. He stood there for a moment, his good hand rubbing his chin, looking for the right way to begin. He began to pace. Above him, the torch hanging from the ceiling crackled as if trying to speak. Drama filled the room.

Finally, he spoke. "The One..." he paused, looking at Judah, then Tre, and letting his gaze linger on me for emphasis. "Our world is slipping into darkness at the hands of the Chaos, all directed by Antioch. It has been for centuries, but it used to be more subtle, cloaked beneath the surface like the molten lava of a building volcano, out of sight, underground. Recently, though, the darkness has come out of the shadows, showing its true colors. It is taking over our world and, unless it is stopped, will destroy everything and everyone that is good and right. Darkness is drawing nigh, but our hope is in the light," he pointed to me and then the torch hanging from the ceiling as he said this. "You may not understand the depth of the chaos, the evil because you've been blinded for most of your life. Your mom and dad knew it existed but tried to shield you and your siblings from it," he paused.

"They were Oblivions?" I asked, feeling conflicted about this revelation.

"*No!*" Thomas said firmly. "Just the opposite. Your mother and father knew the truth but figured if they kept you and your siblings away from it, then you'd be safe. But evil is like water; it finds the path of least resistance and floods the land, destroying everything in its path unless…unless it is stopped."

"Tell him the truth." To my surprise, Tre put her hand on my shoulder as she said this.

What truth? And why does Tre seem to know about it? I thought to myself, getting a little miffed that Tre knew something about my family and me and didn't say it!

She squeezed my shoulder firmly as she knew I must have had a ton of questions. The torch hanging from the ceiling crackled.

Thomas looked down at the ground, grasping for the words to say. He took a step backward toward the other boys. This time as he spoke, in the middle of the room, his words, his story, came to life.

"There was a time, at the beginning, when the ultimate good, Jacob, also known as the Master of Light, ruled the planet. He was the creator and the ruler of everything. Evil did not exist. At all. Light and goodness ruled and reigned. Jacob gave his creatures many gifts like love and peace and goodness, but one of the greatest gifts he gave them, though, was the gift of freedom. Freedom to choose between right and wrong. The freedom to love. The freedom to honor him with the way they lived their lives like their creator," Thomas paused, as did the story that was unfolding before our eyes. "Jacob had created a favored being named Antioch whom he loved dearly. He loved Antioch like a son and gave Antioch much power and responsibility to help oversee our world."

A father and son embracing and sharing a smile emerged in front of us. "For Antioch, though, this wasn't enough. A speck of darkness found its way into Antioch's soul. It was an unwelcome guest at first, but it kept knocking and approaching him as good and harmless and beautiful. Saying things to Antioch like, 'It's not that bad,' or 'Jacob won't mind.' Eventually, these dark thoughts became more sinister, saying things like, 'Why should Jacob have all the power?' The initial unwelcome guest was slowly embraced by Antioch. He took advantage of this freedom and became proud and arrogant, abusing his power and wanting control of everything. Antioch left Jacob and the city of Lucent and began to manipulate humanity. He distorted the creation and its creatures. He distorted the minds and hearts of men and women. Hatred, selfishness, envy, strife, gluttony, greed, and laziness began to take over. And these things were the inward poisons that spawned outward evils: murder, adultery, hatred, racism, divorce, abuse, loneliness, suicide. Like a changing of the tides, the evil began to spread slowly, methodically. He was Antioch no more. He had evolved into something darker and more hideous, the evil, the very definition. Slowly he has built up an army of both willing, like your father, and unwilling, like your mother, minds and souls. He has turned beautiful, majestic creatures into the stuff of nightmares. He's turned handsome men and women into zombies and Wolf Terrors. Others, he has simply tricked their minds into believing that everything is perfectly fine, the Oblivions. And some, who have resisted, have been dragged away to the mines to help fuel his final takeover of Lucent and Jacob. The darkness is spreading quicker than ever before. If not stopped soon, the darkness will win," he paused once again to let this sink in as the story in front of us also came to a halt.

"*Tell him!*" This time it was Judah's turn to chime in. He roared and pointed at Thomas as he said it. He was firm, very firm.

Am I the only one that doesn't know what's going on? I thought exasperatingly. Tre squeezed my shoulder once again.

"Your mom is a direct offspring of Jacob," Thomas said and stopped. "Your dad, however, is a direct offspring of Antioch."

My head began to spin. What did that even mean? How do you process that? *Your mom is a direct descendent of the Light, everything that is good in the world, and your dad is a direct descendent of the Evil, everything that is wrong with the world!* I exhaled deeply, loudly. The torch hanging from the ceiling crackled again as if longing to comfort me.

"The One," this time Hope took over, "the One will be from the seed of Jacob alone. He will be the one, though, that defeats Antioch, the only one capable of doing so, thus defeating evil and restoring the world to its intended state. Your mother comes from the line of Jacob. She was pure and good, and she fell in love with your father, who is of the seed of Antioch. He manipulated her heart and mind. He is not your biological father. He adopted you and your older brother. This is part of your life that has been cloaked from you to protect you." She looked at me, knowing I was processing it all but not getting anywhere. "Your brother left home when he found out the truth. Your father was being used by the evil, Antioch, to keep an eye on you, but he hadn't planned on falling in love with your mom. So they hid you. It's why you never really had any friends. It's why your dad was the only one to go into town. But it's also why your dad left. A Wolf Terror, disguised as the town blacksmith, confronted him in town one day and slipped that he knew who your dad was and what/who he was hiding."

"But…but…why me? Just because of my mom? I'm a nobody! I am not big or strong or brave or significant in any way. I'm clumsy and awkward. And…" I was confused and hurt and mad and angry. I had been lied to, betrayed, misled. My parents, people in this room. I just wanted to take it out on someone. I don't know why, but I lunged from my sitting position and was on top of Hope, my hands around her throat. Everyone just sat there, though, not trying to stop me.

"I know what you're thinking," Hope struggled to say. "You're thinking that you have no one you can trust. No one you can rely on or turn to." She wasn't struggling; she was smiling. "But you do. You have Hope, and when you have Hope, you have endless possibilities, positive possibilities. Your friends, they believe in you. We, in this room, believe in you. We have hope, and so do you. Stop thinking like a chicken and start thinking like an eagle. Stop pecking on the ground, making yourself easy prey for Antioch and his evil comrades, and start owning who you were created to be: a warrior, a predator, an agent of light, a force that strikes fear and terror into the very core of the evil." She was right. I was afraid. I was angry, and I was still pecking along at the ground. I released my grip on her throat and sheepishly tried to help her to her feet.

She continued, "You have a lot to process, but as long as you hold on to hope, you'll be able to figure it out without all of the extra drama that the evil brings: negativity, confusion, anger. Hope and light are synonymous. Light and clarity are synonymous. Freedom and power are synonymous. Remember that."

"I…I…I'm sorry," I stammered, looking her in the eye.

She threw her arms around me and patted me on the back. "It's okay, friend," she repeated over and over again.

She finally let go and looked me in the eye. "You're wondering what's next, aren't you?"

I nodded.

"I have a plan."

My heart skipped a beat with anticipation.

TORCH

RECIPE FOR SUCCESS

"So, I'm supposed to be the One?" I chuckled awkwardly.

Tre, Judah, and I were still sitting on the floor in the middle of the room. The torch above us crackled occasionally. Hope had the boys helping her with something over at the table.

Judah also found this to be funny, "Ya, that's what I thought when my dad and I found you, and you were pretending to be dead!"

Tre chimed in, "You're not the only one, Judah. I couldn't believe it when I first met you in the cabin. I questioned my mother, and I never question my mother." She said with a chuckle making air quotes as she pronounced the word, "one."

"Look," I said, "we're stuck in a basement, underneath a town where we were arrested by silly-looking men wearing silly hats with even sillier sounding voices. Everyone in Helen hates our kind, and even if we get out of here, we have no idea how to get to the mines." I was painting a worst-case scenario for sure.

Judah added to the worseness, "Um, you're forgetting that you and Tre had your weapons confiscated by the silly sheriffs."

Tre made the painted picture of the problematic, worst-case scenario worse still, "And you're forgetting that we have Offspring, Arachne, and Wolf Terrors hunting for us."

Tre won.

Behind us, Hope was directing the boys in whatever it was that they were working on at the table.

I looked at Tre and Judah and thought about what Hope had said. They believe in me. They're willing to die for me. Whoa! But a lingering question was haunting me, "Who has my real dad?"

Tre gave me a smile and a knowing look as if to say, "You'll know when it's time to know."

Hope's voice broke into my reverie, "Easy…easy…Not too much, now, Franklin. We don't want to kill anyone."

I turned to see that Franklin was pouring a powdery substance into a bowl. He had a scarf wrapped around his nose and face. They all did.

"Just a tad bit more…" she mumbled. "That should do it." Hope looked pleased. "Now, Teddy, carefully stir, making sure not to spill any of it." Teddy began to stir slowly, carefully. Hope looked on with much concern, but after a few minutes of slow stirring, Teddy stopped and looked at Hope, who smiled and nodded at him.

"It's time," she said mumbly to the boys who you could tell had been waiting for this moment. A few chuckles escaped as well.

"What time?" I asked, moving toward the table.

"*Stop!*" Thomas said firmly. "*Don't come any closer.*"

I stopped, unclear of what I did wrong.

"You didn't do anything wrong," Hope mumbled. "Let us finish up, and I'll tell you our plan."

I retreated back to where Tre and Judah sat on the ground and continued to watch the scene unfold.

The boys that had actual human hands began to take clumps of the mixture out of the bowl and shape them on a pan. They were wearing gloves and moving very cautiously. They filled a pan with the concoction and placed the pan in the firebox. They repeated this process over and over again, filling pans and placing them in the firebox. When they had finished, Thomas and his twin brother Edison took the bowl and utensils to a side corner of the room. The sound of running water was soon heard. It must have been a sink. With the only light in the room coming from the torch overhead, the basement was filled with dark spots. The sink area was one of those spots.

"Careful," Hope mumbled to the boys.

The other boys carefully and meticulously wiped down the table.

Thomas and Edison joined the group a few minutes later with the newly cleaned bowl and utensils. The table was clean: not a hint of flour to be seen.

"Come," Hope mumbled, motioning for the three of us to join her at the table. "Let's chat," she said, smiling from ear to ear, her tongue hanging out.

We joined her at the table, and the boys brought out a few chairs for us to sit on. They were tall chairs that we had to climb up into in order to sit on them. Once everyone was settled, Thomas took over the conversation.

"Hope's plan, and I concur," he began, "is to get you out of town tomorrow evening. Doing that should be relatively easy. Getting back your torch and sword, on the other hand, not so much. We believe that they are stored at the supervising sheriff's station. Where? We're not sure. We're not even sure if they are stored there." He was looking at us for a reaction. We waited for him to continue.

"So, that's the plan?" Tre asked, unimpressed. "We sneak out at night, hoping not to get caught, and wander around until we find the sheriff's shop who may or may not be in possession of our weapons?" She huffed indignantly and rolled her eyes. I liked it when she was like this, salty.

"Well, no," Thomas replied, a bit flustered. I don't think many people ever talked to Thomas like that, especially a young lady.

He continued, "In order to do this successfully, we need help. First of all, what you saw us bake was a special cinnamon roll recipe designed to induce sleep. It is time-released so that it should take effect eight hours after they've been consumed. In other words, in the middle of the night. That is when we make our move."

"So, we drug the whole town?" I asked skeptically. "Then how do we find the sheriff's station and our weapons?"

"This is the tricky part..." his voice trailed off as he looked over at Hope.

Hope picked up the scenario, looking down at the table and playing with her hands as she spoke, "We need help on the outside. From someone up there," she mumbled, pointing upstairs. "I gave my mother a letter a few days ago when I dropped off the cinnamon rolls. I asked her to deliver the cinnamon rolls all over town tomorrow morning, making special sure to deliver them to the sheriff's station and not to eat any herself. I also asked her to show us the location of the sheriff's station tomorrow night." She was still staring down at her hands.

"Can you trust her?" Tre said in disbelief.

"I'm not sure. But we have no other choice. You need your weapons where you're going, and she's the closest thing that we have to a person on the inside or the outside, if you prefer," Hope finished firmly, but also as if she was trying to convince herself.

"So, we get out of here, get our weapons, and then what?" I asked.

"I come back here," Hope said. "The boys will accompany you. They know the way to the mines. Plus, you'll need all the help you can get."

Looking around the table at the mismatched crew of creatures and human oddities, I thought to myself, *What good would they do in a fight? Somersaulting for cinnamon rolls is one thing, taking on the Offspring, another.* I glanced at Tre out of the corner of my eye and saw she was thinking the same thing.

Tre and I were thinking the same thing.

"Don't let their appearance fool you; they are more fierce than you know," Hope said aloud. "They will fight with you and for you. They are not afraid." She smiled a crooked smile at the boys. Her "boys." "Besides, they have plenty of wrongs they want to right. More than you'll ever know."

"But what about you?" I asked. "Why stay here, stuck in a life of hiding?"

Hope turned to look at me. "My mother needs me. If I leave, there will be no one to make the cinnamon rolls."

Her answer seemed a bit rehearsed. Even if her mother needed her to make the cinnamon rolls, wouldn't Hope long to be free of this place? Was she trying to earn her mother's favor and attention? Why hadn't her mother visited her? She could've come in the middle of the night when everyone else was asleep. So, why the loyalty?

Tears formed in the corner of Hope's eyes. She sniffled. She knew what Tre and I were thinking by our body language. I was right: her answer had been well-rehearsed. She was still trying to win the affection of her mother.

"I…I…I promised my mother I would stay in Helen and make her cinnamon rolls if she helped us," she finally mumbled in between sniffles, tears now streaming down her cheeks.

"So, she agreed to help?" Tre asked.

"Not exactly," Thomas cut in. "Not in so many words. She just slipped a note under the door at the top of the stairwell with the word 'Yes' on it."

"That's it, then. That's the plan," I said into the air. "I guess we'll find out if it works." The torch began to crackle loudly as if it was excited for what was to come.

TORCH

MOMMY DEAREST

The next day we sat around with some pacing, some sleeping, some joking, some playing cards, and some making nervous small talk. The night couldn't come fast enough. The thought of what we were about to do was on everyone's minds. We waited and waited and waited for the cue, a soft rapping on the door at the top of the stairwell.

Finally, we heard the faint knocking. In the cavernous room, it echoed, sending chills down my spine. It was the "go" time. A couple of the boys pounded their chests as the adrenaline started to kick in. Franklin, half man/half bear, led out a roar, and on cue, Teddy, the half ox/half eagle, began to snort, steam, and drool emanating from his ox snout and pawing at the ground. The roars and snorts startled me, and I was immediately filled with respect and fear of these two powerful creatures, grateful we were on the same side.

We waited for Hope to lead the way.

Hope stood in the middle of the room with Edison. Roosevelt, the brown Pegasus, hovered in the air above the hanging torch. Roosevelt used the horn protruding from his forehead to slice the rope of the torch. It tumbled from the ceiling and ended up in Edison's hand. He took the torch and, with a bow, handed it to Hope. The lighting changed drastically from being above us to coming from wherever Hope was. She made her way to the stairs. We all followed.

Reaching the top of the stairs, Hope slowly opened the door and walked through. One by one, we all did the same, with Teddy bringing up the rear. We found ourselves in a small, wonderful-smelling bakery. There were a few chairs scattered around a few tables and a long counter, which also had a few chairs hugging it. A cash register was at the far end of the counter. To the right of the cash register was a display case (probably to showcase the daily cinnamon rolls).

She stood quietly near the door, almost hidden in a shadow. She appeared to be pretty, or at one point was pretty, but life had worn her down, making her appear older than she really was. She had long hair that was more gray than its original color of brown. She was slender but not stick-skinny and was of medium height. Her fingers were intertwined down by her waist.

"Hello, darling," came a sweet soft voice from across the bakery. Who knows how long it had been since Hope had heard her mother's voice?

Hope stopped. She stood there for a moment, the torch crackling in her hand, and we waited. I don't think anyone was breathing.

Hope started. Handing the torch to me, she ran toward her mother, brushing into chairs and tables along the way. She dove into her mother's arms.

"Momma!" she cried out as she wrapped her arms around her in a hug.

Almost immediately, her mother pried her off. Hope was taken aback slightly.

"Not now, Hope, dear. There will be plenty of time for that later," Hope's mother replied, a little more coolly now. "We need to get moving before your little potion wears off." She turned and opened the door for us.

Out on the street, Hope's mother began to walk fast. Very fast. Okay, it was more of a jog than a walk. She was in a hurry. I didn't blame her, though. If she were caught, they'd execute her for sure. If I were her, I would've been sprinting.

Helen was dark. Moonlight was the only light, save for the glow of Hope's torch. Our little party of unusual characters followed Hope's mother around this corner and that corner, occasionally stopping when we thought we heard something or someone coming. We walked until we came to what appeared to be the center of town. A large fountain was in the middle of the street, and the street was flanked on four sides by two-story buildings all butted up against one another. Most appeared to be businesses, with the business on the bottom floor and a small apartment on the top floor. In front of one of the buildings was a yellow star, kinda like on a sheriff's badge. We made a beeline for it.

Standing in front of the yellow star building, Hope's mother gave us some insight, "Now, the sheriff usually keeps a few of his finest deputies stationed here all night to guard the place." Her voice was barely above a whisper, "Hopefully, your little concoction worked."

"Me, Tre, Judah, and T will go in to look for the weapons. The rest of you wait outside for us and keep watch," Hope said in a whispered voice.

Hope's mother slowly turned the handle of the door and opened it for us. Hope entered first, followed by Tre, then me, then... *Where is Judah?* I asked this question in my mind to both Hope and Tre. The three of us turned around to see him staggering across the town square as if he were drunk.

"Teddy, Franklin, go get Judah," Hope commanded.

We slowly entered the building with Hope and her torch leading the way. The room we entered was part office, part lobby/waiting room. There were two desks on one side of the room and one on the opposite side. The place appeared empty. That was until we heard the snores. Three deputies, each sitting at separate desks, were fast asleep. Making our way through the small lobby, we opened a small wooden dividing gate that separated the general public space from the sheriff's. The gate squeaked just enough to make the hair on the back of my neck stand up. We froze. Behind one of the sheriffs was a glass case that also doubled as a safe. That was it! That was where our weapons were. The three of us tiptoed around the back of the desk to the safe. Our suspicions were true. My torch, not lit, was in there along with Tre's sword. How to get in without breaking it?

Tre stood directly in front of the safe with Hope to her left. There wasn't much room between where the sheriff was sitting/sleeping and the safe, so I stood behind Hope next to the sheriff's desk.

"Do you see a key anywhere?" Tre whispered.

I scanned the desktop next to me. It was just littered with a few typed letters. Nothing else.

"Nope. Maybe in a desk drawer," I whispered in reply. The sheriff was sitting too close to the drawers to open them without moving him out of the way.

"I'll just have to smash it open," Hope said in a mumbly whisper. Tre took a step off to the side as Hope wound up to smash the glass safe. I looked down at the desk to avoid the potential flying glass. It was then I noticed it. Hope swung the torch toward the glass safe; I could hear it cutting through the air like in slow motion. My eyes were fixed on the desk, however. Sticking out from under the sheriff's elbow on a piece of paper was a handwritten signature. "Love, Hope." It was Hope's letter to her mom!

I screamed, "*Run!*" at the same time as the torch smashed through the glass case. Everything happened so quickly and yet in slow motion. The sheriff shoved his chair back, pinning Hope against the glass safe, which was now just shards of broken glass. I heard her let out a painful sigh. The other sheriffs were across the room and on top of us before we knew it. They grabbed our hands, tied them behind our backs, and then stood us up.

"This will teach you to trick us!" cried the high-pitched sheriff who had Hope pinned against the wall with his chair.

The door to the building opened. "Where is she?" Hope's mother demanded.

Standing up, the sheriff pushed his chair in and pointed behind it. "Here. Your daughter is over here," he told her in his high-pitched voice, his tall hat perched precariously on top of his head.

Walking over to where Hope was lying in a small pool of blood, her mother bent down and disgustedly said, "This is not my daughter! I don't have a daughter! This is a freak!" And then I heard her spit on her daughter. I could hear Hope weeping. Outside there was more commotion. More sheriff's deputies had shown up and surrounded the boys.

We needed Hope right now, but she was on the floor, and we seemed to be losing her fast.

"What should we do with her?" asked the helium-voiced sheriff.

"The same as the others!" the woman shot back.

"Yes, Ma'am," he responded. Outside there was more commotion. It seemed as if the boys weren't going down without a fight.

The sheriff turned and commanded the deputy detaining Tre, "Junior, go check and see what the fuss is all about outside." It sounded like he meant business, but again, his voice was high, and that ruined the mood. He walked her over so that the deputy holding onto me could try to keep a hold of both of us. Tre and I started to giggle. The sheriff looked on while they did the handoff, scowling at us for giggling. He turned back to see Hope's mother bent over her. What the sheriff did not hear is the whispering between Hope and her mother.

The sheriff approached Hope's mother.

"You're a no good for nothin' excuse for a human being," the woman said to Hope in a vicious tone.

"Ma'am? Isn't that a bit harsh?" the high-pitched po-po said.

"Why, no, sir. I meant it when I said that you're a no good for nothin' excuse for a human being!" As she said this, she stood up and whirled around, catching the sheriff square in the head with Hope's torch. His tall hat flew through the air; his body plopped to the ground. She then bent down and helped Hope to her feet. Mother and daughter shared a hug and a smile.

The sheriff holding onto Tre and me screamed (a high-pitched scream, of course) at the sight of his boss being dropped so easily. We wiggled out of his grip just before Hope's mother cracked him across the skull too. Down he went. By this point, Hope was fetching my torch and Tre's sword from the safe and none too soon. Hope's mother quickly untied our hands.

Using Hope's torch to light mine, we turned to see all of the sheriffs that had been outside retreating inside the building. In an instant, the room was filled with sheriffs. Tall-hatted, high-pitched hooligans flooded in as if running from something…They were running from something…The boys. Tre and I looked at one another and then at Hope and smiled.

"We got this," Tre said to Hope, fully meaning that she and I would take care of it while she sat this one out.

"I know, and I know," Hope responded with a smile, and then she took off, torch blazing. Tre and I stood there, our mouths aghast! What and who is Hope?

"Sometimes Hope is all you need!" Hope yelled with a chuckle as she began to take out sheriff after sheriff. She jumped, she shimmied, she ducked, she dove, all the while taking out sheriffs. They still seemed to be everywhere, so Tre and I joined in.

The three of us, me, Hope, and Tre, closed in from the back of the room. The boys closed in from the front of the room. High-pitched screams and yells mixed with oofs and ows filled the room. Tall hats flew; their owners fell. A couple of sheriffs tried to escape from the fray by holding onto light fixtures or ceiling fans, and still, others tried crawling on their bellies to escape only to be used as area rugs by their comrades. Several minutes later and the high-pitched horde had been reduced to a couple of hangers-on. They weren't about to fight. They were outmatched, so they ran into the night screaming and blowing raspberries.

Standing in the middle of the room on the backs of some fallen sheriffs, I scanned the scene. Hope's mother was holding Hope in her arms and sharing a moment. The boys were standing around talking excitedly about the milieu. Tre stood near me doing the same.

"We need to go," Tre said to me firmly.

"I hate to break up the party, but we need to leave right now!" I said. "The potion will be wearing off soon, and we need to be long gone by then."

We headed to the door of the building and gathered outside on the street. We were pleasantly surprised to see Judah sitting on the edge of the fountain. He saw us and stumbled over to where we'd gathered.

"Hey, guys, bin what up to, um, ya?" His tongue was hanging out with every word, and drool was streaming out of his mouth.

"What?" Hope asked him.

"Yup," Judah replied, "ate delicious one only. Sleepy." He fell asleep standing in front of us but thankfully, Roosevelt, the brown Pegasus, was there to catch his fall. We loaded him onto Roosevelt's back.

"We need to go!" Hope's mom pleaded. "Follow me, I know a shortcut out of town."

Off she fled quickly, in a full run now, down a side street with her sideshow friends in tow. Dawn would break soon.

TORCH

MONKEY BUSINESS

We got beyond the city limits as dawn was breaking. The sky was a hazy orange as the ambient light of the sun made everything appear golden. We stopped to catch our breath and to talk strategy. Hope's mother pulled her aside, and they were talking quietly.

Hearing only bits of their conversation, I could tell that Hope was upset with her mom.

"But I need you, mom!" came Hope's pleading voice.

Her mom's hushed response triggered more pleas from Hope.

"But you need me, mom!" again, her voice was pleading. She buried her head into her mother's chest. They stood like that for several minutes, Hope and her mother sharing a hug and a cry. Finally, her mother broke free of Hope's grip and came over to address the group.

"Friends, you need to leave now. I will go back into town to distract any of the remaining sheriffs. My only request is that you take care of Hope, my daughter." She gave a loving glance toward Hope, who still had tears in her eyes. "It is not safe for her to return to Helen while the town is under Antioch's control," Hope's mother told the group.

"It's not safe for you, either!" blurted out Hope through a stream of tears.

"As long as you are safe, that's a risk I'm willing to take. Besides, you may make one mean baker, but after what I just witnessed, you are an even better warrior!" Hope's mom responded with a smile of pride. "And where you are going, you could use all the warriors you can get."

Hope ran over and gave her mother another long hug.

Her mother was right: Hope was an amazing warrior. Wait, amazing is an understatement. When Hope has her torch in her hand, she is transformed. No longer does she mumble. Her movements are quick and confident. Her mind is sharp. Even her body seems to transform slightly. I know the power of the torch, so I'm not surprised.

"Will I see you again, mother?" Hope asked, looking up into her mother's face.

"I pray so, my special girl. I pray so." She gave Hope a kiss on the forehead and then, backing away, said a tearful, "I love you, my special girl." She turned and started running back to town.

"I love you, too!" Hope yelled/mumbled after her mom through her tears.

The sun had barely broken over the horizon now. We had to move. According to Thomas and Edison, the only ones that knew how to get to the Veiled City, the mines were a few days' journey and the high-pitched police were sure to come after us, not to mention the Offspring, Arachne, and Wolf Terrors. We set off, initially by the main road. That would quickly change.

"Roosevelt, fly up ahead and give us a scouting report on the road," Thomas commanded the brown Pegasus.

Roosevelt took off ahead of us and eventually out of sight. We continued walking on the main road but not too fast as we awaited Roosevelt's report.

The pathway was relatively smooth, indicating that this was a well-traveled road, though we were the only ones on it this morning. The terrain meandered up and down hills, but we appeared to be climbing in elevation. Ahead, a mountain range loomed with snowy white peaks. Ominous-looking forests flanked our sides, trees towering high into the sky. The air was hot and stale with not even a hint of a breeze, and we walked on mostly in silence with only the sound of our breathing or foot/paw prints breaking the quietness. No birds chirping. No mooing of distant farmyard animals. It was quiet. It was still. It was foreboding.

We'd been walking for about an hour when the sun finally crested, and with it came the small vibrations of the ground we were walking on. They were subtle at first, hardly noticeable but slowly got longer and stronger, as did a rhythmic drumlike cadence of wood on wood and stick on leather drumhead. This added to the rhythm of the vibrations.

"What is that?" Judah asked, voicing what we were all thinking but trying to act too cool/brave to say anything.

"Whatever it is, I don't like it!" Tre said through clenched teeth.

The sound and vibrations were coming from behind us and getting closer. Looking back, all we could see was a cloud of dust, like a thick fog moving in from the sea. It appeared that some humongous creature or creatures were demolishing trees on either side of the road as it/they came toward us.

Since we were in the middle of the road, we made for easy targets. If these creatures weren't friendly, we would be in trouble.

"Let's wait over in the forest for whatever that is to pass," Thomas said to our crew.

We all agreed. The crew dashed into the forest just off the road and waited.

The rhythm, vibrations, and dust got closer still to where you could hear the voices of manic-sounding creatures yelling and screaming. There was a distinct beat that was coming from the dust.

The beat went something like:

> Click, click, click, click, thud,
> *boom* (the ground shaking)!
> Click, click, click, click, thud,
> *boom* (the ground shaking)!

Over and over, it rang out as it got closer to our location. I thought that if Simon were here, he'd want to drop some bars (even though this was not the time for such thoughts). The dust was growing thicker and spreading out into the forest like a river that jumped its banks during a flood.

Closer and closer, this mass of sound and rhythm came down the road. They were wider than the road, so again, certain trees were the casualty of this band.

> Click, click, click, click, thud,
> *boom* (the ground shaking)!
> Click, click, click, click, thud,
> *boom* (the ground shaking)!

They were close enough now that not only did the ground vibrate, but it altered my breathing.

Boom (heart trying to beat normally)! *Boom* (trying to catch my breath)!

Dust began to envelop us.

Through my gasps of breath and peeking out from behind a well-concealed bush, I could finally make out specific creatures and shapes. In front, leading the way, was a line of creatures that looked like monkeys but more than just monkeys. They were a hybrid of another animal like a hyena with a mangy frock of hair on their backs. Their legs were more hyenalike as well, but the rest of them definitely resembled a monkey. They were tall, towering, muscular monkeys walking upright and playing some drumlike instrument. They wore masks over their faces, which were attached with a tube to a cylinder on their backs. This seemed to help them breathe when the beat "boomed." They were fanned out across the road and onto the sides. They looked straight ahead and had perfect rhythm. They almost appeared to be in some sort of trance, and they were responsible for the "click, click, click, click, thud."

*Wow…*Here comes *the Boom*!

Directly behind them were three enormous creatures resembling woolly mammoths. These creatures were the biggest I'd ever seen. Humongous hairy bodies, laboring under their own weight, their feet crashed seismically down on the ground creating the *boom* in perfect rhythm! I had to strain my neck to see the tops of their heads. They towered as tall as the tallest trees that surrounded us. These woolly beasts wore breastplates made of metal and strapped around their gargantuan midsections. Atop each mammoth were two muscular-looking hyena-monkeys. One was calling out orders. The other was trying to control the enormous beast by holding onto reins that reached to the mouth of the beasts. Each of the hyena-monkeys that called out orders had brilliant, red-colored plumes coming from silver helmets. They also wore metal breastplates with some red characters drawn on them. There were six rows of these mammoths for a total of eighteen. They were regal and terrifying at the same time!

Atop the middle mammoth, in the front row of mammoths, was a hyena-monkey with a yellow-colored plume. He was wearing a red cape and a breastplate with yellow characters painted on it, and he appeared larger and more muscular than his counterparts. He appeared to be the leader. He was/they were, intimidating, to say the least.

In between gasps, Thomas whispered loudly to us, "Banshees, also known as bounty hunters!" The gig was up.

Thomas continued, "The banshee or monkey in the middle, he goes by 'Slash' and is the leader. His real name is Gregory, and he used to be a professional tap dancer in my hometown." Everybody gasped as the "boom" dropped. Thomas continued, "He found out that tap dancing wasn't good for his image or his wallet and that bounty hunting is better for both. He still loves a good rhythm, and he can really dance! He hates it, though, when people call him by his real name, and he tries to keep his tap-dancing nickname, the Sandman, on the down-low." Everybody gasped as the "boom" dropped.

The rhythmic troupe was nearly upon us now. Breathing was almost impossible. The ground shook, and the trees rattled, sending seeds, leaves, and branches raining down on us. Dust was everywhere: in our eyes, up our noses, on our clothes. It was terrifyingly magnificent!

I looked briefly to my right and left, and I could tell that my comrades had the same feeling. And then, they started to fade into the dust, just barely visible through the haze. Tre and Judah were beside me, but I could no longer see them.

The muscular masked monkey marchers were directly on their mark in front of us now. Besides the drumming, we could also hear their labored breathing coming through their mouthpieces. A woolly mammoth on the far side of the road took out a patch of trees signified by the echoing sound of timber cracking/exploding, and on our side, we could hear trees groaning and straining against the weight of oversized behemoths' bellies as they brushed against them. We froze, not making a sound. We were hardly breathing both from the booming beat and from fear.

The silence on our end was suddenly interrupted.

"*A w w w w w w w w w w w w w w w w w w w w w w w w w w w w—Chuuuuuuuuuuuuuuuuu!*" It was Judah. The dust had gotten the better of him. Would the monkeys get the better of us?

A shout of epic decibels erupted from Gregory, the monkey in the middle.

"*Halt!*" he yelled as a final cadence of

"click, click, click, click, thud,

boom (the ground shaking)!"

finished up.

Gregory, or Slash, or Sandman, stood atop his woolly mammoth and turned his head slowly from side to side, looking as if he was preening his ears and sniffing the air to find out where the source of the sound could be. He seemed slightly baffled. The entire gang of hyena-monkeys and pachyderms stood completely still, just feet in front of where we were standing. The dust had settled in the trees and surrounded us but seemed to avoid Slash and his crew. I could barely make out Tre's position just to my left and Judah just to my right. Nobody moved. Not our crew, not their crew. No one.

The silence was interrupted by Slash's booming voice, "Come out, come out, whoever you are!" he yelled and laughed a terrifying hyena laugh as he looked to and fro. I got the chills. "I'll say it again, 'Come out, come out, whoever you are!'" he repeated, sounding more irritated this time. Again, not a sound was made.

He was still standing atop his pachyderm when the silence was broken once again. This time, by the drummer closest to our position. As if in slow motion, his drumstick slipped out of his hand, and in the silence, it reverberated from one side of the road to the other as it hit the ground, causing everyone from both parties to jump. The drumstick, of course, hit the ground and bounced a few times before finally landing right in front of the bush directly in front of me.

Slash saw it immediately. "Wesley, Wesley, Wesley, you fool! I only forced you to be part of my troupe as a favor to your mother. Now, go pick up your drumstick!" Slash commanded him, punctuating his command with a snide hyena laugh.

The timid banshee scurried over to the edge of bushes to retrieve the rogue drumstick. As he bent over to pick it up, something caught his eye. He stared at the bushes. He stared at me. The torch quietly crackled in my hand. I slowly raised a finger of my opposite hand to my lips, the universal sign of "shhhhhhh." He looked at me, confused.

"What is it?" Slash yelled down to Wesley.

Wesley retrieved his drumstick and slowly backed away. "Nothing..." Wesley stammered, "Nothing." He went back to his assigned spot in the drumline. I could see a trickle of sweat running down Wesley's face.

We all let out a sigh of relief as the gang began to move out...or move in. At that exact moment, Slash looked over to where I was hiding and somehow made direct eye contact.

"Hard left, boys! Let's get them! Daddy wants a big payday!" Slash yelled. And with that, the entire elephant entourage led by the drumming banshees turned hard left and ascended on us. The chase was on (again)!

TORCH

MONKEYING AROUND

We scattered, not knowing where we were heading but just that we were running in the opposite direction of Slash and his gang. Though the fog of dust kicked up by the oversized pachyderms had subsided, the woods around us got thicker. There was no path, and with the thickening of the woods came darkness. Thankfully, I had my torch, and it seemed to be enjoying the chase. My counterparts were running beside me, though the only way I could tell was the breaking of branches and panting.

Behind us, the drummers broke rank and were in an all-out sprint with the woolly mammoths creating a path of destruction right behind them. The banshees screamed and screeched, their inner wild banshees coming out! They were fast, mostly running on all fours like a hyena, and strong. Some scampered along the ground while others went to the trees. Slash yelled out threats to both his gang and us.

"Hurry up, you sloths!" came one of his threats, "We can't let these losers get away! If they get away, you'll have to deal with me!" came another threat.

The torch sent more and more power through my body. A familiar feeling shot through my legs as I ran faster and faster, putting more and more distance between myself and the crazed banshee gang.

Not too far behind me, I heard a melee. Thomas and Edison were scraping it out with a couple of banshee drummers. I heard shouts and shrieks and screams. The banshees sounded as if they were getting the worst of it.

"Edison, come on!" I heard Thomas pleading with his brother. "Get up! We have to keep moving!" There was concern in his voice. Something was wrong.

I stopped on a dime and ran to where I had heard Thomas. Up ahead, in the dim light, I saw Thomas kneeling on the ground.

"Get up, brother! Get up!" he was softly pleading with Edison.

I arrived at a bloody scene. Four dead drumming banshees were scattered about on the ground. Thomas and Edison gave them a whooping, but Edison had also taken some blows. He was bleeding, and all the pleadings in the world from his brother weren't going to help him. I stood there for a moment in silence, knowing that we couldn't stay here. We had to get moving!

I placed a hand on Thomas's shoulder. "Thomas, we have to leave now!" I said quietly but firmly.

The wild banshee screams were getting closer now. These four down drummers must have been the fastest, the front line. Now the others were catching up.

"*No!*" snarled Thomas. "I'm not leaving him!" he said as he knocked my hand away.

"If we don't go now, then we'll all die out here!" I said more forcefully this time.

"If you want to leave, then leave!" he shot back. "I am not leaving my brother!" he didn't look at me, just at his beloved twin laying in a pool of blood at his knees.

Branches snapped nearby. I couldn't tell if it was from the ground or the treetops, and I surely couldn't tell how many. We had to move. I tried one more time.

"Thomas, you've got to let your brother go! If there is any hope of saving this planet from the darkness, from Antioch, I need you in this fight!" I implored.

The ground began to shake as the woolly mammoths got closer. I could once again hear Slash's voice calling out threats to his gang members. I stood over Thomas, who knelt over Edison, waiting for a response from him.

Branches and banshees came raining down from above, and instantly, the moment was interrupted. They were screaming and foaming at the mouth and wasted no time in attacking us, or rather, me. Thomas just continued kneeling above his brother, oblivious to what was happening. The torch and I went to work. I ran directly at the closest banshee and jumped high in the air, somersaulting over him as he tried to grab me. Landing directly behind him, I swung the torch and hit the back of his head, knocking him to the ground in an instant. He didn't move. He wouldn't. Two other banshees, however, were fast and on me in no time. I managed to get a few blows in on one of them, but the other grabbed me from behind, knocking my torch to the ground. He immediately began to bite my shoulder. Through my pain, I looked over to see Thomas, still kneeling over his brother, get kicked in the head by the fourth monkey, sending him to the ground and landing face down in his brother's blood.

The banshee still holding me continued biting down on my shoulder when the first pachyderm arrived, taking down trees and kicking up dust. It stood over us. A second and third and fourth woolly mammoth arrived. They formed a circle around us. Several banshee drummers arrived as well and began to play a low, ominous rhythm. A clearing had been formed, allowing streaks of sunlight to stream through the dust. More and more banshee drummers began to arrive on the scene. I looked over and noticed that Thomas's eyes were open. At least he was alive. The banshee biting my shoulder still had a firm grip on my hands but had stopped biting once Slash and Co. showed up.

A shuffling of feet, a couple of grunts, and a bit of frenetic activity, and suddenly, Slash was standing in front of me, having dismounted his steed. His hands were out to the side as if for dramatic flair. In the distance, I heard a banshee yell out, "Jazz hands!"

Slash immediately put his hands down and yelled, "I heard that!" Faint hyena chuckles were heard from the banshee gang members. Slash turned his attention toward me, though, as I was thrown toward his feet. I stumbled slightly and noticed my torch was a few feet away, but I dare not make a move. We were clearly outnumbered.

"Well, well, well," Slash said, looking me up and down. He was quite taller than me and even more muscular this close up. He bent down and grabbed me by the throat and lifted me off my feet like I weighed nothing. I was staring at him eyeball to eyeball. His breath smelled like rotten cabbage, and he had yellow teeth, like when someone's a smoker. His eyes were manic and bloodshot, like he'd been drinking or smoking something.

"What do we have here?" he asked rhetorically, a crazed yellow-toothed grin spreading across his face and laughing the eerie laugh of a hyena. And then he just stared at me for a long time, not saying a word. I didn't breathe because I couldn't. I felt the blood begin to drain from my body.

"Mm-hmm…" he finally said. I was about to pass out. Slash released his grip, and I fell to the ground, rubbing my neck and breathing frantically. "I don't see it," Slash said, looking down at me. "But what do I know? Look, kid, I don't know who you are or what all of the fuss is over you, but apparently, someone thinks you're a pretty big deal." He bent down to address me. "You're worth a lot of money to someone. Your friends, not so much. They're what I call 'expendable,'" Slash said using air quotes. "So, while we're going to take you with us, your friends, on the other hand, well, let's just say they're the price of doing business."

"What do you mean by 'the price of doing business'?" I asked with a little venom in my voice but still somewhat hoarse from Slash's hand.

"Ha, ha, ha!" Slash cackled a hyena cackle. "You aren't very sharp, are you?" he asked rhetorically. He continued, "Let me explain it like this: we're going to kill your friends," he said with delight. "In fact, we're going to rip them apart and eat them for dinner!" he said, laughing.

"I don't think that's going to happen!" I said matter-of-factly but still a bit hoarse.

"Wha…wha…what did you say?" Slash replied indignantly as he strode toward me.

He hates being called by his real name. Thomas's words suddenly came back to me.

"You heard me right, *Gregory*. Or should I say, Sandman?" I said with forceful sarcasm.

All around, banshees started to snicker like hyenas. In fact, the woolly mammoths looked like they were laughing as well.

"Why, if you weren't worth so much, I'd finish you right now!" Slash yelled at me, a hairy finger in my face. "My name is Slash, leader of the Honkey-Monkey gang, and I will not be disrespected!"

"Whoa, what are you going to do, outdance me, Sandman?" I said much more sarcastically, this time pretending to tap dance.

At this, the banshees and elephants lost it and began to laugh hysterically. Some of them started "dancing" too, mocking their leader. The scene was getting more raucous by the second. Mammoths and monkeys were laughing and stomping and carrying on. And then, from the back of the pack (these things always start at the back), the chant, "Dance! Dance! Dance!" made its way through the entire gang and got louder and louder until it was almost deafening. Drummers were banging on their drums and woolly mammoths stomping on the ground.

"*Quiet!*" came the roaring shout from Slash. The noise trickled to a stop. "Fine. You want me to dance; I'll give you a dance," Slash said emphatically, not one to ever miss an opportunity for a good show.

He stood there for a second, closed his eyes, and held his hands out to his side. "Rhythm. I need a beat. A hot beat. Some four-on-the-floor action." On cue, a few of the drummers started drumming. It was upbeat, with a few woolly mammoths providing the base. Slash took a deep breath and waited for the right moment. Hands out to the side, he started to dance to the delight of his gang members. They cheered him on, hooting and hollering their approval. The Sandman was in the zone.

I have to say he was a really good dancer! But I wasn't here to watch him tap dance; I had to escape. This was my chance. With Gregory in a full-blown tap dance mode trance, I dove over to where my torch lay and, in one fluid movement, grabbed it and ran straight toward Thomas. I reached down and grabbed him with my free hand, pulling him to his feet. He was still feeling the effects of the foot to his head, so his feet were unsteady at first. I could feel him feebly reaching back toward his slain brother. Edison wouldn't be going with us. We ran together, me supporting Thomas, through the banshees and mammoths on the opposite side of where Gregory was dancing. There was only one banshee and mammoth left to contend with, and they were so entranced at Gregory's dancing that they didn't notice us.

We got a two-minute head start on them before they even realized we were gone. I willed the torch to help give me more power and strength.

In the distance, the beat stopped, and I heard what sounded like a war cry. The banshee band was after us again.

The woods were thick, Thomas was heavy, and our pursuers were gaining momentum. The closer they got, the louder they were. Up ahead, though, it appeared to be lighter. A clearing? This could be good news. Even better news, Thomas suddenly snapped out of his trance and was running on his own! We approached the clearing, running at top speed. The trees behind us were falling and shaking the ground, which made every few steps difficult. We were nearly there!

We broke into the light! Into the clearing! But it wasn't a clearing. I mean, it was, but it wasn't. It was more of a cliff than a clearing. We stopped on a dime at the edge of the cliff. In no time, Gregory/Sandman/Slash and Co. joined us. In front of us, a semicircle of mammoths and banshees, and behind us, a sheer drop-off.

Slash dismounted from his pachyderm and made his way over to Thomas and me.

"Well, well, well," Slash started, "you thought you could outsmart ole Slash, did you?" he asked rhetorically, smugly striding over to us.

"He basically did," came a distant banshee's voice once again from the back of the gang.

"I heard that!" yelled Slash, head up in the air.

The air on the edge of the cliff was cool, very cool, and there was a stiff breeze blowing. The sun was high in the sky, and hardly a cloud could be seen. If not for my current situation, this would make a great spot for a picnic with Tre. *Stop thinking about Tre*, I berated myself.

The banshees and behemoths continued snickering as Slash turned his attention back to Thomas and me.

"So, here's what's going to happen," Slash said, walking toward us. "I'm going to kill your friend," he said, looking at Thomas, "and then I may or may not kill you! Money or no money, nobody embarrasses Slash and lives to tell about it!"

"It's easy to do!" came a distant bantering banshee's voice. More laughter.

"I heard that!" Slash said, a bit peevishly this time. He looked at us, "This is what I get. They always want to monkey around," he said with a wry grin and a chuckle.

"Dad joke!" yelled a different banshee.

"I heard that!" Slash yelled in reply. "It was better than a dad joke! Anyways, I have killing on my mind, and I'm not thinking clearly." He turned and walked up toward Thomas, putting a hairy finger in his face. "Sorry about your brother. Nothing personal. I'm sure he was a great guy and yadda, yadda, yadda…Who am I kidding? I don't care about you or your stupid disfigured brother," he said to Thomas as he walked toward him.

That's when I heard the faint flapping of wings from Teddy, the half ox-eagle, coming from just below the cliff but out of sight. Slash was so caught up in his threats he couldn't hear it. I made my move.

"Your brother deserved to die!" I said to Thomas. I charged, shoving Thomas with my full body weight, sending him careening over the edge of the cliff. He landed safely on Teddy's back.

Slash was stunned. He stood there for a moment, not sure what to do. His big moment was taken from him!

Snapping out of it, Slash lunged for me, but I was too quick. I jumped off the cliff and fell down, down, down, somersaulting ways before landing on the back of a hovering lion-boy, *Judah*!

"Great catch!" I hollered at him. He turned over just enough to give me a fist bump.

"Glad you're safe, but we need to catch up with the others," Judah said. In the distance, I could see Teddy and Thomas flying away to safety.

"Before you do, let's head straight up!" I said. "I have something I need to do."

Judah shot straight back up in the direction I had just fallen from. And just like I imagined it, Gregory was staring over the edge of the cliff. And also like I imagined it, we were on him before he knew it.

As we closed in on him, I stood up on Judah's back and, with a shout of "Jazz hands!" swung the torch at his confused face. Judah banked hard left, and we bolted away from the cliffs to the cackling of banshees and behemoths. That was the last I, or anyone else, would see of Gregory.

TORCH

BREWING

It took a minute for Judah and me to stop laughing as we thought about the surprised look on Gregory's face. As we flew, though, a feeling of sadness swept across me as I remembered Edison's body lying on the forest floor. I wondered how many more of our comrades encountered the same fate. Judah sensed something was wrong, and he focused on flying, lost in his own thoughts. We flew high and fast in order to catch up to the others. The sun was still high in the sky but was starting to set when we alighted on a barren cliff. Once on the ground, Judah led the way. We walked down until we came to a thin canopy of trees. Other than the trees, which were skinny and completely white and some ground cover, there wasn't much else, just the same cool wind I had felt on the cliff with Thomas, which gave me a slight chill. We made our way through the trees for some time before we came up to a fast-moving stream where the air seemed even colder. The same ground cover flanked either side of the stream with an occasional rock and an even more occasional boulder peeking out from the water's surface. We followed the stream for long enough for the sun to set. Out of nowhere, the comforting smell of a campfire wafted through the air.

Up ahead, I could see a small plume of smoke dancing up into the crisp mountain air. We walked into a scene of quiet conversation as the rest of our mates sat around the campfire, chatting. I thought we'd receive a hero's welcome. We did not. Nobody even acknowledged us.

Hope and Tre sat next to each other on one side of the fire while Thomas, Franklin, the black bear-man, and Teddy, the half ox-eagle, were on the opposite side of the fire. They were all listening intently to Roosevelt's story. Roosevelt had flown ahead of us to gather strategic intel before we got attacked by Gregory and Co. Roosevelt was speaking slowly and methodically, and his speech sounded almost slurred. As we neared the fire, I noticed that he didn't look too good either. In fact, he looked awful.

I stood back for a moment, trying not to interrupt. Judah didn't get the hint and went right on in.

"Hey, guys, I got him," Judah said cheerfully.

Everyone turned to look at me. The silence was broken a second time by Thomas, who jumped to his feet and ran directly at me. In one instant, he was standing in front of me; the next instant, I was flat on my back, rubbing my jaw. Thomas stood over me.

"I don't care if you're the One; he's dead because of you!" He kicked me in the side and spat in my face for emphasis.

"Thomas," Hope yelled, "that is completely uncalled for." She chastised him to his back as he walked away from the group.

Standing up, I admitted, "No, Hope, Thomas has every right to be angry. I couldn't save his brother and forced him to leave him. If it wasn't for me, Edison would still be alive."

Hope got up and went after Thomas. After all, he was one of her "boys."

I walked over to the campfire but couldn't sit. No one said a word, each lost in his or her thoughts. The fire crackled, the wind bit down. My thoughts swirled around the insane events of my day. Almost kidnapped. Almost killed. Witnessing Edison's death. Rescuing Thomas. Being saved by Judah. It all began to sink in. I began to sink. First to my knees. Onto my hands. And finally, facedown in front of the fire. A mix of exhaustion and trauma washed over me. I found myself weeping. I found myself begging for forgiveness (from whom, I don't know). Guilt and anger consumed me. Flashes of my father attacking my mother came rushing back. Thoughts of my little sister Em being taken away. *Who would ever call me the One? I'm just a screwup who gets everyone close to me either hurt or killed. And here I am, lying face down, crying. So much for saving the world. I can't even save myself!* I reprimanded myself.

"There's more," Tre said, interrupting my pity party.

"I don't care," I replied through sniffs and sniffles.

"You need to care!" she fired back. "The world needs you to care."

"I'm done. I'm not the One. I just want to find my mom and sister and go back home," I responded bitterly.

"I guess you're right. You're not the One. But you can't run and hide from the impending war, and in order to save your mom and sister, there's more you need to know." She tried to reason, "Roosevelt has some news you need to hear."

"Roosevelt, can you tell T what you saw?" Tre said to the brown Pegasus.

He shook his head as if trying to get rid of a bad memory. When he spoke, it sounded painful.

Wiping away dirt and tears, I sat up and gave Roosevelt my full attention.

"I went ahead as Thomas requested, and just over the next range from where I left you, I ran into swarms of Arachne. I flew high over them for miles, their numbers in the millions. All heading in toward the Veiled City. I saw towns that were completely destroyed. Fields that were scorched. I saw little children weeping outside of their homes, their parents having been dragged away by the Offspring. I was on my way back to meet up with you when a regiment of Arachne saw me and gave chase. There must've been a hundred Arachnes in this regiment. I could outfly all but a couple of them. Those I had to fight. They were vicious and unrelenting. The only way they would stop fighting was if they were dead. I was nearly back when Judah and Teddy spotted me and helped me with the last Arachne. I barely escaped." He let out a long sigh.

"We escaped Slash and his gang the same way you did, T," Tre said. "We were pursued to the edge of the cliff when the three boys showed up in the nick of time. We jumped just as a posse of banshees ran full speed at us. They didn't make it. We did thanks to Judah and Teddy."

"So Antioch is gearing up for war?" I asked, already knowing the answer.

"Yes. The troops appear to be marching toward the Veiled City and, at their current pace, will arrive in a day or two," Roosevelt said somberly. "We've got to get to the city before they do if we have any chance of rescuing your mother and sister."

"How are we going to get into the city?" Franklin asked.

"Thomas," Teddy said, "Thomas knows how to get in."

"When do we go?" Judah asked.

"First light," Tre.

Hope and Thomas came walking up.

"Thomas has something he'd like to say," Hope said as they approached the group.

Thomas began, "T, you may be the One, but after what happened to my brother, I cannot go with you to the Veiled City." He paused and then continued, "I will take you to the outskirts of the city, and then you will be on your own. This is not my battle," he finished.

A long pause. Everyone found something on the ground to stare at.

"Battle, no. War, yes." It was Tre. She stood up and started walking toward Thomas. "You can weep for your brother. You can be angry. You can be sad, but nothing will change the fact that if we don't stand up to the darkness, evil will win. Let the dead bury themselves, for now is the time for action! Now is the time for good men and women to stand up for truth. To shine a light in the darkness."

Tre was practically glowing now. My heart skipped a beat. On the ground, my torch crackled, as did Hope's. Thomas turned and started to walk away. "We leave at first light," he said angrily as he stalked off.

TORCH

WAITING

First light came, thankfully, interrupting a myriad of nightmares we were all having. I walked down to the stream to get some water to drink and splash on my face to help me wake up. It was peaceful. It was beautiful. If you didn't know any better, you'd think all was right in the world. You wouldn't see any hint of an impending war. Nope. This was nice—a gift from Jacob, no doubt, before our final journey. I sat there for a few minutes, soaking up the scene. It took me a while before I realized that she was sitting beside me. And when I realized it, I just soaked up the scene even more.

Finally, she spoke, "The speech that I gave to Thomas wasn't intended for Thomas," Tre paused, "that speech was for you." She turned and looked me dead in the eye. "Each of us has been created with a purpose. If we live out our purpose, if we pursue it, we're doing exactly what we were created for. That's the sweet spot of life. A place fueled by passion, driving the direction of our lives. If not, we have wasted our lives and have taken up precious space in this world. Those people, the ones that Antioch has taken hostage, the ones he's duped and the ones who willingly gave everything to him, they've forgotten this. They have to be reminded that they've been created for more, they've been created with a purpose, that they matter! They're not mistakes. They weren't created to be miserable. They weren't created to be slaves to fear and anger and hatred and deceit and lies and loneliness," she paused again and turned her face toward the water, "I would not be here, if I didn't think, no, if I didn't *know* that you are the One, T. So, go rescue your mom, but what about all the other moms?" She got up, and as she walked past me, she paused to give me a kiss on the cheek.

Wait a minute! What? One minute I'm getting a lecture; the next, I'm getting a kiss on the cheek. I don't get girls, I chuckled to myself, but the reality of what Tre said was starting to kick my tail. *Why me? Why am I considered the One? I didn't sign up for this. The world needs a hero, and somehow Jacob, out of the billions of people on the planet, chooses me? I don't get it. I don't believe it.*

In the distance, I heard the rumble of thunder and, looking in the direction of the mountains Roosevelt spoke about, could see storm clouds brewing.

"We need to move out!" came Thomas's voice. He yelled loud enough so that everyone in our scattered little group could hear him. We gathered at the cliff face that Judah and I had landed on the previous day. Thunder boomed in the distance.

Roosevelt was looking much better, which was a good thing because we needed an extra flyer. Teddy, the half ox-eagle, would have Franklin, the half bear-man, fly with him since he was the only one strong enough to carry Franklin's weight. Thomas and Hope would be with Roosevelt, and Tre and I were with Judah. We set off with great speed and height, soaring high above the undulating mountain range below. The mountain range gave way to an expansive valley that was lined with row after row of crops. We slowed to a stop abruptly. Something had caught Franklin's attention. We hovered for a minute to try to see why Franklin stopped. He started to descend ever slowly like a dandelion (or dande-eagle). We all followed suit. We descended just low enough to confirm what Franklin had seen. The hair on my neck stood up. Suddenly, I could feel the cold. Thunder boomed in the distance but sounded closer.

Below us, what looked like rows of crops were really just rows of Offspring marching in place. Not going anywhere. Just marching like they were in a trance. The wind changed direction, and with it, we could hear the rhythmic pounding of the Offspring's feet. We needed to get moving.

"The Veiled City isn't too far now," Thomas turned and snapped at us.

We climbed back high into the sky so we wouldn't be detected and soared toward the city. As we neared, the landscape slowly changed from the rural countryside and rolling hills to being flat. Fewer and fewer trees and grass could be seen because these had given way to smooth rock surfaces. A few horseless carriages made their way down the smooth rock pathway. Everything looked so neat and tidy from where we were. Homes and businesses seemed to be in perfect condition. Nothing out of place.

Once again, we slowed to a stop and hovered.

Thomas addressed our crew, "We will descend behind the school down there, just off the main road. The main road will take you into the Veiled City. You need to stay out of sight. Move in the shadows. Don't get caught."

We made our move, drifting swiftly out of sight behind the school. We touched down and proceeded with our farewells to Thomas.

"Are you sure?" Hope asked Thomas, pleading. "We could really use you."

"If the kid is the One, you won't need me," Thomas replied. At this point, he was getting a full-blown Hope hug.

"Okay, friend," she said, "you'll always be one of my boys."

"And you'll always be my Hope," he said and almost sounded like he was about to cry. "You guys better wait here until nightfall. It should be easier to get around. Just watch out for the night watchman. He is not your friend. And one last thing," Thomas gave as a final piece of advice, "don't let anything happen to Hope!"

Final farewells ended, and Thomas started to make his way around the corner of the school building. He stopped and turned to us before disappearing out of sight and said, "I will try to send help if I can, but no guarantees." And then he was gone.

We hunkered down to wait for nightfall, grateful we made it to the Veiled City ahead of Antioch's troops. In the distance, though, we could hear the faint sound of war drums. They were getting closer. This time, we couldn't wait for darkness to make our move.

TORCH

ROGER THAT

Nightfall couldn't come fast enough, and when it did, we were all anxious for action. Our crew set out around the back of the school and proceeded toward the Veiled City. We walked along the sides of the road, sticking to the shadows, which was made more difficult because of Hope's and my torches. Amazingly, the torches seemed to know that we needed some anonymity, so they dimmed almost to the point of going out. They appeared to be glowing embers atop a stick.

The buildings and houses lining the road all looked alike. They were made of smooth stone, and they were all white or off-white. No grass. No trees. Three identical houses faced each other, followed by businesses of some sort, which also faced each other. In fact, if it weren't for the additional lights up ahead, you would've thought we were either walking in circles or walking in place. Every fourth block stood a flagpole with a black flag hoisted high atop with the letter "A" emblazoned on it in crimson red. The "A" was in the middle of a crimson circle but was bigger than the circle. For some reason, each time we passed these flags, I got a chill. Apparently, I wasn't the only one as I looked over at Tre, and she nodded as if to say, "I feel it too." This scene played itself out over and over again until the entrance to the Veiled City came into view.

There wasn't a soul on the streets when we made it to the city entrance. A towering stone wall surrounded the city. Standing at its base, you couldn't see the top of it as it disappeared into the sky. The wall was made of a white stone that was completely smooth and looked almost glassy. It practically glowed against the dark night sky. Surprisingly, there was just an opening in the massive wall through which the main road passed. No guard tower. No beefed-up security. No gate to open and close. We strolled through the opening, noting the thickness of the walls to be thicker than three woolly mammoths lined up end to end.

Once through the entrance, Tre motioned our group over to a shadowed overhang.

"No one has been here before, right?" Tre asked in hushed tones. We all shook our heads, no.

"I don't get it," Tre continued. "This is the Veiled City, right?"

"Yes," Teddy spoke up with confusion in his voice.

"What makes this place the 'Veiled City'?" Hope asked. "It's practically glowing!" she said in a whispered bewilderment.

"And this place is so, so clean and not very evil-looking," said Franklin, also confused.

"And where are the mines?" I asked. It was a rhetorical question, a statement of the obvious since none of us knew where the mines were. Usually, though, mines were dirty and smelly, normally accompanied by clangs and clinks but not here. The city was completely silent, almost like a noise vacuum.

"This place is huge. Let's divide and conquer," Tre proposed. In front of us, the main road continued. To the right and left were smaller streets that followed the curvature of the wall. "Me, T, Judah, and Hope will take the road that follows the city wall to the left. Franklin, Teddy, and Roosevelt stick together. Follow the wall to the right. Whoever gets to the mines first, wait for the others." And then, for added measure, Tre said, "Don't get caught!"

We split up. The road along the inside of the wall was fairly narrow and studded with smooth cobblestone. An occasional streetlamp threw off sparse amounts of light, casting undulating shadows. In our case, this could be good—we could hide in them—or bad—so could the enemy. It was still quiet. Eerily quiet. On one side of the road, the wall towered high into the sky; on the other, perfectly squared buildings, one after the other, lined the road. Every fourth building, there was a small road that connected to other identical buildings. Each building had a single door and a single window which was covered by a curtain. A white curtain. After walking for some time and passing many identical blocks, we came to another larger road which appeared to go from one side of the city to the other. Halfway down this road was an open area, like a town square with a towering flag and pole in the center similar to the ones outside of town. Everything in the Veiled City was massive. We stared at the flag from a distance, noticing the crimson red "A" on it. The flag was being illuminated. A sense of dread and awe came over us while we were staring at the flag. This silence was broken.

"Psst..." came a sound behind us in the shadows. It broke through the silence like gunfire, and we jumped like we'd just been shot at. Someone was there! "Psst..." came again.

We looked at each other. Do we run? Do we attack? Maybe they know where the mines are?

"Hey, kids, come over here," came the voice in the shadow.

If we ran, they could sound an alarm, so we had no choice. Slowly, we made our way over to the shadow. We stepped into the shadow, and I thrust out my torch to see the source of the voice. In the torchlight stood an elderly man of about eighty years old. Small and bent over, he had a cane for balance. He had the remaining patch of white hair atop his head and a stray hair coming out of his nose. His ears were pointy and hairy, maybe even more hairy than his head. He reminded me of an elf. He was wearing a plain white button-down shirt and brown suspenders, which were holding up a tan pair of trousers. A pair of brown sandals adorned his feet. He looked every part of a kind and fragile grandpa, or peepaw, or pawpaw, whatever you prefer.

"My name is Roger," the old man began, "Roger the night watchman, and I've been expecting you," he said with a grin, his voice strong and clear for his age.

My heart skipped a beat, and the torch crackled as he said this. At times like these, the torch gave me comfort and confidence. I can't explain it other than it seemed to know my emotions, and most of the time, it counteracted them. If I was anxious, it gave me peace. Doubtful—confidence. Desperate—hope. Right now, it was reassuring.

"Actually, we've all been expecting you," Roger said, still grinning.

He stepped forward and, on his tiptoes, steadying himself precariously with his cane, stared hard at my face. This lasted more than a minute. No joke, it was awkward.

The inspection over, Roger took an unsteady step backward. "Yep. You're the One. The spitting image of your mother for sure but with your father's height. The others will be so delighted when I tell them!" he said with the glee of a child.

"You know my parents?" I asked, a little too strong.

"Yes, son. I've known them for a very long time," his voice was trailing off as he said it.

"Others?" I said warily, looking at Hope, Judah, and Tre. They were thinking the same thing.

"This isn't the place to discuss this," Roger said. "Follow me." He started to hobble down the road running along the wall.

We looked at each other. What do we do? Thomas told us to watch out for the night watchman, but he seemed to know my parents, and maybe he knows where my mom and sister are? I started after him. The others followed.

"Is this a good idea?" Tre whispered.

"Yah, is this smart?" Hope echoed.

"It's the only thing I know to do," I whispered in reply.

We followed Roger, walking the full distance down the left side of the city, sticking close to the wall for quite some time. Roger occasionally ducked into one of the shadows as if something or someone was coming. We did likewise but could never quite figure out what he was afraid of. Finally, we came to a stone building identical to all the others we'd passed, just smaller. Roger opened the door for us and ushered us inside. The room was dark except for the light from our torches. Roger went over and closed the curtains, making sure no one could see in. He then went over to a small wooden table and turned on a lamp. This was it. This small building, identical to the others, looked more like a cold prison cell. A small cot was against one wall and a small dresser against another. There was a sink and a toilet side by side and a mirror above the sink. It was depressing. Roger made his way over to the cot and sat down.

"I would offer you a place to sit or something nice to eat, but, well…" again, his voice trailed off. He scanned the paltry room and tried to come to its defense. "It's not much, but it's all I need," he paused for a second, seemingly lost in thought. "Please, sit," he motioned to the cold stone floor.

Judah plopped right down on the floor. Hope sat down as well. Tre and I decided to remain standing.

"Why should we trust you, Roger?" Tre said what we were all thinking. "We heard that you aren't to be trusted," she said almost defiantly.

Roger chuckled. "The legend of the night watchman lives on!" He continued to chuckle. "Wait until I tell the others!" He slapped his bony knee at that one. "Let me guess. It was Thomas who told you that! He's had something against me ever since I caught him sneaking around the city after curfew one night. He said he was looking for his father, who'd been taken here. Of course, I had no idea what he was referring to, so I escorted him to the city entrance and told him not to come back. Thomas was going to get himself killed."

"*You* escorted Thomas?" Judah asked, pointing at Roger.

"I know I look feeble, but I can be very persuasive when I want to be." He winked at Judah.

"Why should we trust you?" I asked the question again.

"The truth is you shouldn't. You shouldn't trust anyone in times like these." Roger picked up his cane and pointed it at me. "But I know where your mother is. You need me." He put down his cane.

"And the others you keep referring to?" Hope asked.

"Ah, yes, the others. We call ourselves 'the Remnant,'" Roger said using air quotes. "I don't know how many, but I know that there are those fighting from the inside, waiting for the moment when the One comes to free us. All of us." He grinned at me.

"The Remnant? Fighting from the inside?" I wasn't tracking, none of us were, and Roger knew it.

"I was supposed to be eliminated about twenty years ago. That's the age your usefulness runs out, according to Antioch. You're dead weight. A blight on society. In my persuasiveness, though, I was able to talk my way into this job. I patrol the streets all night long. At sunrise, I report to the city center for Liberation Ceremonies, and then I return here and sleep most of the day. I know the city better than anyone else. Those fighting from the inside are a resistance force. We've been expecting you for some time, T. Freedom is so close now I can taste it," Roger said, looking up to the heavens.

"But how?" I said in a bit of shock at the confidence the old man had placed in me. "There are but a few of us, and Antioch is powerful. We saw the troops amassing outside the city, and more are on their way!"

"True," Roger said, "those troops, however, aren't on their way here. No, this is just a staging area. But, if you're the One, then none of that will matter."

"So, how do we do this?" Tre asked Roger.

"I never thought you'd ask," Roger said. "I've had a long time to think about this. Let's walk." He got to his feet and headed to the door. We followed.

Outside, the city was still quiet. We followed the wall again. We stopped when we were at the complete opposite end of the city from the entrance. From where we stood, we could see the enormous flag and pole still waving in the night sky.

Roger pulled out a watch from his pocket.

"Watch," he said, pointing toward the flagpole. He counted down on his fingers, five, four, three, two, one…*Beep! Beep! Beep!* Went an alarm that blared throughout the city, breaking through the silence and causing us all to jump.

A voice was heard next over a loudspeaker:

"Night school pupils, night school pupils. Please report for the Liberation Ceremony."

Next came the sound of doors opening all throughout the city. They opened in unison and sounded like the opening of prison cells. This was followed by the slow, orderly march of men and women. Not a word was said. They looked straight ahead. All were wearing white canvas-looking material: long trousers and long-sleeved shirts. All had the same hair-do: short, very short, almost buzzed. A group of more than a hundred marched right in front of us and didn't even notice us. From all parts of the city, they assembled around the flagpole and stood at attention.

"*Now!*" said the voice over the loudspeaker. Trumpetlike horns blasted, and, on cue, the sea of people dropped to their knees, faces to the ground. Over and over, all around the flagpole, they bowed down. They did this for five minutes. Over the loudspeaker, the same voice was chanting something low and in some other language. It sounded alien. It sounded ominous.

"It's an ancient prayer in an ancient language giving praise to Antioch over and over," Roger said with a wry grin.

We looked at each other, and a chill came over me. I noticed that Tre's arm was barely touching mine. Judah's mouth was wide open.

The chanting and bowing finally stopped with the blast of another trumpet.

"Together!" the voice commanded.

The crowd rose and, saluting the flag, in unison said:

> "*Freedom is the absence of rules.*
> *Rules exist to hold us back from our true potential.*
> *We seek perfection by eliminating the imperfect.*
> *Antioch is our liberator.*
> *We pledge our lives to Antioch!*"

They repeated this three times in a row, completely monotone. We were all feeling the chill now.

I looked over at Tre to get her reaction. Her eyes were closed, and a tear seemed to be caught in the corners. And then I noticed it. Her lips were subtly moving as if she were praying. Her eyes squeezed, closed tighter, like she was really concentrating even more. This was the second time I witnessed this. What was she doing? My hand started to reach out to comfort her but was interrupted by another message…

"*Liberation learning time,*" blasted the voice over the loudspeaker.

With that, everyone in white turned and started to march straight toward where we were standing. They were in a trancelike state. Roger motioned for us to stay put. He walked a little way down the wall and pulled out a large key. Just as the first group in white made their way to where we were standing, Roger inserted the key into a spot in the wall and turned it just in time as the group was just about to walk into the wall. To our shock, we were standing beside massive doors which were concealed in the wall. These doors were almost as tall as the wall itself and opened slowly but smoothly, allowing the group to pour in. They just kept coming and coming.

Wait a second, a thought exploded through my mind, *What if my mom is part of this crew?* Frantically, I began to scan the almost identical-looking faces. It was still dark out, and only the slightest of light highlighted certain facial features. It was too hard to tell.

The end of the line was approaching, all still in a trancelike state. No emotion. Nothing. Another question raced through my mind: *Why are there no guards? No one is forcing these people to march, and yet they are marching, nonetheless.* No pointed guns. No chains. No yelling or shouting. On they marched, though. As the final line marched past, Roger motioned for us to follow them. We saw him turn the large key and the enormous doors began to close. He hobbled in just behind the last line of marchers, and we followed him just as the enormous doors closed.

TORCH

MINER DETAILS

It took a minute for our eyes to adjust to the lighting (or lack of). The only light was from sporadic torches on the walls. We found ourselves in a labyrinth of tunnels that split off in different directions. The only sound was the soft padding of the marchers' feet. The ground was made of the same smooth cobblestone, and the walls looked like they were hewn out of the middle of a mountain. They had a wet appearance, almost as if the walls were weeping. Ahead of us, the marchers peeled off, going down different tunnels. We followed what appeared to be the main corridor, a group of marchers directly in front of us. We heard a noise up ahead. A familiar noise in an unfamiliar setting. The sound was of a door opening. And then another. And another. And another. All throughout the labyrinth, doors were opening, similar to when they opened outside. Like prison cells.

Ahead of us, we could see the doors opening and marchers entering rooms that were embedded in the rock. They were in groups of about twenty. We stopped and waited. The same doors closed all throughout the labyrinth, clanging and echoing off the stone walls. We slowly moved down the hallway, trying our best not to make much noise even though, honestly, I don't think it would've mattered. There were no guards, and the people were in a trance. My guess is we could've run up and down the hallway screaming, "Antioch's a lowlife who smells like stinky cheese!"

and no one would care. I decided against doing that, especially after the look I got from Tre.

We came to a room with an oversized window. We froze. Roger didn't. He stopped right in front of the window and turned to address us.

"It's okay," he chuckled. "They have no idea we're even here." To punctuate this, Roger turned and began blowing raspberries at the window, waving his hands wildly in the air, and yelling, "Antioch's a lowlife who smells like stinky cheese!" We stepped forward to look into the window ourselves. Sure enough, no one flinched. No one paid us any attention. The room, like the rest of the Veiled City, was very sterile. Perfectly aligned rows of desks faced a blackboard. A few lights hung from the ceiling. They cast a harsh light in the room. At the head of the class stood a tall old man, or woman—it was hard to tell because their hair was cut short like the others. This person didn't look entirely human. They wore a long flowing black robe that was hooded but not over their heads. Their skin was ghostly white. The pupils in this room were all boys, and all appeared to be my age. There were just three boys in this classroom. Skin color, size, and weight were the only things that distinguished them from each other. They were, like the rest of the people, dressed exactly alike: identical clothes and hairstyle. I heard the teacher say the word "brothers" several times while we stood there. Roger noticed my curiosity and explained, "You see, as part of the transformation process, Antioch gives everyone who is part of his kingdom a new family made up of new brothers and sisters. Parents aren't important; that's Antioch's role. This group here," Roger continued referring to the boys in the room, "was part of the resistance, fighting to overthrow Antioch. They arrived yesterday, and this is one of their first lessons."

Suddenly, a short and stocky dark-skinned student stood up and ran straight at the professor, yelling, "My name is Takeshi, and I am a warrior of light!" The teacher grabbed Takeshi by the throat and slammed him to the ground in one swift, effortless move. As if on cue, the other boys stood up and charged the teacher!

"I am Salam, and I am a warrior of light!" a very dark-skinned boy screamed. He, too, was slammed to the ground.

Bringing up the rear was a heavy, very heavyset boy charging the teacher! "I am Twitch, and I am a warrior of light!" With a little more effort this time, the teacher slammed Twitch to the ground. I cringed as his head hit the ground, and blood began to flow. He looked right at me, Tre, and Hope.

"We're here to free you," I saw Tre mouth to the boy on the ground.

"Are we done now?" we heard the teacher say. The boys sheepishly went back to their seats.

"Oh dear," said Roger, an embarrassment in his voice, "I'm sorry you had to witness that."

On the blackboard at the front of the classroom were words like "truth," "relative," "natural selection," and "perfection." There were also some symbols above the blackboard that seemed ancient or alien. I turned to ask Roger what the symbols meant, but he beat me to it. He was glad to change the subject.

Roger explained, "The symbols above the blackboard are indeed ancient. Antioch has used this language throughout the millennia. It comes from the Twilight Age, a transition time from when Jacob's pure light blended with Antioch's darkness. When Antioch broke free from Jacob, he needed to create a new language unknown to Jacob." The way he said it sounded like he'd been there when it was created. He was quite excited. In fact, he sounded almost giddy.

"What does it mean?" Tre asked.

"It means, 'The mind and heart are interconnected. Control one, control both.'" Roger said with a sense of pride. Once again, his tone was not lost on me, Hope, and Tre. Judah, as usual, was clueless.

"Come," Roger said, "there's something I need to show you," as he turned and hobbled down the hallway. We followed him, passing room after room of marchers and ghostly-looking teachers. The first few rooms were identical, with the same things written on each of the blackboards. The further down the hallway we ventured, though, the sayings changed. Words like "accident," "mistake," and "elimination" were right next to "positivity," "equality," and "ignorance." In these classrooms, the professors' faces were cloaked by their hoods, and a veil of blackness concealed their identities. I got the chills. The torch in my hand crackled in agreement. The torch had remained relatively silent as we made our way through the Veiled City, but now, it was crackling quite loudly. Roger turned to look at me, or rather, the torch. It was a brief glance but enough for me to notice. And then another loud crackle. This time it was Hope's torch that had also been quiet up to this point. Roger turned back again, shook his head, and kept going.

The walkway got wider and wider and eventually opened up to where all the other labyrinth tunnels converged into a large open room. The room was huge. We were definitely inside a mountain. The ceiling disappeared into a black abyss, the walls towering who knows how high. I felt very small in this place. As before, there was very little light. A couple of torches hung on the distant walls but were mostly ineffective, creating almost a haze in the oversized stone room. We made our way across the room, noting that the smooth cobblestone beneath our feet was now slick like the weeping walls of the cave. The closer we got to the other side of the room, the faster Roger walked. He was either in a hurry or excited.

Maybe we are finally heading to the mines where I'll find my mom, I thought to myself but, in my heart, I had a feeling of despair. I think we all felt that way.

By the time we reached the other side of the room, we were in complete darkness. Cave darkness. Were it not for my and Hope's torches, we would have been completely blind. We came to a back wall and stopped. Roger began fumbling for keys.

"Fiddlesticks," he said, trying to find the right key in such bad lighting.

"Here, use this," Hope offered helpfully.

"Why, thank you," came a cheerful reply from the old man as he took Hope's torch.

"There you are," said the old man to the rogue key. Again, he put the key in an almost hidden keyhole and turned. The door opened. "This is gonna be great!" Roger said as he limped through the door opening. We stepped inside and collectively gasped.

TORCH

NO WAY OUT

We entered a round, high-ceilinged room. It had the same weeping walls and floors as the other part of the cave. This time there was only one solitary light in the room. It was a torch that hung down from a chain in the center of the room. I still had my torch, and Roger still had Hope's. We stopped just inside the entrance. The door slammed close behind us. Roger walked to the other side of the room and disappeared into the dark shadow on the opposite side of the room, the darkness consuming Hope's flame.

"I'll give you a minute for your eyes to adjust," he said with a chuckle from deep inside the shadow.

The light was so poor that our eyes were indeed having trouble adjusting. We just stood there, our eyes desperate to focus.

"You know," came Roger's voice from across the room.

Something clanked and slid across the floor and landed at our feet. I bent down to inspect it. A cane. More despair overcame me.

"You should've listened to Thomas."

Out of the shadows came a tall old man, nearly identical to the teachers but taller. Much taller.

"Have your eyes adjusted yet?" he asked, this time goading us and thoroughly enjoying himself. "It doesn't matter."

He crossed the room in a blink. Towering over us, he must've been eight feet tall, he said, "Let's play a game, shall we?" he smiled a maniacal smile, knowing that we were trying to process what was going on, "It's called three questions."

"First, do you know who I am?" Roger asked with a devious chuckle.

"Roger the night watchman!" Judah said enthusiastically, thinking this was a game, game.

"*Right and wrong!*" Roger said with a demonic laugh. "No, my name is not Roger. My name is Belshazzar. Yes, I am the night watchman. I am from the line of Cyrus."

"Second question, what is my role?" asked Belshazzar.

"To kill us," said Hope matter-of-factly.

"*Right and wrong!*" Belshazzar said with another demonic laugh. "Kill you, yes. But the reason I'm going to kill you is nothing personal. You see, I work for the overlords whom Antioch has placed over various parts of the planet. There are four overlords in all who carry out Antioch's wishes. My job is to make sure nothing and no one gets in the way including, the One."

"Four overlords? What were those leading the troops? I thought those were the overlords?" Tre asked.

"There are only four overlords. Those you saw were just their generals. You thought you were coming here to rescue your mother and sister and that Antioch would be hanging outside in the open, sipping tea!" he laughed a maniacal laugh at the thought. "You have no idea how far from the truth that is! Your friend Sampson was right. Maybe you are the One or now, were the One, but all you see is what's right in front of your face. You keep looking with your eyes. That's your problem. That's why you and your friends are going to die." He walked back and forth in front of us, really enjoying himself, like a cat toying with a mouse. He still held Hope's torch in his hand.

"Final question, do you know who the 'we' are that I've been referring to when I said, 'We've been expecting you?'" He moved out of the way and, in the middle of the room, stood my mother and my sister, Em. Instinctively, I ran to them.

"T, what are you doing here?" my mother asked with tears in her eyes as she reached for me. Em just stood there looking at me, quite displeased. "You shouldn't be here," my mother continued.

"I've come to rescue you," I said, trying to sound confident.

"This place...this place is evil. It is the evil," she said, trembling.

"Now, now, now. That's not very nice!" said Belshazzar, approaching us. "I guess our classes haven't been working on you. Let's see, for those who don't comply, we either eliminate them or, better yet, use them. So, what will it be, elimination or transformation? Hmmm..." Belshazzar said, his long boney fingers scratching his chin as if thinking. He knocked me out of the way, sending me tumbling across the cold, wet floor as he walked over and picked up Em. "What do you think, princess? Should we eliminate your mother or transform her?" he asked Em as he stroked her blonde hair.

She grabbed Belshazzar's gaunt, pale face between her little three-year-old hands, looked him in the eye, and said, "Well, she didn't comply, so I say we should eliminate her!" Em shot my mother a look of disgust. My heart sank as her words cut mother and me to the core. My mother let out a sob.

"Well, that might be a bit harsh," said Belshazzar with fake sincerity. "After all, that is your mother."

"Not anymore!" the tiny three-year-old said. "Antioch is all I need!"

My mother wept openly, hearing her three-year-old say such things.

"Now that's a good girl," Belshazzar said, patting her on the head before lowering her back to the ground.

"I've decided," Belshazzar said, looking at my mother. "Transformation it is!"

"Help is coming. T, get Hope's torch. Hope, grab Em and run for the door," Tre whispered into the darkness. Somehow, I heard her from clear across the room, and so did Hope.

"Arachne or Offspring? Hmmm...Arachne it is!" cried Belshazzar. He turned and handed Hope's torch to Em, who had trouble holding it for its weight. Standing over my mother, he began some indiscernible incantation while she cowered on the slick cobblestone ground. My mother was shaking and crying. As Belshazzar laid his hands on her, I laid my hands on him. I jumped in the air and brought my torch crashing down on his head. It was enough to get him to remove his hands but only stunned him. I ripped Hope's torch out of Em's hands and tossed it over to Hope, who dashed toward us. Tre ran toward us, too, her sword out, waiting for her shot at Belshazzar. Hope grabbed a squirming, fighting Em, and fled toward the closed door where Judah stood waiting. Belshazzar turned toward me and thrust out his hands. He didn't touch me, but whatever power came out of his hands sent me flying into the wall. I lay there for a moment, dazed, as I watched him put his hands on my mother once again. It was Tre's turn this time, who was running full speed into Belshazzar with the end of her sword. He fell to the ground and began to bleed on his white rob. Tre helped Mom to her feet, and they started toward the door. Belshazzar made his way back to his feet and started toward the door, too. He was fully focused on my mother and Tre. I made my move and caught him halfway. This time my blow hit him square in the same spot as Tre's wound. He doubled over in pain. I came down on his head again with my torch again, sending him to the ground. His body hit the ground with an oof.

"Come on, T, let's go!" yelled Tre.

I made a beeline to the door…It was locked! The key! Where was the key? Roger had it, but Roger wasn't around. Belshazzar had transformed on the far side of the room in the shadows. Maybe it was there! I ran across the room, stepping on Belshazzar's head for good measure as I ran past him and right into the shadow. With my torch low to the ground, I searched the area before finally spotting a large key ring hanging on the wall.

"Hurry, T!" came my mother's plea as Belshazzar moaned and began to stir. I grabbed the key ring and bolted for the door, making sure to once again step on Belshazzar's head as I went by. Getting to the door, I had to figure out which key would do the trick. There must have been fifty keys on the ring! I began fumbling. Which key? Which key? I was panicking! Belshazzar let out a guttural sound of pain behind me. Em continued to fight Hope.

Which key?

"Hurry, T, he's getting up!" yelled Judah.

Belshazzar was on his feet now and slowly starting toward us. He sounded like an enraged animal. Roger was no longer.

The keys fell out of my hands and clanked hard on the ground. I was shaking. *I can't do this!* I thought to myself, the weight of everything crashing down on me. Rescuing my mom and sister, being "the One" that was supposed to free the world of evil. I can't even open a stupid door! I can't even save myself!

"*Your problem is that you only see with your eyes.*" It wasn't Belshazzar's voice. No, it was Sampson's voice. "*Stop looking with your eyes!*" came the roar of a memory.

Belshazzar was almost to us now.

Flash!

Time stopped. Whiteness. Whiteness was all around. I wasn't in the cave. I was alone; at least, I thought I was alone. A voice called out to me, "You are the offspring of Jacob!" A familiar, unfamiliar voice said with fire, "My offspring!" A man who looked to be about the age of my dad was sitting at a table with a cup of coffee in front of him. He motioned for me to sit across from him. He looked strong and kind at the same time. Powerful yet meek. His eyes were a fierce blue. His hair was brown with a slight curl to it. His chin was chiseled, his biceps sculpted. His skin was almond colored, neither black nor white but perfectly in between. I had never met him, but somehow, I'd known him my whole life. Jacob.

"Yes, T, it is me. Yes, you've known me your whole life even though we've never met before. Sit." He motioned for me to sit across from him. I sat.

"I love how much you look like your mother." He grinned. "I'm not going to keep you long because you have work to do. You are my offspring. You may not feel equipped to win the war, but you have everything you need to win this battle because I will be with you. I will be in you. You are my offspring. My DNA flows through your body, and when you realize that, T, you will be an unstoppable force for good! No stronghold of the enemy will be able to touch you, and those that will dare to try will regret the day they were born! Claim your name as my child and take the victory before you!"

Flash!

He was gone.

The door was in front of me. I closed my eyes. "What do you see now?" came Jacob's voice. I slowly opened my eyes. My heart skipped a beat, and the torch roared, for in this moment, I realized why this was called the Veiled City. Whoa. A fight indeed. I smiled to myself and then thanked Jacob.

TORCH

SACRIFICE

Before me, the door. Behind me, Belshazzar. He was still slowly approaching, wounded but approaching. To the others, he looked like a tall, wounded old man. But I could see him for what he really was, an Offspring (I would find out later that he was, in fact, an imperial Offspring meaning that he was the father of the Offspring). He was enormous and, like his smaller minions, just as grotesque as all the others I'd encountered. His wings slowly unfurled, seeming to fill the entire room, and with each staggering step he took, he seemed to gain strength. We had to get out of here.

I turned back to the door. It was glowing and sealed shut by some sort of ancient curse. Doors. Some are meant to be opened, some are meant to stay closed, and others, well, are meant to be destroyed. "Okay, torch, it's go time!"

"*Are you ready?*" I screamed to my teammates, Hope, still holding Em, Tre, Judah, and my mother.

I didn't wait for a response. Gripping the torch, I breathed a deep breath and felt the warmth and power of the torch surge through my veins. Jacob's power. "*Yaaaaaaaaaaaaaa!*" I yelled as the torch slammed into the door, shattering it into a million pieces. We bolted into the great room just as Belshazzar let out a hideous demonic cry.

We started back across the enormous great room when an announcement came over the speaker system. "Class dismissed," said a monotone voice repeatedly along with an alarm, which was accompanied by the sound of dozens of cell doors opening.

Halfway across the great room, we encountered our first wave of marchers. They came flooding into the great room from all sections of the tunnels. A few turned into a few thousand.

"*Now!*" came the voice over the intercom.

At that moment, they went from neat rows of slow, methodical marchers to running in an all-out crazed sprint toward us. They were marchers no more; they were Offspring. We had to make it to the other side of the great room, but there was no way of avoiding them. And behind them stood the professors. I could see them for who they really were as well, imperial Offspring. They were large like Belshazzar and appeared to be directing the Offspring. They were blocking each tunnel entrance! In some ways, this reminded me of the time when Keith the molve and I were attacked. We had to fight.

The first wave of Offspring came at us, and Tre and I took the lead, followed by Judah and Hope. My mother was now carrying Em, who was still struggling to break free. We beat them down, punches, torches, and claws. Wings and limbs went flying. The noxious odor of burning demon flesh. But they kept coming, growing in numbers. We were holding our own, but something had to be done.

"*Hope, Tre, follow my lead!*" I yelled, seeing the Offspring in front of us growing. "*Mother, grab onto Judah!*" I glanced back to see my mother struggling with Em, but it wasn't the little sister I knew. She was changing before my eyes! Becoming more Offspring than human.

I turned back to the fight and took a deep breath, and felt the warmth and power of the torch surge through my veins. Jacob's power. "*Yaaaaaaaaaaaaaa!*" I yelled, running full speed, faster and faster. Offspring went flying. Any Offspring that came in contact with the torch was immediately decimated. My troop was hot on my tail, destroying any Offspring that approached. Even Judah, with my mother and sister on his back, was fighting more ferociously than I'd ever seen him fight. Out of the corner of my eye, I think I saw him bite the head off an Offspring (disgusting and awesome at the same time). We were making progress and were nearly across the great room when the first of the imperial Offspring professors ascended on our group. He left his post in front of one of the tunnels and decided to put an end to our lil' rebellion. I had no choice but to fight him while the rest of the group held off the Offspring.

"Keep pushing the herd closer to the tunnel entrances while I take on the big one!" I yelled to my comrades.

They flanked to either side of me and continued annihilating any Offspring in our path. I raised the torch, took a deep breath, and harnessed the power of Jacob as I attacked the imperial Offspring in front of me. He was strong and fast, catching me a few times with blows to the head and body. He raised his hands and used his dark magic to knock me off balance, but he was no match for the power of Jacob. I quickly regained my balance and charged as he threw a wild clawed punch at me. I took off his hand with one swing of the torch and his head with another. Acrid green stench exploded out of his body. He gone!

I joined my teammates in driving back the herd, and by driving them back, I mean they were completely destroying the herd.

We were nearly there now. Imperial Offspring still blocked all but one of the tunnels, so to get out meant we had to go through them. I was still fighting and surveying our next move when…

Flash!

Time stopped. Everyone was frozen. A hand was on my shoulder, and, instinctively, I turned quickly and swung the torch. The person moved out of the way of my blow, disappearing and then reappearing. It was Jacob.

"T, you are fighting bravely and harnessing my power to gain the victory. But I have one question: Who is your enemy? Your real enemy." Jacob walked over to the nearest frozen Offspring and put his arm on its shoulder affectionately, and a tear came to his eye.

"This is Peter. He used to be the town baker. Has a wife, or had a wife, and two kids. Good father but got duped." He let go of Peter and began to point, "That's Sam, the best hunter in his village. And that's Mary, a skilled nurse. And over there is Olivia. She used to be a singer."

I had looked in the eyes of an Offspring before and wondered what had happened. They were real people with real lives who had gotten hoodwinked by Antioch and his deceptive ways or simply sold out to him for some cheap, beautifully adorned lie.

"T, you know what the difference is between them and you? Light. Somewhere along the way, they succumbed to the darkness. They gave themselves over to lies…lies about themselves, their kids, and their marriages. And these lies gave way to darkness. Have you ever thought, 'Why a torch?' It's a pretty dumb weapon if you think about it, especially if you're fighting flesh and bone. But it's the perfect weapon if your enemy is the embodiment of darkness." He walked straight toward me with his eyes peering into my soul. "So, I ask you again, 'Who is your enemy?'"

"Antioch is the enemy," I said, trying to sound confident.

"And what about these?" Jacob asked, motioning to the Offspring.

"They are collateral damage," I ventured uneasily, turning my gaze away from Jacob.

"No. In my book, no one is collateral damage. Everyone deserves a second chance and a third chance and a fourth chance. These are my kids, my creation whom I love. But to Antioch, they are a means to an end. They are not his 'children,' as he claims. They are his slaves, and slaves have no value other than what they produce for their master. To Antioch, they are expendable," Jacob said, scanning the faces of the Offspring.

"But can they be changed? I mean, look at them?" I said, a bit flustered.

"Not all. But some. And some is more than none," Jacob responded, sounding hopeful.

"But how? How is that even possible?"

Jacob walked over to another Offspring and put his hand on the Offspring's shoulder. "When a person is sick, we don't blame the person and say, 'Well, it's his own fault for getting sick, we might as well put him down.' No, we've got to root out the cause of the illness. The person is the host for the disease," Jacob stopped to let this sink in.

"So, these people have an infection, as simple as that?" I asked, a little put off and thinking about the destruction they'd caused.

"Yes. The infection is the darkness that has penetrated their minds and their hearts. It manifests itself in evil. The infection might be the flu, but it manifests itself as coughing, sneezing, runny nose, etc.," Jacob replied. "Darkness is the infection, and you are here to destroy the darkness."

"So, what do I do with these?" I asked.

"Help them see the light and destroy as few as you have to. We will need them to help in the fight. The imperial Offspring, though, are a lost cause. Destroy them." He put his hand on my shoulder. "You came here on a rescue mission, so go save them all!"

Flash!

Like on a turn of a light switch, the battle was back on. I stepped over the body of the imperial Offspring as Hope, Tre, and Judah continued to fight. "Help them see the light…" *How? How do we get out of here without destroying too many Offspring?* My mind was racing. We had to get to a tunnel entrance, we had to go through the Offspring without destroying too many, and we had to destroy the imperial Offspring.

The torch roared suddenly, almost violently in my hand. It sent a bolt of fire through my body as if it were taking over. "Help them see the light…" I felt like I was on fire but not burning, and it appeared as if my body was glowing. In an instant, the torch and I were becoming one. But this time, the light came from within me, raging to escape.

As the battle continued around me, I began to see the faces of the people that Jacob had pointed out. People who had succumbed to the evil. To the darkness. Bakers and hunters and singers but more than that, parents and sons and daughters. Real people whose lives had been decimated by the evil.

Holy indignation longed to escape my body. A white-hot fire of light! I was angry, not in an evil, prideful way that is just misplaced angst. No, this was anger that is reserved for only the worst, most grotesque kind of injustice! It was time to act!

Holding the torch with both hands, I crouched down and pushed off the floor of the cave. I raised the torch to the sky, soared straight up over the heads of those fighting, and then rocketed toward the ground, thrusting the end of the torch into the ground. The ground quaked, and immediately, the most brilliant wave of light began ripping through the darkness. The fighting slowed, starting with those closest. Peter, Sam, and Olivia had stopped their fighting and, though they were still disfigured, they had changed. And those directly behind them too. And the next row, and then next.

It was working. Slowly. But it was working. If I could hold onto the torch long enough for the thousands in this room to see the light, they would be free!

"*T, watch out!*" Tre yelled.

Belshazzar was approaching from behind us. The ground shook as he got closer and closer. I had to hold onto the torch as long as I could!

I could smell Belshazzar's hideous odor and feel the darkness approaching, but I couldn't let go of the light. Though many were transformed, still, many more weren't. I could see that Tre and Judah were looking for a way out, but the imperial Offspring still stationed themselves in front of the tunnel exits. And though there were many Offspring who stopped fighting, there were still others that were pressing in to fight. I still held fast to the torch.

Suddenly, Tre and Judah came running straight toward me. What? They were going the wrong way! I could hear a commotion behind me. There was another voice…Hope. Hope was there, and the three of them were battling Belshazzar! Meanwhile, in front of me, the Offspring who turned were fighting the Offspring who hadn't. I could hear my three friends battling bravely behind me, and then Judah and Tre landed in a heap in front of me. They were okay but battered. It took them a second to get up and get their bearings, but when they did, they screamed in unison, "T! Turn around!"

Still on my knees, I ripped the torch out of the ground and spun around, ready to take on Belshazzar. He had grown into such an immense size that he shook the ground with each step. This is why this room was so massive: so that Roger, aka Belshazzar, could fully show who he really was. Hair all over his body, his long, sharp claws on his hands and feet were swinging away at my friends. His teeth were gnarly and protruding from his mouth like the smaller versions we'd been fighting, and his eyes were bulbous and manic-looking. They tend to run hunched over, appearing to look hunchbacked, on all fours like a wild animal. He did not. In fact, he had a set of wings, an enormous set of wings! A long black claw came straight toward me.

I saw her out of the corner of my eye. Without the torch, she was the special girl: slurred speech, awkward, slow. But with the torch, she was transformed from special to extraordinary: articulate, nimble, and fast. Her torch came across my face and then her body as she dove on top of me. I felt a blow, like getting punched in the stomach, and heard a gasp and a scream from Hope. She rolled off me and onto the cave floor, blood pouring from her midsection. In an instant, my torch arched through the air, cutting off the offending claw, sending Belshazzar reeling in pain.

Time stood still. Sure, the battle was raging around me, but I was oblivious to it. I grabbed Hope in my arms and just held her for a moment. I was processing what just happened. Hope sacrificed her life for me! Who does that? I bent over to look at my broken special friend. Hope does that. Hope shows up just when you need it. Or when you need her. She was alive, but barely.

Her eyes were still filled with fire as she mumbled, "I love you, T. Save them all." And then she closed her eyes.

"Love you, too, special girl. I will save them all!" I vowed to her.

A powerful paw squeezed my shoulder in comfort and to get my attention. Judah took Hope from my arms and gently put her on his back.

"T, we need to go! Help is here," Tre yelled above the noise of the battle. She grabbed my arm and pulled me to my feet.

They were right. We needed to leave, and help had arrived. An explosion and a burst of light came from the front of the cave, immediately taking out the imperial Offspring in front of the cave tunnels. There, at the entrance to the middle cave, stood Anni and Sampson along with Franklin, Teddy, and Roosevelt.

The Offspring were so stunned by the light that they stopped fighting.

"If you desire freedom, follow the light!" Anni yelled to the room. A torch was now visible in her hands, and she waved it back and forth with rays of light rocketing through the cave. Offspring turned and started toward the tunnel. Anni turned and started running through the tunnel toward the exit. Sampson stayed at the entrance waving them through. The Offspring still embracing the darkness, though, were slowing down progress because they were still fighting, still very full of evil. Tre and I made our way to where fighting was taking place. Franklin, Teddy, and Roosevelt were already there, and right beside them, I saw the three boys from the classroom fighting their hearts out! The eight of us (Me, Tre, Franklin, Teddy, Roosevelt, and the three boys, Takeshi, Salam, and Twitch) created a barrier so that the freedom seekers could get to the tunnel. We blocked and punched and fought until the last of the freedom seekers could get to the tunnel.

"*Let's go!*" Sampson roared at us. We didn't hesitate. We ran toward Sampson, Franklin in the lead, me in the rear.

Somewhere in the darkness, Belshazzar shrieked. He wasn't done yet.

TORCH

COMMENCEMENT

The Offspring that hadn't turned were closing in on us as we made our way toward the tunnel exit. So was Belshazzar. We were just about to the exit when I felt a white-hot pain on the back of my leg. I tumbled to the ground as Belshazzar let out a horrific yell of triumph. Whatever he used to impale me was like nothing else I'd been hit with. My friends were oblivious to what just happened and continued into the tunnel with Sampson. They bolted down the tunnel with Offspring in hot pursuit. The Offspring that were still in the cave began to close in around me. Lying on my back, I held them off as best I could, but the pain was almost unbearable. *I have to get to my feet, or I am going to die*, I tried to will myself to stand, but there were so many of them! For some reason, the torch had trouble healing me from whatever this pain was.

And then, miraculously, one by one, the Offspring began to get ripped off me. Okay, maybe not miraculously…Belshazzar was doing the ripping. A few of the Offspring turned their attention toward Belshazzar, futilely trying to bite him, but he made quick work of disposing of them.

Now, standing over me, Belshazzar addressed them, *"Children, you can have your way with him once I'm done!"* The Offspring were agitated, and some were foaming at the mouth, but they shrunk back, waiting for their turn at me. Belshazzar bent down and stared at me with his grotesque face. This close, I could clearly see every gnarly feature. His face was pockmarked with random long hairs; he had huge bulbous bloodshot eyes with midnight black oversized pupils, holes in the place of his nose, and a pointy mouth with fangs extruding from it. He looked like a blend between an Offspring and an Arachne. He had six arms, or he was supposed to. (The arm that I cut off still oozed a black bloodlike liquid.) He smelled of sulfur and rotting flesh. The air was heavy with darkness as he grinned at me with a sick, distorted, evil grin.

"Do you know, boy, that right now, piercing through your body is a lethal toxin? It's a little concoction that I created myself with the help of some ancient forms of nasty poisons. I slowly collected enough over the millennia to lethally infect anyone who comes into contact with it, including 'the One.' I've been waiting for this day for quite some time!"

In other words, he had been planning for this exact moment for thousands of years.

He cracked another diabolical smile as he continued, "So, that nasty little cut on the back of your leg *will* kill you. Actually, the toxins in the cut will kill you, not the cut itself. With every beat of your heart, it is being distributed throughout your body. The more effort you exert, the faster you will die."

Toxins or no toxins, I was not going down without a fight! I struggled to my feet with the world spinning around me.

"You could just lie down and take a forever nap and not feel a thing, but that would make a horrible ending to this story," he goaded me. "Oh, well, suit yourself." He grabbed me with one hand and threw me high into the air, batting me clear across the huge cave, causing me to hit a wall. I slid down the wall and landed on the ground with a thud. The toxins were taking over, and I was slipping away. I looked up to see Belshazzar on top of me again. He grabbed me once again.

"Jacob, I need your help," I whispered in desperation.

"*I am there with you, inside of you. Be strong and courageous. You have the power, my power, because you are my child. Use it!*" Jacob replied to my mind and soul.

Belshazzar threw me hard to the ground this time, and I landed on my back, blacking out momentarily.

"I was going to let my children have fun with your carcass once I was finished with you, but I've changed my mind!" A maniacal, sulfur-filled laugh vomited out of his mouth.

I looked up just as his fanged teeth came toward me. I gripped the torch, and with all the energy I had, and with fangs bearing down on me, I swung the torch at his face, knocking one of his fangs clear out of his mouth. He reeled slightly but kept coming. Once again, I willed myself to move the torch upward, praying that Jacob would guide the torch. Belshazzar's mouth was wide open, but it wasn't his mouth that my torch embedded in...It was one of his bulbous eyes! He shrieked in pain! The torch was firmly in his eye, and the light, the flame from the torch began, to slowly make its way through Belshazzar's disgusting body, starting with his head and moving all the way down. I gripped the torch harder now as I felt a rush of righteous fire flowing out of my soul and into Belshazzar's dark heart. I heard a sound like a roaring wind, low and intense rumbling wind that was coming from the torch. In that moment, we became one, the fire and the flesh. And then, the first of two explosions.

The first was Belshazzar's body. Decaying flesh and liquid shot out like shrapnel in a million different directions covering me and the Offspring that surrounded me. The smell alone made me want to vomit, but I was too weak, even for that. The Offspring were coming for me!

The second explosion sent the Offspring scattering as a flash of white-hot light lit up the room. I suppose it was a magnificent scene, but I was too weak to enjoy it or completely understand what was happening. The scattered Offspring, though, quickly recovered but were still eager to rip me to shreds. They would be disappointed.

Someone was standing over me with a torch in their hand. A torch like I'd never seen before. This stranger handed me my torch and said, "Try holding on to this; you'll need it later. By the way, my name is Sabre," he said with a bow and a salute. He picked me up over his shoulder. And then I succumbed to the blackness.

TORCH

POSTLUDE

Thump…thump…thump…thump…thump…ever louder, faster.
Thump…thump…thump…thump…thump…ever louder, faster.
Thump. Thump. Thump. Thump. Ever louder, faster.

The rhythm is building. It's growing louder, faster as it does every morning. The most intense, the most sacred, the most awe-inspiring wake-up call.

With my new "brothers" by my side, I opened the door to our room and stepped outside, and once again, as I had every day since I got here, I had to catch my breath. You see, even in this dawn-breaking hour, with silhouettes and outlines filling our view, the scenery was almost too beautiful to comprehend. Too majestic to describe. It is the city of Lucent. The city of light. And the rhythm is calling us! The rhythm is calling me, calling me to save them all!

To Be Continued…

CPSIA information can be obtained
at www.ICGtesting.com
Printed in the USA
BVHW041755190122
626634BV00017B/332

9 781637 698600